A LOVE WISH

She must not let him know. She must maintain her dignity at all costs. She should back away at this very moment.

As he stood intimately close, looking down at her, his ragged breathing gave him away. She wasn't sure before, but now she knew it wasn't her imagination: he wanted her. She noticed how an uncommon quiet had filled the room. But was it quiet, or just that for this moment they were in their own little world, so acutely aware of each other no other sounds or sights could penetrate?

Suddenly, his hands clasped her shoulders, causing her flesh to tingle beneath the blue chemise gown. Even in the semidarkness she could see a bright flare of desire in his eyes. He was hers—she knew it. She had only to give the slightest hint of her own desire and she'd be tight in his arms. . . .

Three Wishes for Miss Winthrop

Shirley Kennedy

A SIGNET BOOK

SIGNET
Published by New American Library, a division of
Penguin Group (USA) Inc., 375 Hudson Street,
New York, New York 10014, U.S.A.
Penguin Books Ltd, 80 Strand,
London WC2R 0RL, England
Penguin Books Australia Ltd, 250 Camberwell Road,
Camberwell, Victoria 3124, Australia
Penguin Books Canada Ltd, 10 Alcorn Avenue,
Toronto, Ontario, Canada M4V 3B2
Penguin Books (N.Z.) Ltd, Cnr Rosedale and Airborne Roads,
Albany, Auckland 1310, New Zealand

Penguin Books Ltd, Registered Offices:
80 Strand, London WC2R 0RL, England

First published by Signet, an imprint of New American Library,
a division of Penguin Group (USA) Inc.

First Printing, August 2003
10 9 8 7 6 5 4 3 2 1

Dedicated to the memory of Elizabeth Fry, 1780–1845, who fought for years to bring about England's much-needed prison reforms.

Queen Victoria took a close interest in her work and the two women met several times. Victoria wrote in her journal that she considered Fry a "very superior person." It is claimed that Victoria, who was forty years younger than Elizabeth Fry, might have modeled herself after this stalwart woman, who successfully combined the roles of mother and public figure.

Chapter One

London, June 1815

*O*n the day before Mrs. Emma Montgomery was to be hanged, a carriage bearing two plainly dressed women rolled at a fair pace through the hustle-bustle of afternoon commerce on Bridge Street toward the Palace of Westminster, wherein both the House of Lords and the House of Commons were accommodated.

An occasional gentleman's head turned as the carriage passed by, although surely no one could have found any interest in the carriage itself. A gig of ancient vintage, it was much in need of paint and minor repair. Nor was the horse in any way remarkable. Although obviously well cared for, it was swaybacked and well into middle age. The gentlemen's attention most certainly could not have been drawn by the older and larger of the two women. Stern-jawed, dressed in black, she wore a formidable scowl and sat ramrod-straight, gripping the reins in a manner suggesting no sane person would dare grab them away.

It was the younger woman sitting beside her who drew from every man who saw her a reaction ranging from furtive glance to admiring stare. Slender but full-bosomed, she, too, sat ramrod-straight, although without the uncompromising rigidness of her companion. Her dress and bonnet, both humdrum gray, suggested the dull attire of a governess, yet bright auburn curls peeked from beneath her bonnet in a most ungovernesslike fashion. There was something about her delicate face, though currently set in solemn mode, that gave a sense that change could be imminent. Her wide-set gray eyes could easily sparkle with merriment. Her full red lips, presently pressed in a cheerless line, could easily tilt into an enticing smile. She was twenty-eight or so, not especially tall, with creamy skin, roses on her cheeks, and an air of confidence about her, although a worried frown had just flitted across her forehead.

Miss Lucy Winthrop was unaware of the admiring stares she attracted, if, in fact, she ever paid attention to men's calculating glances. Rather, she was listening intently to her sister, the formidable Mrs. Augusta Winthrop-Scott, who was currently exclaiming, "The trouble with you, my dear Lucy, is you don't take life seriously enough."

Lucy bit her tongue. No use protesting. Augusta, who was ten years older and considered herself twenty years wiser, was the most stubborn, obdurate woman Lucy had ever known. She was also the most generous, kind, understanding woman Lucy had ever known. When Lucy was eight, Augusta eighteen, and their widowed mother died, Augusta unquestioningly took on the responsibility of raising Lucy and their younger brother, Montague. For that, and other reasons, Lucy's love for Augusta knew no bounds. She would never forget the sacrifices her older sister had made for her.

Still, Augusta could be most trying at times.

"I'm here, aren't I?" responded Lucy, careful not to add that once again she had forfeited one of her precious, and few, free days. "You know very well you have my full support. That poor woman, I cannot believe she's being put to death over what amounts to a minor offense. So unjust! I fully agree you should address Lord Sidmouth. My only problem is—"

"I sent a note ahead," interrupted Augusta, eyes suddenly blazing. "Lord Sidmouth must give me an audience immediately. I cannot bear to think that tomorrow morning Mrs. Emma Montgomery goes to the gallows. We must do everything we can to spare her life." As if to accent her words, Augusta sharply flicked the reins. "Time is of the essence," she exclaimed as the horse momentarily picked up its pace. She slanted a gaze at her sister. "What were you saying?"

Lucy suppressed a sigh. "You know I'm only too happy to

accompany you to Parliament. How could I say no? But I devoutly hope I don't catch sight of my employer. More to the point, I hope he doesn't catch sight of me."

"Lord Darwood?" Augusta looked down her nose. "Humph, that ninny, that Whig! Didn't you say he'd gone fishing at his estate in Scotland?"

"Yes, else I wouldn't be here. The problem is, I've worked for him for three years, so I know he has a penchant for suddenly changing his plans. So ninny or no, Whig or no, he is my employer, and if he returned early and saw me here with you—"

"You mean he's still not aware I'm your sister?" Augusta looked surprised and duly insulted.

Lucy returned a wry smile. "I've managed to conceal that fact thus far."

"I am aghast."

"You can be aghast all you want, but I must be practical. Lord Darwood loathes reformists. As far as he's concerned, those beneath his station do not, in essence, exist, and most certainly do not have any rights. If he discovers I'm related to the champion of the downtrodden, I would lose my position fast as light."

Augusta thrust her chin forward, in what was commonly her highly indignant pose. "But I'm the so-called rabble-rouser, not you."

"It doesn't matter. Do you think Lord Darwood would allow me to tutor his children if he knew you were my sister? It's guilt by association if nothing else. Believe me, if there's one thing he cannot abide, it's those who advocate just laws for the poor."

Augusta bristled. "Such as universal suffrage? Such as speaking up for those poor, suffering women in Newgate Prison? Such as trying to save Mrs. Emma Montgomery from the gallows?"

"Well . . . yes." Lucy realized she was waffling. Never one to avoid an issue, she hastened to make her position clear. "You devote your energies to those in need, Augusta. I admire you immensely for it. Last year when you came to Parliament and addressed the House of Commons Committee on London Prisons, I thought I'd burst with pride."

"For all the good it did me," grumbled Augusta. "Those heartless wretches strongly disapproved of my views on capital punishment. What do those nodcocks care that over two hundred offenses are punishable by death? You would wonder who in their right mind would put someone to death for stealing clothes or forging a banknote. Yet here, in supposedly merciful England, it's done all the time."

"You don't have to convince me," Lucy hastened to answer. "Your presentation was splendid. By the time you finished, only a fool would not have seen we should revise our laws regarding capital punishment. And who would approve of the wretched conditions that exist for women at Newgate?"

"Yet they chose to ignore me." Bitterness edged Augusta's words. "In the end, they did nothing except accuse me of not knowing my place. I'm only a woman. Therefore, I should stay home, scrub floors, and tend to my children."

Lucy's heart went out to her widowed sister, mother of three, who lived in a leaky-roofed cottage in Harford Lane, with only one servant, eking out a bare existence from the small stipend her husband had left her. But despite the constraints of poverty and having to raise her family, she had truly devoted her life to noble causes. "But they did listen, Augusta, despite what they said. I suspect you did more good than you know."

Augusta appeared not to notice Lucy's words of comfort. After a short silence, she burst, "Those politicians! Selfish to the core, every last one of them. They know they've got the power. They, with their servants and fancy clothes and fine country houses. They don't give a farthing for the needy and destitute of this world and never will."

They had reached the Palace of Westminster. As Augusta guided the carriage to the curb and reined in the horse, she briskly nodded toward an elegantly dressed gentleman who was approaching the ornate, wrought-iron gates guarding the entrance. "See that man? The one in the drill trousers and fancy frock coat? There's your perfect example of upper-class decadence and sloth."

Lucy dutifully turned her attention to the object of Augusta's wrath: a dark-haired man in his early thirties, of medium height, slender, yet well muscled. She was struck at once with how attractive he was, not only because of his physical appearance but because of the self-confident way he carried himself and the way he moved, not plodding along heavy-footed as many men did but light-footed, full of grace. "Who is he?" she asked.

Augusta sniffed in disdain. "That, my dear, is John Weston, Lord Granville, head of one of the richest, most influential families in England. Look at him. You can just see the smugness oozing from his pores. And why not? He's been privileged and petted since the day he was born."

"He's a member of Parliament?" Lucy asked.

"Indeed, yes, and likely to be prime minister one of these days. Represents the borough of Weymouth, if I'm not mistaken. No doubt his father bought it for him. A Whig, of course, and—"

"Oh, no." Lucy slammed her hand to her mouth.

"What is it, sister?" Augusta called, alarmed.

Lucy's heart raced as she answered, "The man headed for the gate now—it's my employer, Lord Darwood. He's supposed to be in Scotland."

"Then he must have arrived home early. How unfortunate. You could duck beneath the seat if you like."

"If he looks this way, I shall."

Augusta looked puzzled. "But surely you won't lose your position simply because you're related to me."

"I fear you don't understand," Lucy answered, forcing a laugh. For three years now she'd held her position as governess for the Earl of Darwood, grateful each day she'd had the wits to leave her previous position with Mr. Joseph Weeton, a rich manufacturer from Manchester, where she'd been treated like a lowly servant. Since the Weetons considered her of too lowly a status to eat with the family, she'd been forced to dine alone. No room of her own, either. She'd slept on a trundle bed in the room of the two eldest daughters. Not only that, the Weeton children had all been unruly, without the slightest desire to learn, and had plagued her constantly, knowing she'd never dare complain.

So different from Stanton Manor, the Darwoods' principal country home where she and the children spent much of their time. Despite Darwood's autocratic nature and arrogant attitude, she was given a lovely room of her own and was treated with respect. Best of all, the children, though lively, were eager to learn. The girls especially, and if she slipped a bit of Pythagoras and Newton in with their watercolors, and pianoforte, then Lord and Lady Darwood, who were mostly taken up with their social life anyway, were none the wiser. "I should hate to lose my position, Augusta, for more reasons than one."

Augusta gave her knee a reassuring pat. "Don't worry, you can always come live with me."

What a horrible fate. Lucy shut her eyes a moment. She loved her sister dearly, but with her noble goals and just causes, Augusta was like an avalanche: unstoppable when started, sweeping every obstacle from her path. Lucy had no desire to entangle herself in Augusta's life. She had her own goals, her own just causes. "That's very kind of you, Augusta, but—oh, look, he's joined Lord Granville."

"Good, he's distracted. Perhaps he won't notice you. If he does, and he comes this way, you can pretend you don't know me."

Lucy could almost laugh. Augusta was such a force that denying knowing her would be like denying the ocean was wet or the sky was blue. "Look, they're starting to talk. Let's slip past. If my luck holds, Lord Darwood won't see me."

"Glad I caught you, Granville," said Percy Godwin, Lord Darwood, a stocky man of middle age with bulging eyes. "I'm dying to have you meet Mrs. Ponsonby. What a woman. I shortened my sojourn in Scotland, just so I could be with her."

John Weston, Lord Granville, was not a man to tolerate any kind of artifice, including his own. He replied bluntly, "I'd gladly meet your latest mistress, Darwood, but I wager by the time I do you'll have a new one."

"But this one's special." A smile wreathed the short man's

ruddy face. "She's smooth of skin and on the plump side, like a juicy peach ripe for the picking. I've already leased her a house in Montpelier Square and got her a smart cabriolet." A wicked twinkle lit his eye. "Next week I plan to drive her down to Brighton for some . . . shall we say, amorous relaxation."

Granville made no effort to conceal his annoyance. "You're just back from fishing in Scotland and now you're off again? I trust you're not planning on skipping the remaining sessions of Parliament."

Darwood rolled his eyes. "Damme, Granville, *must* you always be so conscientious? Thank God, Parliament meets only a few months a year or I should be bored beyond all belief. What do I care about the tedious passage of laws? I've much better things to do with my time."

Granville lifted a sardonic eyebrow. "Spoken like a true member of the aristocracy."

Darwood drew himself up. "My dear boy, I may be a member of Parliament, but I don't consider it a life sentence, nor should you."

Granville knew all too well the futility of arguing, but he couldn't resist asking, "Don't you give a thought from time to time to the problems of the common man?"

"Please." Darwood held up a protesting hand. "My principles are no different from the fundamental canons of the Whig Party. I believe in ordered liberty, low taxation, and the enclosure of land. What else is there?"

Granville returned a wicked grin. "Not long ago, the French aristocracy held similar views. If memory serves, many of them are now without their heads."

"Good point." Darwood laughed good-naturedly. "I doubt that'll happen in merry old England, although anytime they want to set the blade to that fat neck of Prinny's, I shouldn't be too displeased. Well, you're young yet. I give you a few more years in Parliament and you'll care for the rabble as much as I do. As for me, my life is splendid and satisfying, and I don't intend to . . . oh, my word."

Lord Darwood's gaze had wandered to the curb where two women, both in plain dress, were alighting from an ancient carriage. "There's that wretched woman . . ." His forehead furrowed in concentration. "What is her name? I cannot—"

"Augusta Winthrop-Scott," Granville promptly replied. "Don't you recall, she spoke before the Committee for Prison Reform last year, addressing the horrendous conditions for women in Newgate Prison. She made an excellent presentation. I was quite impressed."

Darwood sniffed. "The rest of us were impressed at the brazenness of the woman. Whatever possessed her to appear before Parliament when she should have been home looking after her family?"

Words of reason formed on Granville's lips, but before he could utter them, he saw his friend's mouth drop open and his brow furrow in puzzlement. "What is it, Darwood?"

"I bloody well cannot believe this. Do you see that woman with Augusta Winthrop-Scott? The pretty one in gray?"

"Of course I see her. Even from here one can see she's quite attractive."

"It's my governess, Miss Winthrop."

"So?"

"What do you mean, so?" Darwood looked a trifle wild-eyed. "Whatever is she doing with that rabble-rousing woman? If there's any connection between my governess and that . . ." Sudden realization lit his face. "But there must be. Miss Winthrop . . . Mrs. Winthrop-Scott . . . my God, they must be related." His jaw jutted with purpose. "If they are, out she goes."

"But didn't you once tell me you were more than pleased with Miss Winthrop? That your children couldn't be in better hands?"

If Darwood heard, he paid no heed. Instead, scowling fiercely, he started toward the two women. "I shall get to the bottom of this, and if there's a connection—any connection at all—Miss Winthrop shall summarily be dismissed."

"It appears he's headed this way," Lucy said. A sick feeling pervaded her stomach as she watched her employer approach with purpose in his step and castigation in his eyes. Following behind, reluctantly it appeared, came his companion, Lord Granville.

"Good afternoon, your lordship," Lucy said as her employer arrived. She dipped a curtsy, willing herself to stay calm. "You must be just back from Scotland. I trust you enjoyed the fishing." She gestured toward Augusta. "I would like you to meet—"

"Might I ask why you are not home with my children?" Lord Darwood interrupted. He kept glaring at Lucy and had yet to cast a single glance at Augusta.

"Sir, it's my free day." Lucy felt pleased she'd managed to quell her instant annoyance and sound utterly tranquil.

"Oh." Darwood looked abashed but only for a moment. He shot a look at Augusta and said with thinly veiled sarcasm, "Ah, if it isn't Mrs. Winthrop-Scott."

Augusta drew herself up in what Lucy always liked to call her battle stance: chin high, shoulders back, her considerable bosom thrust forward. "You know me, sir?"

Darwood returned a slight taunting bow. "I remember you well, madam, from your visit to Parliament a year or so ago. You, as I recall, are the champion of good causes. So tell me, what draws you to Parliament this fine day? Let me guess. Could it be another selfless mission to help all those poor, downtrodden women in Newgate?"

Lucy's throat tightened with anger. How dare this man address her sister in such a mocking fashion? She spoke up sharply, "I take it you've never seen the conditions under which women live at Newgate Prison. Well, I have, sir, and I can tell you they're appalling. Picture three hundred women all crammed together, some with babies. They're sleeping on the floor without nightclothes or bedding. They're living in filth, cooking and washing and sleeping all in the same cell. My sister is right. It's a disgrace. Something must be done." Surprised at herself, Lucy drew a deep breath and marveled at her outburst. Always in perfect control of herself, not once had she ever thrown caution to the winds and defied her employer. He looked taken aback. In fact, he had actually flinched.

No doubt she would be immediately dismissed.

Augusta joined the conversation. "We are both here on

what you call a selfless mission, Lord Darwood. We're trying to save the life of a poor woman sentenced to hang tomorrow."

Lord Granville, who had been standing relaxed, hand on hip in the background, listening intently, stepped forward. "Is that the woman accused of forgery?"

Augusta asked in surprise, "You've heard of her?"

"Not an hour ago I was talking to Lord Sidmouth. He mentioned you had sent word you were coming to plead the poor woman's case."

"Never in the world has there been such a miscarriage of justice," Augusta hotly declared. "Mrs. Montgomery was forced to pass those forged banknotes under pressure from her husband."

Lucy added, "He abused her constantly. No doubt she would have been beaten severely had she refused him."

"It does seem unfair," commented Granville.

Lucy, who had been gazing intently at Lord Darwood, waiting for his words of dismissal, turned her attention to the man by his side. Up close, she found him even more handsome. His shoulders were broad, his waist trim, his stomach flat. A careless lock of wavy, dark, long hair fell over his forehead, giving him a dashing, devil-may-care demeanor. "Unfair is an understatement," she replied as she looked into two of the warmest brown eyes she'd ever seen. Something uncommon flared within her. "Do you think Lord Sidmouth will be amenable to a reprieve for Mrs. Montgomery?" she asked, hoping her discomfit didn't show.

Before Lord Granville could answer, Darwood burst into derisive laughter. "Not likely. Sidmouth considers reformers dangerous. He firmly believes crime will run rampant in the streets if you remove the dread of punishment from the criminal."

"What nonsense," declared Augusta. "We are here to talk some sense into Lord Sidmouth's head. I vow, we'll do everything we can to spare the life of that unfortunate woman."

"We can but try," Lucy added with quiet firmness. Her heart skipped a beat as she looked into those brown eyes again.

Lord Granville smiled back. "I wish you luck," he said softly, in a voice that held infinite compassion.

"It'll take more than luck, I'd wager," said Darwood. He turned to Lucy. "I note your last name is Winthrop. Are you in any way related to Mrs. Winthrop-Scott?"

Here it comes. Lucy felt a nudge in her side from Augusta's elbow—a reminder, no doubt, that Lucy need not admit a thing. But that was nonsense. Lucy had never been less than honest. This was no time to start lying now. She swallowed her anger, managed a pleasant smile, and laid an affectionate hand on Augusta's shoulder. "How perspicacious of you, Lord Darwood. I'm proud to say this lady is my sister."

Lord Darwood's face immediately flushed red. He sputtered a moment before he answered, "I had no idea. You should have told me. This makes all the difference in the world. I shall not, under any circumstances—"

"We must be going, Darwood," interrupted Lord Granville. "The debates are about to begin. You *do* want to be there, don't you?" He shot a meaningful look at his companion.

For a brief moment, Darwood looked nonplussed, as if he had forgotten where he was. "I . . . er . . . oh, well, yes. Certain matters can wait. So let us be off, Granville. Good day, ladies." His features hardened as he focused on Lucy. "We shall discuss a certain matter later. Obviously now is neither the time nor place."

"Of course," Lucy managed, weak with relief that for the moment she'd been spared. As the two men moved away, she turned to Augusta. "I was positive he was going to dismiss me on the spot."

"Lord Darwood was angry," Augusta answered. "He'll soon come to his senses. When he calms down, he'll realize he'll never find another governess as capable as you." She paused, then asked accusingly, "Liked him, didn't you?"

"Liked who?" Lucy asked, all innocence.

"Lord Granville, of course. I saw the way you pushed your chest out and sucked in your stomach when you knew he was watching."

"I did no such thing." Lucy thought a moment and realized there was no fooling perceptive Augusta. "You must admit, he's an extremely attractive man."

"I'm surprised you took notice," Augusta replied with more

than a trace of irony. "I thought you'd all but forgotten the ex-istence of men."

"Not entirely." What an understatement, thought Lucy. During her ten years as a governess, her several employers would have deemed it extremely improper if she'd shown an interest in anything other than her duties. Still, sometimes at night when she'd climbed into her bed, exhausted after caring for small children all day, her thoughts drifted to a fantasy of a faceless man, warm of voice, confident and strong, who would sweep her into his arms and whisper he loved her. Idiocy, of course. She had long since resigned herself to stop looking for love and concentrate instead on being the best governess she could be. Eventually, if she ever saved enough money, she would open a school for girls and become its mistress. Either way, there was no room for a man in her life and she would remain a spinster until . . . She laughed to herself because one of Augusta's favorite phrases had popped into her mind: *until I dry up and blow away.*

"I still think you should have married Thomas Craig," said Augusta, referring to the shy schoolmaster in the village where they'd been raised.

"I didn't love Thomas Craig." Lucy tried to curb her impa-tience. They had gone through this exchange many times.

"Foolishness." Augusta grimaced. "I told you years ago you'd dry up and blow away if you waited around to marry for love. As for Lord Granville, I cannot think of a man who would be more unsuitable."

Lucy laughed in reply. "Well, I haven't dried up yet, have I? Don't worry, Augusta, just because I find a man attractive doesn't mean I shall go cakey over him. As for Lord Granville, 'unsuitable' is hardly the word."

"I'm glad you see that. Lord Granville is one of *them*, Lucy. He lives in a world of privilege and luxury, a world that cares not one whit for the common man."

"I know, but still . . . is he entirely without compassion?" Lucy genuinely wondered. "I had the distinct feeling he was sympathetic to our cause. And at the end, when I could have sworn Lord Darwood was about to dismiss me, I suspect it's by design Lord Granville lured him away."

Augusta awarded her a fierce scowl. "Granville's a wid-ower, you know, but if you're thinking—"

"Are you daft?" Lucy could not control another burst of laughter. "I'm merely a poor governess, whereas Lord Granville is wealthy, titled, and from one of the grandest fam-ilies in all England. What folly to think he'd even look twice at me."

"Don't forget, our father was a baron," said Augusta.

"A poverty-stricken baron. Rest assured, I know my place."

"Good." Augusta nodded with satisfaction. "Bear in mind, Lord Granville may seem sympathetic to our cause, but like the rest of the aristocracy, when the chips are down, he'll side with those elitist friends of his. Now, enough of your prob-lems. Don't forget why we are here. Come along."

Augusta headed at a brisk pace toward the Palace of West-minster. Lucy followed behind, feeling properly guilty. Her sister was right. The most serious of Lucy's problems paled in comparison to the plight of Mrs. Emma Montgomery. Still . . .

Lucy knew in her heart Augusta was wrong when she said Lord Darwood would come to his senses. He would not. The man was most extremely arrogant, treating his inferiors with a patrician insolence that seemed almost the reverse of good breeding. What a pity that he, as a member of Parliament, di-rected England's destiny when all he cared about was satisfy-ing his own selfish vices. Of course he was going to dismiss her.

Lord Granville—what a handsome man he is. The uninvited thought thrust its way into Lucy's head as she trailed behind her sister. Then she felt guilty again for her callousness in thinking of an attractive man when tomorrow Mrs. Emma Montgomery, penniless, mistreated, and completely undeserv-ing, was destined to meet her fate on the gallows.

Chapter Two

$\mathcal{A}$ugusta was correct when she described John Weston, Lord Granville, as a man who lived in a world of privilege and splendor. He had been born into one of the wealthiest, most influential families in all England. Grounded in classics by a tutor, then sent to Eton, followed by Oxford, he'd been given the best possible education, finished off by two years abroad where, besides pursuing the classics, he'd learned French and impeccable manners. A first son, he had largely been ignored by his parents when he was a child—a common custom among the *ton*. Instead, his care had been placed in the hands of servants. They were no substitute for his parents. Not only was Lord Granville not in the least spoiled, he had learned compassion for others from the loneliness he himself had suffered growing up a neglected child. He was twenty-nine when his father died and left him vast wealth, which he accepted with indifference. After all, a life of luxury and ease was all he'd ever known so how could it be more so? Many first sons became members of Parliament, and Granville was no exception. He accepted his comfortable career as his due. And why should he not? As a Whig member of Parliament, firmly entrenched in the aristocracy, he lived in the most agreeable society England had ever known. The easy, unassertive confidence he possessed was made possible only because he'd never had cause to doubt his social position—or, for that matter, anything else in his pleasant, smooth-running life.

Tragedy had touched him only once when his wife, Jane, of whom he'd been extremely fond, died in childbirth, leaving behind his son and heir, William, now nine; Mary, now seven; and the baby, Winifred, who was now five. He didn't see much of them. They lived quite contentedly, or so he assumed, at Penfield Manor, his estate in Surrey. Currently they had no governess. For reasons Granville could not quite fathom, governesses were hard to keep. He was not especially concerned, though. His mother, the supremely capable Sophia, dowager Countess of Granville, doted on the children and supervised their upbringing.

Now, standing with Darwood in the Commons lobby waiting for the debates to begin, Granville turned his attention to his friend, who, it seemed, was still in a bit of a rant.

"That wretched woman should be transported," Darwood declared. He flicked a piece of lint from his impeccably tailored frock coat. "Now she's about to descend upon poor Sidmouth. Really, there should be some sort of law. "

"How unworthy of you, Darwood," Granville evenly replied. "Whether you like it or not, the time for reforms is upon us. Don't forget the French peasants."

"Rabble."

"Rabble, perhaps, but they won their point concerning liberty, equality, fraternity. If we don't listen, the same could happen here. Reforms are coming, whether you like them or not. It's best to allow Mrs. Augusta Winthrop-Scott to speak in support of her cause."

Lord Darwood forgot his indignation and looked mildly amused. "What has gotten into you? If your mother heard you talk that way—"

"My mother has nothing to do with this," Granville answered sharply. He wondered why he should feel annoyed, considering he had long since detached himself from the dominating influence of his mother. Perhaps the chance meeting with Mrs. Augusta Winthrop-Scott and her sister had something to do with this unsettled feeling that had suddenly overcome him. *The very pretty sister* . . .

"You needn't snap at me." Darwood sounded sulky.

Granville was well aware his friend's dealings with his servants were none of his affair. Still, he felt compelled to ask, "You're not really going to dismiss your governess, are you?"

"I most certainly am." Darwood smiled jovially. "If not for you, I'd have dismissed her right there at the curb in front of the Palace of Westminster. Course, it would have created a bit of a scene, especially if the poor girl had started to cry. You were right to drag me away. I shall sack her in private. Better yet, I shall have Lady Darwood do the dirty deed. Why should I have to bother?"

Lord Granville felt a rush of sympathy for the pretty young woman with the spark in her velvet gray eyes who had spoken so fervently for her sister's cause. "But why dismiss her? What exactly has she done wrong?"

Darwood drew himself up. "I cannot countenance in my employ anyone who is even remotely connected with those lunatic reformists who seek to change our way of life. Prison reform, bah! Coddling criminals is against all reason. It's against England! Didn't I just say Mrs. Augusta Winthrop-Scott should be transported? On second thought, they ought to toss her in the Tower."

"They don't do that anymore."

"Pity."

"Ah, Darwood, your compassion shines through once again." Granville accompanied his remark with an ironic smile. "I suspect I cannot change your mind."

"Indeed not. The governess must go and that's that. Pity, the children rather liked her. But let's get on to more pleasant subjects. Are you planning to attend Lady Spencer's soiree tonight?"

"I suppose."

"Ah, and are you bringing your betrothed?"

Granville felt his patience snap again. But he concealed his hostile reaction and answered easily, "Lady Camilla Harvey is not my betrothed. At least not yet."

"She soon will be if your mother has her say. Oops." Darwood looked unconvincingly abashed. "There I go again, mentioning your mother, who we all know has no influence over you whatsoever."

"Quite true," Granville answered equitably, raising a meaningful eyebrow. He was in no mood to argue. Instead, a question burned in his mind. "Your governess . . . where will she go? Does she have resources? Will you give her a character so she can obtain another position?"

Darwood shrugged. "I've no objection to giving her a character, providing my wife wishes to write one. But why would you care?"

"She's a human being, after all. I should hate to see her tossed penniless onto the streets."

Darwood spread his hands wide, as if explaining a basic reality. "Good grief, man, she's only a governess."

Granville knew further argument was useless. And why, indeed, should he trouble himself over the problems of a mere servant?

"Will your mother attend the soiree tonight?" asked Darwood.

Mama. Granville's mood darkened as his thoughts returned to the latest crisis with his mother. He liked Lady Camilla Harvey well enough. What he did *not* like was his mother's blatant efforts to persuade him to propose to the oh-so-willing belle. Of course, he was going to marry her . . . eventually, but why should he rush? Though quite beautiful, she wasn't perfect. Most definitely, he was not enraptured by the sound of her rather high-pitched, nasal, whining voice. Still, her family was firmly entrenched in the *haute ton.* They were, in fact, one of the three hundred great landed families of England, as was his own. Mama liked that. She firmly believed in keeping with one's own, avoiding those of lesser rank as much as possible.

He wasn't going to be pushed, though. He would propose to Lady Camilla in his own good time. He'd been a widower five years. With only one son, he assuredly needed more, for safety's sake, but he didn't need his mother to goad him into marrying again.

Darwood nudged him. "Come, the debate is about to start."

As Granville headed into St. Stephen's Chapel, where the House of Commons met, thoughts of Miss Lucy Winthrop flitted through his mind. She had spirit. He liked that in a woman. He wished he could help her, although . . .

His three children were currently without a governess. No doubt his mother was already seeking another. Why not Miss

Lucy Winthrop? What a splendid idea. He had never interfered in such matters, but there was always a first time.

But Mama won't like it. Granville's lips twisted into a cynical smile. *She won't like it at all.* His mother had a penchant for choosing drab, homely governesses. Lucy Winthrop most certainly didn't qualify.

He dreaded those occasional scenes with his mother, wherein he was compelled to remind her he was head of the family, not she; that powerful though she was, he held the real power. Thank God, such occasions were rare. He suspected, though, that were he to express a desire to hire Miss Lucy Winthrop he'd be facing such an occasion again.

But perhaps . . . on second thought . . .

What had he been thinking of? Why should he go out of his way to hire a governess? Let Mama handle it. He hated scenes.

Face it, Granville, you don't win with your mother every time. The forced admission to himself depressed him. Why couldn't he have a mother like Darwood's mother, who was amenable, if not downright subservient, and always seeking to please? Instead, his life was a constant battle as he sought, time and again, to keep the upper hand.

Barely polite, lips twitching with impatience, Lord Sidmouth refused to grant clemency to Mrs. Emma Montgomery. Further, he gave Augusta short shrift, barely allowing her to speak before announcing he must attend to pressing business elsewhere.

In all her twenty-eight years, Lucy had never seen Augusta in such a state. She felt terribly sorry for her sister, who was ordinarily so feisty but now downhearted in defeat. Strangely silent, shoulders slumped, Augusta seemed to have lost her spirit as they departed the House of Commons. Finally, as they reached their carriage, Augusta resentfully declared, "He hardly listened." She climbed wearily to the seat. "That poor woman will die and he doesn't care."

Searching for words of comfort, Lucy climbed in beside her. "There was nothing you could have done. Obviously his mind was made up before we even arrived."

"I shall go to Newgate and see if I can sit with her tonight."

"I'll go with you."

"No you won't. You're due back at your employer's."

Lucy gave a wry laugh. "Of course. I should hurry home to be dismissed."

Augusta ignored her sister's acerbity. "There is no sense in the both of us having to endure the misery of Newgate."

Lucy hadn't the heart to argue. She had seen Newgate once, when Augusta had taken her on a tour, and that was enough. It was a horrible place. To see those pitiful human beings cold and hungry, forced to live in dark, cramped fetid quarters, was almost more than she could bear.

"I shan't argue, Augusta. You're right, I should go home." She let out a wistful sigh, thinking of what lay ahead.

"It'll be all right," assured Augusta. "You're the best governess Lord Darwood ever had. How could he possibly dismiss you?"

"I hope you're right," Lucy replied wistfully. "Working for Lord Darwood hasn't been easy. He's so demanding. But at least he pays a fair stipend, and you know how important that is to me."

"So you can save your money and someday open a school for young ladies." Augusta smiled gently. "I haven't forgotten your dream."

More than a dream, thought Lucy. Growing up, she and Augusta had received an excellent education, thanks to their mother who taught them the classics, history, mathematics— all the subjects normally taught only to boys. Such an education was rare for women. As a governess, Lucy was required to teach demanding academic subjects only to the boys. Other than a smattering of reading and writing, Lord Darwood's three girls were expected to conquer such subjects as dancing and watercolors. What an injustice. What a waste of good minds. Years ago, Lucy vowed that someday she would own a school where girls could receive as fine an education as boys. Because of her limited finances, she knew such an objective was far in the future, yet now it was her prime goal. Perhaps love would find her someday, but at the age of eighteen, with her mother gone and the family in dire financial straits, she put dreams of love behind her and went to work as a governess.

Despite the hard work, it was a position she truly loved. Of course she was lonely sometimes, but for the time being her happiness lay in the satisfaction of knowing she was an excellent teacher, helping young minds to grow.

"Augusta, will you be all right? I hate to see you so depressed."

Augusta drew herself up, seeming as she did so to regain some of her pluck. "I may not have saved Mrs. Montgomery, but I am not done yet." She waggled a finger at Lucy. "Change is coming, mark my words. Those high-and-mighty Whigs want to keep the status quo, but their selfish little world will soon start to crumble."

Unbidden, an image of Lord Granville filled Lucy's mind. He was looking down at her, standing, hand on hip, in that easy, masculine stance of his that proclaimed his confidence in himself and his disdain for all that didn't suit him in what Augusta called his selfish little world. Lucy doubted very much Lord Granville was aware his world was crumbling. She thought of poor Mrs. Montgomery and suddenly wished he did. Resentment boiled within her. As Augusta pointed out, Lord Granville was indeed one of *them. How could I ever have found the man attractive?* Lucy wondered. She should put him out of her mind and not think of him again.

"Ah, John, there you are."

It was early evening as Granville's mother, Sophia, dowager Countess of Granville, swept down the main staircase of Cheltham House, the Granvilles' palatial London mansion, to where he stood in the marble-pillared entry hall.

He bowed slightly, noting his mother's no-nonsense black bombazine ball gown, made slightly less severe by her beautifully coiffed silver hair crowned by a modest tiara of diamonds. "Good evening, Mama. You're looking exceptionally lovely tonight."

"You are far too kind," Lady Granville testily replied. "How could I possibly look lovely when I am practically at death's door?"

Damned if there was a good answer to that, thought Granville with an inward sigh. Mama had been at death's door for years. He would ask what was wrong but knew he'd receive one of her customary vague replies. Sometimes she complained of her heart, sometimes "stomach problems." Other times, her problem was simply a mysterious malaise that threatened to carry her off at any moment. When he was a child, he constantly worried about his mother's imminent demise. That she had reached the age of fifty-five and was still alive seemed some sort of miracle, although he had long since suspected that most of her illnesses were in her head. Still, there was always a small part of him that remained concerned about his mother's health. "You're as beautiful as ever," he told her with a smile.

Indeed, she had been a beauty once. Not anymore. Her once-magnificent figure was now too thin, with skinny arms and collarbones too prominent. Despite her age, the angular features of her face were not marred by drooping jowls and double chin, but the bloom of youth had faded. She had that inevitable look of brittleness about her that came with thinness and advancing age.

Frowning, she tapped him on the shoulder with her small ivory and black fan. "You must hurry and change. In case you forgot, we are attending Lady Spencer's soiree tonight." Voice dripping with meaningful overtones, she continued. "Lady Camilla Harvey will be there."

Granville was suffused with instant irritation. How many times had his mother and he played out this little scene? She, bound and determined to be in command; he, once again forced to assert himself. "I am not in the least concerned whether Lady Camilla will be at Lady Spencer's tonight. And furthermore—"

"Oh, and one more thing," his mother went on as if she hadn't heard a word he'd said. "I have found a new governess for the children. She's a Scottish woman, rather on the dour side, but comes with an excellent character. I hired her this morning."

"Then unhire her."

"What?" Mama's head went back. The cords of her neck stood out and her eyes bulged. "What do you mean, unhire her?"

No wonder she looked thunderstruck, thought Granville. Since Jane died, his mother had been almost completely in charge of raising the children. His own choice, of course. Pressed by parliamentary matters, he had gladly relinquished his responsibilities. Mama had done a fine job. At this late date, he had no good reason to interfere. Still, his domineering mother's insufferable attitude annoyed him no end. She would ride roughshod over him if, now and then, he didn't let her know she could not always have her way.

"Forget the Scottish governess. I am about to hire someone else."

The words were no sooner out of Granville's mouth than he wondered whatever had possessed him. True, the thought had crossed his mind that Darwood's Miss Winthrop would make an excellent governess for his children. At the time, though, he'd no intention of pursuing the notion.

As expected, his unflappable mother concealed her anger and immediately changed course. Forcing a smile, she sweetly inquired, "Do tell me about her, John. I am all ears."

What had he gotten himself into? Now that he thought about it, the easiest course by far would be to let his mother have her way. He had chosen to take a stand, however. Honor decreed he could not back down.

"Her name is Miss Lucy Winthrop. She's Lord Darwood's governess, or was. She's quite competent, I understand."

"Was she sacked?"

"Er, I'm not sure what the circumstances were." A lie, but unavoidable.

"Have you definitely decided to hire her?" Try as she might to hide her irritation, his mother couldn't fool him. The angry glint in her eyes gave her away.

"I plan to hire her tomorrow. Good night, Mama."

"What do you mean good night?" his mother called after him as he started up the stairs. "Aren't you coming to—?"

"Lady Spencer's soiree?" Granville paused and turned. "I think not. It's been a trying day. I plan an early supper, then straight to bed."

"John, dear, I shall be *crushed* if you don't go."

It was his younger sister, Florinda. Slender, dark-haired,

with even features, she was pretty enough, but as usual, she was dressed to the nines. Overdressed in his opinion—in one of her many ball gowns, this time a white beaded lace over purple affair with towering, sequined plumes of purple in her hair. The diamonds sparkling from her neck, ears, wrist, and fingers were much too pretentious as far as he was concerned. Worst of all, the bodice of her gown was cut so low her breasts were in imminent danger of popping completely out. Not that she'd much care, he supposed. His spoiled, giddy sister did as she pleased. He had long since learned to keep his mouth shut and let Mama handle her.

Florinda feigned a pout. "What's this I hear? You're not coming with us to Lady Spencer's?"

"No, I am not."

"But you must come, you naughty boy. Dear Camilla is expecting you to propose tonight." She giggled and raised her brows. "Well, we all are."

"Not tonight, I'm tired."

"What an excuse! That is so *de trop*." She was fracturing her French as usual.

"John, you must come," his mother said, "I demand you fulfill your obligations."

"My main obligation is to myself. Now if you'll excuse me, Mama, Florinda, I'm off to bed."

His mother called after him, "John, won't you at least reconsider hiring that governess? I don't think—"

He never even paused. "I'm hiring her tomorrow," he called over his shoulder.

As he continued his ascent, Granville guiltily reflected that while he was right to defy his mother, his noble stance had just brought him a whole lot of trouble. He'd had no intention of hiring Miss Winthrop.

Now he had no choice.

Tomorrow, whether he liked it or not, he would find Miss Lucy Winthrop and offer her a position as his governess. Of course, she'd be thrilled. Doubtless she'd jump at the chance to work for the prestigious Granvilles. He might even increase her stipend. Forty-five pounds would be more appropriate than

Darwood's no doubt stingy amount. Perhaps fifty. The woman would be beside herself with joy.

Granville smiled with self-satisfaction, mightily pleased with himself. Not only had he found a competent governess for his children, he had shown his mother yet again she was not in charge.

Before retiring, Granville tapped lightly on the door of his older sister. It was his custom if the evening was not too far gone. "Regina?" he called.

Matilda, Regina's dour-faced, elderly servant, opened the door. "She's not up to having visitors. She's much too tired."

"John, is that you?" came his sister's voice. "Come in if you must."

Moving past Matilda, he paid no attention to his invalid sister's customary, acerbic reply, having learned long ago to ignore her prickly disposition. She was in her usual place on the couch, book in her hands, legs covered by a warm wool coverlet. "I cannot believe you're home," she snipped, tilting her pretty nose. "I thought you were going to attend Lady Spencer's soiree tonight. Aren't you supposed to propose to that silly, simpering Lady Camilla?"

He slung himself into a chair beside the chaise and stretched his legs comfortably, as he had done countless times before. "Changed my mind. I'm staying home tonight."

"I'd wager Mama didn't approve."

"She was a trifle miffed."

They laughed companionably, recognizing the enormity of his understatement.

He asked, "How are you feeling?" regarding his pretty, red-headed sister with concern. Regina had been sick all her life. Most of her childhood had been spent in bed, what with lung problems, her heart, and he knew not what. She'd been in bed a good part of her teen years, too, an invalid when other girls her age were experiencing all the fun and excitement of coming out. She never came out. Now, at age thirty-five, she showed no sign of improvement. She spent most of her time in her room except when one of the footmen carried her downstairs to the grand salon for special occasions.

Her green-flecked, luminous eyes lit with amusement. "The doctor has a new elixir for me. It tastes so terrible I'm quite sure if my illness doesn't kill me the elixir will."

"Don't talk that way." He knew she was joking but couldn't laugh. He didn't even want to think about losing his beloved sister. When he was younger, he never doubted that Regina would somehow recover from whatever ailed her and lead a normal life. Now that he was older, he realized how foolish he'd been. Time and again, his mother dashed his hopes.

"John, you must realize, Regina is so frail she'll always be an invalid. She is doomed, I fear, to a short life, although God knows the sacrifices I've made to care for her and prolong her stay on earth."

Mama was right in one respect. Whereas he had grown up lonely and ignored in the country, Regina had suffered the opposite fate. From early childhood she was kept in London, Mama hovering nearby, and was poked and prodded by an endless procession of doctors who bled, purged, blistered, and leeched her; forced her to swallow the most unspeakably ghastly tasting potions imaginable, all of which did not help one whit.

Regina said, "I have a question."

"Ask away."

"One of the gentlemen you brought home the other day? The tall, blond one with the broad shoulders."

"I believe you mean Viscount Kellems, the Earl of March's oldest son."

"He's rather blunt."

"That's Kellems all right. A fine fellow and a good friend of mine. Met him at White's, although he's not one to gamble. Not an intellectual but a sharp mind, nonetheless. Why do you ask?"

"He sent me a note. Said he'd like to come calling."

"Well, well, so you caught his eye. It's time you had a beau. I think you and he would hit it off just fine, considering you're as blunt and bullheaded as he is."

Regina's tinkling laughter filled the room. "I? Become involved with a man in my condition? Mama would . . ."

"Be furious?"

They both laughed again.

"Do you like him?" Granville asked.

"Oddly enough, yes. We chatted only a short time, but I found him most entertaining. He doesn't share my interest in history and the classics, or poetry, yet I found his enthusiasm for sports and the out-of-doors to be most . . . well, stimulating."

"Ah, yes, Kellems is mad for horses, hunting, fishing, that sort of thing."

"He's younger than I."

"Five years or so, but what difference does that make?"

"I don't want him thinking of me as his mother."

"Don't be ridiculous. Will you allow him to call?"

Regina shrugged in defeat. "What would be the point?"

"You could be friends, couldn't you? Just because he asked to call doesn't necessarily mean he wants to marry you. Come on, don't be so stubborn. Write the man a note. Give it a try."

"Oh, very well, as a favor to you."

"I had better let you get some rest." Granville arose and kissed his sister on the forehead. He left, but poked his head back in. "Oh, by the way, you'd be interested to know Kellems is available, not married or betrothed. He's quite a catch, considering he'll inherit his father's title and fortune one of these days."

With a devilish laugh, he ducked as a pillow hit the door. "Just joking," he called.

In the hallway, his smile swiftly faded. Never before had Regina expressed an interest in a man. Obviously she was taken with Kellems, but in her condition, what good would it do to entertain thoughts of any kind of romance? God, if only she'd get well.

Chapter Three

*N*ext morning Lucy's mood was somber as she led her five small charges from the Darwoods' London mansion in Arlington Street, down Piccadilly, and into Green Park. Poor Mrs. Emma Montgomery. Hangings took place early in the day, so she must be dead by now. Poor Augusta. How utterly selfless she was to offer to sit with the condemned woman during her final hours on earth. What an endless night it must have been.

Lucy had not forgotten Lord Darwood's obvious displeasure when he informed her he would speak to her later. So far, he had not. Of course, he'd been out all night and hadn't come home until dawn. She had heard enough of servants' gossip to know he'd been either tossing massive amounts of money away on the tables at White's or dallying with his latest mistress. Either way, despite Augusta's assurances, Lucy doubted he had forgotten.

"Daniel, wait! Don't run off into the park by yourself," Lucy called to the inquisitive youngest Darwood, who at six needed to be watched every moment. She glanced around. No one was in sight. Picking up her skirt, loosening the ribbons of her gray sarcenet bonnet so that it hung down her back, she started running. She ran to catch Daniel, of course, but he was a convenient excuse. She also ran because away from watchful eyes, her staid governess demeanor quickly slipped to reveal a lighthearted, vivacious woman hidden underneath. She was a woman who, on an average day, was happy, and though not completely content, coped without complaint with her lot in life. It was not an easy one. From seven o'clock in the morn-

ing until half past seven or eight at night her time was totally
taken up with the children. She could not lie abed later than six
in the morning. If she had anything to do for herself, such as
sewing or writing letters, she must rise even earlier. At seven
she went to the nursery to hear the children say their prayers
and assist the nursery maid, in their dressing. She remained
until after they had breakfasted when they all went out to play,
as they were doing now. Then schooling until twelve. Then on
with the hats and bonnets for play or a short walk. At one
o'clock, they all dressed for dinner, where they all sat down at
a quarter past, the children always dining with their parents, if
they were home. Then back to school to remain until five, after
which she saw the children eat their supper, played with them,
heard their prayers, saw that they were washed with the maid's
help, and at long last, put them to bed. Then she, weary from
the long day, must herself go to bed soon after.

Every day was grueling, yet she had grown accustomed to
hard work. Her happiness lay in the satisfaction she derived
from watching her five charges grow, both in mind and body.
That this was true was a tribute to her love of teaching.

Lucy's gown was plain but could not disguise her full-
bosomed, small-waisted figure nor the natural grace with
which she moved as, finally trapping Daniel, she led him back
to the path to join the other children.

Will this be the last time? she wondered as she escorted the
children back to Arlington Street. But perhaps Augusta was
right when she said Lord Darwood wouldn't dream of dismissing such a fine governess. Lucy prayed that was so.

Her hopes were dashed when the butler met her in the entryway.

"Her ladyship wishes to see you in the study, Miss
Winthrop." The butler, who had always been her friend, wore
a pained expression on his usually pleasant face.

I am doomed and done for, thought Lucy as her legs, now
suddenly trembling, took her on a shaky path to the study and
the Countess of Darwood.

"Do sit down, my dear," said the kindly, gray-haired countess as she seated herself behind her walnut writing desk.
Lucy's stomach tightened. Like the butler, the countess's ex-

pression was pained. She appeared not at all her usual easy-going self this morning but kept compressing her lips and shifting her eyes upward, as if searching for some sort of divine intervention from above.

Lucy seated herself across, mindful that her posture was correctly straight. She smoothed her skirt and rested her hands loosely on her lap. Striving to look every inch the proper governess, she was careful to conceal the pounding of her heart and her deep concern. "This is about yesterday, is it not, your ladyship?" She was never one to vacillate.

"Oh, dear." Lady Darwood compressed her lips again, looking as if she would rather be anyplace but there.

Lucy inquired, "It concerns his lordship's objection to my being related to Mrs. Augusta Winthrop-Scott, does it not?"

Inadvertently, the countess wrinkled her nose, thus revealing her distaste for her husband's many prejudices. "I'm afraid it does," she said. "You see—"

"Just tell me what his wishes are," Lucy interrupted. She could not endure the suspense.

The countess heaved a sigh, resigning herself to the uncomfortable scene that lay directly ahead. "It would appear you are Mrs. Augusta Winthrop-Scott's sister, so in my husband's eyes that makes you . . . well, guilty of all sorts of monstrous crimes."

"You don't agree with him?" This was all so unjust. Lucy could hardly squeeze out her words over the lump that had formed in her throat.

"Whether I agree or not is not the point, is it?" She shook her head in dismay. "I hate to lose you. Believe me, I pleaded mightily with his lordship. I pointed out you are by far the best governess the children ever had, that you are dedicated, loyal, honest, and I sincerely doubt I shall ever find a governess to compare with you." The countess threw out her hands. "I regret my pleadings were of no avail. His lordship wants you dismissed. He's adamant. There was nothing I could say or could ever say that would make him change his mind."

"I see," Lucy managed, trying not to show her despair. She swallowed hard and inquired, "Will I receive a character?"

"His lordship didn't say. However . . ." The countess nodded decisively. "Of course I shall give you a character. You deserve it. Also, I shall do my utmost to find you another position. Although . . ." Unexpectedly she smiled, and reached into a drawer from which she withdrew a large cloth bag. "Many times you've mentioned that someday you would like to own a school for young ladies." She shoved the bag across the desk. "Perhaps this will help." Still smiling, she settled back in her chair and waited for Lucy to open the bag.

Lucy reached for it, tugged on the drawstrings at the top, and peered inside. "Gold sovereigns!" She reached into the bag and fingered the coins. There were so many.

"Around four hundred."

"Oh, madam, this is much too generous. I cannot accept."

"Of course you can."

"But his lordship. Surely he would object—"

"You deserve every farthing," firmly replied the countess. "What his lordship doesn't know won't hurt him in the slightest. This money comes from my own private funds which he has nothing to do with. Quite frankly, he should be grateful I am not like the Duchess of Devonshire and her ilk, who choose to toss away their fortunes at the gambling tables. Nor do I squander my money on French gowns and furbelows. So if I want to make a gift to a deserving governess, especially one who has been unfairly treated, then I shall do so."

For a moment, Lucy sat dazed. Up to now, she had been resigned to the fact that years would pass before she could realize her dream of opening her own school. Of course, she saved all the money she could, but part of her stipend went to Augusta and her children, and lately, part to her brother, Montague, who seemed unable to hold any sort of position. The school seemed farther and farther away, but now, if she accepted Lady Darwood's offer . . .

And why shouldn't I? Lucy wondered. The countess wanted her to have the money, and besides, she most definitely had been treated unfairly. "If you're sure, your ladyship?"

"Quite sure."

A shadow lifted from Lucy's heart. "Then I accept with my deepest thanks."

"Wonderful." Lady Darwood breathed a sigh of relief and smiled broadly. "And where will this school be?"

Lucy instantly answered, "At first, I planned to open a school in my home village. However, I've seen there's a great need for a girls' school right here in London." Lucy pulled the drawstrings on the bag and clutched it tight. "I cannot tell you how happy I am. This money is a godsend." She allowed herself a wry smile. "Almost worth the misery I've been through since yesterday."

"Most unfair," chimed Lady Darwood. "I must remain loyal to his lordship, of course, but between you and me, I strongly support your sister's efforts to help the women at Newgate Prison."

"I am more grateful than you'll ever know, your ladyship."

"You have a place to stay?"

"My sister's house in Harford Lane." Pride prompted Lucy to add, "It's quite comfortable there." Not true, of course. Lady Darwood needn't know she would doubtless be sleeping on the sofa. Her brother, Montague, who had arrived a few weeks before for an indefinite stay, was occupying the only spare bedchamber.

Lucy said her farewells to the countess. Her feelings were mixed as she mounted the staircase to her room to pack her things. On the one hand, she was seized with a sense of outrage. After three years of giving her utmost efforts to the care of the Earl of Darwood's children, how could he have seen fit to dismiss her over a matter she could not control? Worse, the coward had not had the nerve to face her, instead leaving her dismissal in the hands of his reluctant wife. And the poor children would be forced to endure an abrupt change, too. So terribly unjust. But then, this was an unjust world. She'd learned that sad fact years ago, first, when her father died and left the family near-penniless, then when her mother died, leaving the family not only without a farthing but deep in debt.

If it hadn't been for Augusta, they'd all have ended up in the workhouse.

But on the other side of the coin . . .

Lucy's outrage was receding fast. Although she'd been relatively happy working for the Darwoods, she was only just be-

ginning to appreciate the joy of knowing she wouldn't be a
lowly governess anymore. Thanks to Lady Darwood's largess,
she would instead have the respect of the community as owner
and proprietor of *Miss Winthrop's Day School for Young
Ladies*. Or would she call it, *Miss Winthrop's Select Academy
for Young Ladies*? Oh, the delicious decisions she would have
to make! She must be careful, though. Money-wise, even com-
bining what she'd saved, plus Lady Darwood's sovereigns,
she'd barely have enough. She might have to start small, but
she *would* have her day school for young ladies.

Her spirits soared. By the time she reached her room, she
had ceased to dwell upon the humiliation of her dismissal. Instead, she rejoiced that after years of serving others, she was
about to have a life of her own.

Later that day, in Augusta's small parlor, Montague
Winthrop slouched in Augusta's best chair, his long legs
stretched before him. He looked extremely amused. "So my
saintly sister got sacked," he said. "Hard to believe. What did
you do, bed the butler? Steal the silverware?"

"Enough, you cad." Lucy, who had just finished relating to
Montague and Augusta the sad fact of her dismissal, made a
face at her handsome younger brother, welcoming a chance to
laugh. "I wouldn't talk if I were you. At least I held a position.
How many positions have *you* held lately?"

"Touché." Montague struck a hand to his heart. "Cruel girl,
you've cut me to the quick. You know how I've tried."

Augusta gave a disdainful sniff while Lucy replied good-
naturedly, "I know no such thing."

Although the family was poor, Montague, the only son, had
been pampered all his life. Mostly an indifferent scholar, he
lived at home until he was twenty when an uncle died and left
him a small inheritance. Both Lucy and Augusta pleaded with
him to invest his money wisely, not toss it away in the gambling hells of St. James and Jermyn Streets. Their advice fell
on deaf ears. Montague moved to luxurious lodgings and
began the life of a London dandy. In less than three years, he
was rolled up. Forced to give up his valet and fancy lodgings,
he moved back in with ever-generous Augusta. Since then,

he'd conducted a desultory search for, in his words, "some sort of position," but with no luck. This unfortunate turn of events was no surprise to his two older sisters. Nothing could change their enduring love for their younger brother, but charming and endearing though Montague was, they recognized he not only lacked depth of character, he also had no idea of the meaning of hard work.

Montague gave Lucy his most ingratiating smile. "Don't worry, Jermyn Street has seen the last of me."

Lucy replied, "Excuse me if I'm not totally convinced."

"No, really." Montague grew serious, a rarity for him. "You think I don't realize what a fool I've been?"

"For squandering your inheritance? I daresay the thought might have occurred to you that you'd been a tad foolish."

Lucy expected Montague to hurl back one of his customary cutting ripostes, but to her surprise he gazed at her with his soulful blue eyes—the same gaze she knew had melted many a female heart—and said, "My gambling days are behind me. I'm dead serious about seeking a position." He stood and started to pace, worriedly shaking his head. "You think I like being penniless, living off my sisters' charity?"

"You won't be living off me any longer," Lucy replied. "I've no money to spare now. You'll have to make do with just Augusta's charity for a while."

"Ah, Lu, I'm terribly sorry." Montague swiftly sat beside her and took her hand. "How could Darwood have dismissed you when you're the best governess in the world?"

Lucy smiled. She had not yet told Montague and Augusta the good part of her news. "Believe it or not, all is not lost." She went to the mahogany couch table where her reticule lay, and beside it the bag of sovereigns. She picked it up and in a sweeping gesture poured them onto the table where they lay gleaming. "See?" She gestured triumphantly at the golden heap of coins and proceeded to tell Montague and Augusta of Lady Darwood's largesse. "So you see, from disaster comes triumph. I shall have my school for young ladies after all."

"That's wonderful. I am so relieved," exclaimed Augusta. "You don't know how guilty I felt knowing you were dismissed because of me."

Montague's eyes glowed with approval. "I'm delighted, Lu. No one deserves a bit of luck more than you."

"Isn't it wonderful?" A sudden joy swept through her as the knowledge of her good fortune sank in. She clasped Montague's arms and joyously waltzed him around the room. "I'm going to have my school!"

When they stopped, Montague gave her an exuberant hug. "Have you thought of hiring me as a teacher?" he asked. "You know how good I was at numbers."

Augusta nodded affirmatively. "That's true, he was, though not much else." She cast her brother a meaningful gaze.

"I hadn't thought of it, but . . ." Lucy remembered what a terrible scholar Montague had been, yet he was right, he'd appeared to have a natural love of mathematics, and in that one subject had always excelled. "You'd do it?" she asked.

"Of course I'd do it." Montague gave her a lopsided grin. "Not only that, I shall demand but a pittance for a wage . . . at first, anyway."

"Then you are hired and my happiness is complete," Lucy said, marveling at how a day that started out so bleakly could end so well.

That afternoon, Augusta, who had always been an outstanding scholar, also agreed to teach. The two sisters were sitting in the kitchen discussing plans for the school when Nell, Augusta's one and only servant, announced a gentleman had come calling, asking for Miss Lucy Winthrop.

"Did he give you a name?" asked Lucy.

"Lord Granville, ma'am. I put 'im in the parlor."

"What on earth?" Augusta appeared flabbergasted. "Why is that man here? What gall. A woman was put to death today and all because of politicians like Lord Granville and his ilk. No doubt they all applauded Lord Sidmouth's decision not to pardon Mrs. Montgomery."

"You're right." Lucy, too, was incensed at the very thought of what had happened to the doomed woman. "As you've pointed out, Lord Granville is one of *them*. Whatever he wants, I have no desire to see the man."

"I say, send him packing."

"Absolutely. Nell, go to the parlor and tell . . ." Lucy stopped, her thoughts in disarray. *But why is he here?* called a little voice inside her head.

"Well?" Augusta asked. Judging from the eagerness in her voice, it was obvious she was keen on removing a notorious Whig from her home as quickly as possible.

For a long moment, Lucy mulled her dilemma. Augusta wanted Lord Granville gone. So did she, of course. But on the other hand . . . "Aren't you curious to know what he wants?"

"Not in the slightest." Augusta's mouth was grim.

"I grant you are right, but if I allow him to leave without speaking to him, I shall always wonder what brought him here."

Augusta threw up her hands. "I, for one, do not give a fig why he came here, but the decision is yours."

At the risk of displeasing Augusta, Lucy made her decision. She addressed Nell. "Inform Lord Granville I shall join him in a moment." She turned to her sister. "I cannot help but be enormously curious to see what the man could possibly want."

Despite her antipathy toward Lord Granville, before Lucy entered the parlor she went to a mirror and rearranged the tiny auburn curls that ringed her forehead and patted her piled-up hair. She bit her lips and pinched her cheeks to make them red. Thank goodness, she had changed from her dreary governess gown to her favorite white cotton batiste, trimmed with lace frills and pink satin ribbon bands around the hem. The gown was a hand-me-down, courtesy of Lady Darwood, but that was something he needn't know. She smoothed her skirt. Profoundly puzzled as to why a man as rich and illustrious as Lord Granville had come to Augusta's humble cottage, she went to greet her guest.

Resplendent in polished Hessian boots, beautifully tied cravat, a tan frock coat over a waistcoat and nankeen breeches, Granville sat in the faded parlor of Mrs. Augusta Winthrop-Scott. That he felt uneasy was an understatement. He recalled his conversation with Darwood this morning when he'd checked to make sure his friend had indeed dismissed his governess. He shouldn't have been surprised when Darwood con-

firmed that Miss Winthrop had been informed early that morning that her services were no longer required and she had
promptly packed her belongings and left. Still, that Darwood
could be so callous surprised him. Miss Winthrop had seemed
so . . . well, capable. Aside from Granville's desire to thwart
his mother, he found himself actually wanting to help the poor
woman.

Wanting to be sure of his facts, he had gotten Darwood to
admit Miss Winthrop was indeed a competent governess. It appeared her dreadful reformist sister was her only flaw.

And no, Darwood would not mind in the least if Granville
offered her a position.

"She'll leap at the chance to work for one of England's
greatest families," Darwood assured him. "By the way, I paid
her thirty pounds per annum."

"Not a vast amount," commented Granville. He refrained
from further comment concerning Darwood's reputation for
stinginess.

"Her wage was sufficient," answered Darwood. "I suggest
you offer her the same and not a farthing more."

"We shall see," Granville told his clutch-fisted friend. That
settled it. He would offer forty pounds at least.

"I believe she went to her sister's," continued Darwood.
"From what I understand, Mrs. Winthrop-Scott lives in some
wretched hovel in Harford Lane. My coachman knows where
she lives. If you like, I'll send for her."

"I shall visit her myself."

"You'd trouble yourself to that extent for a mere governess?" Darwood frowned with suspicion. "See here, you're
not smitten with the wench, are you? I must admit, she's quite
attractive. Matter of fact, I've been tempted a couple of times
to have a go at her myself."

"I trust you managed to control yourself," Granville told his
thick-skinned, sometimes impossible friend. "If you will simply be so kind as to supply me with her address?"

Darwood had done so. Now here Granville sat, cooling his
heels, nothing better to do than casually examine Mrs.
Winthrop-Scott's parlor. Shabby was the word that came to
mind. Rickety chairs, faded draperies and sofa, what a pity

anyone had to live this way. It was downright depressing. Well, he would conduct his business with dispatch and leave as soon as possible. He hoped she wouldn't be too overwhelmed by his offer. He had a sudden vision of Miss Lucy Winthrop, thankful tears in her eyes, gratefully murmuring her appreciation as she tried to kiss his hand. He intensely disliked that sort of thing. He hoped she would control herself.

"Lord Granville?"

Her soft, melodious voice swept over him. He stood and gazed upon her as she entered the room. She was prettier than he even remembered. The dull gray dress was gone, replaced by a gown of soft white, trimmed with lace. Her hair, previously mostly hidden under her bonnet, was now piled in soft, shiny curls atop her head and circling her face. It was a most glorious shade of auburn.

"Good afternoon, Miss Winthrop," he said with a slight bow.

She returned his greeting, dipped a curtsy, and leveled a puzzled gaze at him. "Won't you sit down? I must admit I am curious as to why you are here, sir."

As they settled into two well-worn armchairs situated on either side of the fireplace, Granville cleared his throat, searching for the correct words to say. This was, after all, a rather delicate matter. He would be compelled to allude to the fact that she had just been dismissed. She must be distraught, although she was certainly concealing it well. In fact, the young woman gave the impression of extreme serenity as she sat, posture-perfect yet seemingly relaxed, loosely resting her palms upon her lap. One would never guess she'd just been summarily dismissed.

A moment of silence went by. Her soft gray eyes examined his curiously. "Well?" she asked. He caught a barely definable caustic edge in her voice as she continued. "Surely you haven't come to our humble home simply to pay a call."

He immediately saw that honesty and straightforwardness would be best, since the woman was obviously well in control of her emotions. "I spoke to Lord Darwood this morning. He informed me that you had been . . . er—"

"Sacked," she pleasantly supplied.

"Er, yes." Amazing, how self-possessed she was, and hiding her devastation extremely well. He cleared his throat again, wondering why he was feeling so uncomfortable. He, the unflappable Lord Granville, known for his suave demeanor no matter what the situation. For some reason, this woman was throwing him off balance. Ridiculous. He could not imagine why. "As it happens, I, myself, am in need of a governess and I thought of you."

"Do tell," she remarked with barely polite interest.

He plunged ahead, feeling more insecure every moment. "I have three children whose mother unfortunately passed away five years ago. William, my son and heir, is eight. My daughter, Mary, is six, and my youngest, Winifred, is five. I must tell you, William is rather a willful child but quite bright."

She looked at him strangely. "And your daughters? Are they bright, too?"

"Very bright, the both of them," he hastened to assure her. "Their grandmother has taken charge of their education. According to her, Mary already shows great promise on the piano."

"And Winifred?"

"She's an adorable little creature. No doubt she'll set many a male heart aflutter when she's grown."

"How nice," she replied in a chilly tone. "However, I wonder what their grandmother has in mind for your daughters' academic achievements. Are they going to learn history? Foreign languages? Mathematics?"

"Er . . . I'm not sure." *Good God.* Actually he hadn't given a thought to his daughters' education. Only William's mattered, after all. This conversation was not at all going as he had planned. "Actually, since I've been quite busy . . . Parliament and all . . . I've more or less left the rearing of my children to my mother."

"I see." She was just sitting there, her face a mask.

"But they're quite pleasant, the both of them," he finished lamely. Why was he on the defensive? Along about now she should be on her knees in gratitude. But she wasn't. Ah, perhaps it was the stipend. "I will pay you fifty pounds per annum."

Not only did she not look impressed, she raised an amused eyebrow. "Did you not check with Lord Darwood first? He paid me only thirty."

He was shocked at her frankness, longed to give her his opinion of his clutch-fisted friend but refrained. Instead, irritated, he replied, "I don't necessarily follow in Lord Darwood's footsteps."

She tilted her head to one side. "Speaking of Lord Darwood, something puzzles me."

"Might I ask what?"

"Lord Darwood dismissed me because Mrs. Augusta Winthrop-Scott is my sister. You are a friend of Lord Darwood's. You are also a Whig, just as he is, and doubtless hold the same views. Why, then, do you wish to hire me?"

"Because you're an excellent governess," he promptly replied. "Darwood admitted as much. Frankly, I consider him a fool for letting you go. However, his loss is my gain, if you accept my offer, of course. I haven't the least concern about your sister."

"But what about your family?"

Mama. He could just imagine the furor she'd create if she knew about the sister, but that could all be avoided. "We shall simply keep it quiet. My family need never know you're related to Mrs. Augusta Winthrop-Scott." That should bring her around. Pleased with himself, Lord Granville gave Miss Winthrop a smile he saved for those rare occasions when he wanted to melt a woman's heart. "Will you accept?" He sat back in the shabby chair and waited for her to say yes.

"No."

Her answer jarred him so much he sat straight again. "No?" he echoed.

Lucy almost laughed aloud. *If he could see the look on his face,* she thought as she flashed her most radiant smile. "I do thank you for your kind offer, Lord Granville. However, I have other plans. Even if I didn't, I have vowed that never again will I hide my sister in the shadows. I am proud of everything she stands for. Her beliefs are my beliefs. I shall never again live in a house where my sister is reviled and ridiculed."

"I can see you mean what you say."

"I do, and will never be persuaded otherwise."

He seemed almost dazed. "So you're turning down my offer?"

"Absolutely, unequivocally, my answer is no, I do not wish to accept your offer, m'lord."

He cleared his throat. "Well, then . . ." He rose to go.

She could almost feel sorry for him, he seemed so . . . dashed, she supposed. She rose, too. At the door she said pleasantly, "I do hope you'll find a suitable governess soon, Lord Granville."

"I daresay I will," he replied, seeming to have recovered some of his composure.

What a handsome man he was, and quite charming, although from the way she'd treated him just now she knew he'd be astounded that she thought so. What would he have thought if he knew the whole time he'd been here she'd fought a mad desire to push back the errant lock of hair that fell over his forehead? That wasn't all, but she wouldn't even permit herself to recall the crazy thoughts that had run through her head.

She opened the door and spied his gleaming black coach awaiting at the curb, liveried coachman atop; four matched, spirited horses pawing the ground; elaborate Granville family crest emblazoned on the side. That it looked out of place in this shabby neighborhood was illustrated by the number of inquisitive neighbors poking heads out of windows or out on the street, all agog, gazing at the curious sight.

Just as I would be out of place in his world, she thought with a sigh, knowing she'd been absolutely right to say no.

Chapter Four

*F*ired with enthusiasm, Lucy arose early the next morning. "There's so much to think about," she said to Augusta as they settled at the kitchen table to discuss plans for the new school. "My own school at last. I still have a hard time believing it."

Practical Augusta scowled. "You know I'm happy for you, but let's not allow the euphoria of last night to cloud our vision this morning. Running a girls' school is a huge responsibility. I hope you know you're letting yourself in for years of hard work."

Lucy raised her chin. "I cannot say I shall love every minute of it, but I shall feel fulfilled, knowing I've bettered some girls' education."

"And you won't regret you rejected Lord Granville's generous offer?"

Lucy laughed aloud. "You should have seen the look on his face when I told him no. He couldn't believe anyone in their right mind would turn down his so-called splendid offer."

"Fifty pounds a year *is* a splendid offer."

Lucy nodded agreeably. "Which I would have accepted if not for Lady Darwood's generosity. But I shall have my school, so let's start planning, shall we? I don't want to waste another moment thinking of Lord Granville. We're going to need another sign under the main sign. What do you think of *Young Ladies Boarded and Educated*, and I *do* mean educated. I detest this current trend where lessons are conducted for females in the form of questions and answers."

Augusta nodded. "Especially when no explanations are either asked or given."

Lucy gave a disdainful sniff. "The theory being they can learn the answers by rote, then their poor little female brains won't get overexcited. Well, that will change. Latin, French, the arts, sciences—those are the subjects we'll teach, not watercolors and embroidering."

"Let's not forget chemistry, botany, logic, mathematics." Augusta's eyes glowed with excitement. "Our young ladies will be the best educated in all England." A thought struck her and she frowned. "Are you sure you have enough money? Exactly how many sovereigns did Lady Darwood give you?"

"She said four hundred, but I'd better count."

Lucy arose from the table and pulled her chair to a high cupboard where last night she had tucked the bag of sovereigns into the tea caddy where Augusta kept both her household money and her own savings. *How light it feels,* she thought as she brought it down. A feeling of foreboding came over her as she placed the caddy on the table. She removed the lid and peered inside. Empty. "It's gone." She felt the blood rushing from her face.

"It can't be gone." Augusta leaped to her feet and gazed into the caddy. "It's totally empty," she cried, "your sovereigns—my nest egg. Whoever could have—? Oh, no." A stunned look of horror crossed her face. "Montague."

"But it cannot be Montague," Lucy protested. "Or if it was, perhaps he simply wanted to put the money in a safer place."

"You believe that?" asked Augusta, skepticism written all over her face.

"He was utterly sincere last night, wanting to help me with my school. I could never believe he took our money."

Nell, Augusta's servant, entered the kitchen. When asked, she immediately denied any wrongdoing, distress written on her plain, honest face. " 'Twasn't me, mum, nor the children either. None of 'em could even reach that high."

Lucy said in disbelief, "I just cannot believe it was Montague."

"So do you think some thief broke in during the night?" Augusta asked bitterly. "Is there a door jimmied, a window broken? No, it was Montague. He knew the money was there. Our own brother. Oh, what a rogue he is. What a fool I've been."

"There must be some explanation," said Lucy, still reluctant to accept the truth. "I'll go see if he's here." Her numbness growing, she went to the spare bedchamber and opened the door, telling herself Montague would be snug in his bed, sleeping soundly, innocent of all wrongdoing.

The bed was empty.

Worse, it had not been slept in the night before. She returned to the kitchen where Augusta sat, head in hands. "He's not here." Over her growing dread, she added, "That was all the money I had. He knew it was for the school."

Augusta miserably shook her head. "He's a gambler, and gamblers have no shame nor honesty."

"It cannot be." But the harder Lucy tried to ignore the truth, the more it persisted. "You don't suppose he's run off with our money?"

Before she could answer, the back door swung open. There stood Montague, clothing rumpled, hair in disarray, his fair face pale and strained.

"Did you take our money?" Lucy asked without preamble.

"Where have you been all night?" demanded Augusta. "It's eight o'clock in the morning. Were you out gambling?"

Seeing the tea caddy, lid off, in the middle of the table, Montague slumped against the door frame. In a supplicating gesture, he extended his hands, palms up, toward his sisters. "I thought I was going to win."

"God in heaven," said Augusta.

"You went back to St. James's Street?" Lucy felt screams of frustration at the back of her throat.

Montague nodded dismally. "Last night, after the two of you retired, I had what seemed like a revelation. A tiny voice kept saying to me, take the money, go to Boodles, it's your lucky night. You'll double Lu's money, as well as yours, Augusta. Finally I had to give in. The voice was like a sign from above. I was positive I couldn't lose."

Montague stumbled to the table and slumped into a chair, head in hands.

"Did you lose all of Augusta's money?" Lucy asked.

His face still hidden, Montague silently nodded his head.

"And the money for my school?"

"Gone. It's all gone."

"What were you playing?" Lucy asked. As if it mattered.

"Faro." Montague looked up at his sisters with imploring eyes. "Don't you understand? I'm good at faro. Actually, I was ahead for a while. I kept telling myself I should leave, but I simply couldn't rise from my chair. It was as if some outside force was keeping me there. Part of me kept thinking, just a little longer and I'll win more. And then . . ." A sob shook him. "I am *so* sorry."

Augusta asked in a harsh, raw voice, "Do you realize you've taken my last farthing? How will I feed my children?"

"I don't know," Montague answered in utter despondency.

As she listened, Lucy grew increasingly numb. It was hard to comprehend this sudden plummet from euphoria to despair, but the cold, hard truth was dawning fast. "So you gambled all our money away."

"To the last farthing. But I didn't mean—"

"That does us no good now," Lucy cut in sharply. "How could you? Bad enough, I won't have my school, but you've taken food from the children's mouths. Did you stop to think we'll all be living on bread and potatoes? What do you plan to do about it, Montague?" Feeling herself tremble, Lucy waited for an answer, knowing full well her question was futile.

"What can I do? The money's gone. I can't get it back." Montague slammed his fist dramatically on the table. "But by God, I promise I shall never do this again."

Lucy opened her mouth to speak, intent on further chastising her brother, but changed her mind. "What's the use?" she whispered as she sank down at the table again. She felt sick. The golden dream was gone. In the space of a few minutes her promising, bright new world had shattered. She looked toward Augusta, who always remained stalwart through any adversity. Now she sat slumped and dejected in her chair. Only for a moment, though. Sitting tall again, Augusta announced, "We shall get through this, Lucy."

"How? Our money's gone."

"At the moment, I don't know how." Grimly she added, "I

know I've always been the strong one. I shall remain so. Now, though . . ." Bitterly she added, "I could take in washing, I suppose."

"That won't be necessary." Gently Lucy took her sister's hand. "You've always come through for me. Now it's my turn to come through for you. You can stop worrying. If you recall, yesterday I was offered a position."

"No." Augusta's head jerked back. "I won't have you working for that rich fool."

"He's not a fool, although I don't care for the thought of working for him any more than you do. We must be practical. I don't have time to advertise or go to an agency, I need a position immediately. Not only that, where else could I possibly find an offer to match fifty pounds?"

Augusta thoughtfully pursed her lips. "You have a point. I loathe the thought of your working for the high-and-mighty Granvilles, but we don't have much choice, do we?" A thought occurred to her and she frowned. "But will he hire you? Judging from what you told me about your conversation yesterday, you weren't exactly cordial to the man."

"Of course he'll take me," Lucy answered with a confidence she didn't feel. "I shall call on him this very day."

An hour later, having hitched horse to carriage, Lucy, with a grim grip on the reins, headed toward the Granvilles' palatial London mansion. Though her face wore a mask of serenity, her mind was in chaos. Why had she not been more cordial to Lord Granville? Although he hid his feelings well, she knew he'd been offended by her chilly indifference. Of course he *had* been arrogant, but he was born to be arrogant, as all the *ton* were, so why did she feel compelled to be so rude? Ordinarily, she was the soul of propriety and discretion, but perhaps . . . yes, it was the events of the day that had influenced her. Although the Tories were in power at the moment, the Whigs were the powerful opposition. Lord Granville was a Whig. Therefore, he was in part responsible for Mrs. Montgomery's wrongful execution. *I had every right to be angry at the man,* Lucy thought dismally. Still, she wished she'd been more discreet and not burned her bridges. Her attitude had been so disdainful she wouldn't blame him if he refused to see her. But if he did deign to see her . . .

She must force herself to be very, very humble, a state of mind that would be most difficult to maintain because there was nothing she valued more highly than her pride. How she hated the thought. *I cannot do it*, she told herself one moment, and then the next moment, *but I must*.

At Cheltham House, Sophia, Countess of Granville, dressed in a ruffled muslin morning gown, lacy white cap atop her gray head, eyed her only son with mild curiosity as, frowning, he joined her and Florinda at the breakfast table, nodding briefly. "John, you appear to be out of sorts this morning."

"Look, he's just an old, grumpy bear," gushed Florinda. "You should have come with us last night."

Granville resigned himself to being at least polite. "Did you enjoy your evening at Lady Spencer's?" he asked.

"You are so *du vieux temps* not to have been there," Florinda replied, the little sausage curls around her face bobbing with feigned reproach. "I danced every dance as did my dear friend, Lady Camilla. You'd better watch out, John, she was positively knee-deep in beaux. She has *such savoir vivre.*"

If his flighty sister with her wretched French thought she was going to make him jealous, she was whistling in the wind. Granville uttered a noncommittal "Hmm," and bent over the plate of eggs, toast, and ham the butler placed before him.

"Well?" Mama regarded him with her near-lashless eyes that were set close together and smallish against her narrow flange of cheek.

"What do you mean, well?" he asked, in no mood to talk this morning. He heartily wished his mother would keep quiet and just let him eat.

"I mean, where is the wonderful new governess you hired yesterday? Naturally I'm dying to meet her."

Hell and damnation. "There's been a change of plans."

"Oh, really?" his mother asked with exaggerated interest.

He had to force the words out. "It appears Miss Winthrop will not be coming with us after all."

"Do tell." His mother could not keep the smug satisfaction from her voice. "Might I ask why?"

"No, you might not."

Undismayed, she continued. "It only goes to show that I know best, John. You should never interfere with my plans for the children. I shall hire the Scottish woman." She added sharply, "*If* she's still available."

"Do that." John turned his attention to his meal, devoutly hoping his mother would do the same. Uninvited and unwelcome, a vision of Miss Lucy Winthrop filled his head. Despite himself, he'd been thinking about her since that galling interview yesterday wherein she'd treated him worse than she would treat a beggar on the streets. Why he still thought of her he could not imagine, but he kept seeing the beguiling way her soft red lips curled when she'd given him that churlish "no" in response to his splendidly generous offer. He kept seeing, too, the defiant spark that dwelled in those gray velvet eyes. *Most* unservantlike. Of course, a governess wasn't exactly a servant. Nor did she belong with the *ton* either but instead in that undefinable nether land between. Who cared where she belonged? At any rate, the girl did not know her place.

"I did not sleep well last night," his mother complained in the high, whiny voice she reserved for discussion of her medical disorders.

Granville considered a mumbled answer, something that would elicit no response. But on the other hand, she did look tired this morning. And it could very well be she was truly unwell. The least he could do . . .

"Why did you not sleep well, Mama? Was it your heart acting up again?"

Granville settled back in his chair, prepared for the at least ten-minute discourse that was sure to follow. As it turned out, her answer lasted fifteen benumbing minutes, during which she reviewed every ache, pain, and illness, both major and minor, she'd ever experienced.

He, having decided to indulge her, fell into his usual pattern of listening only half attentively, letting his mind wander where it wished. Problem was, despite his efforts to block it, that dreadful scene of yesterday kept running through his head.

Why could he not think of something else besides how he had been affronted by that impudent, ungrateful girl?

At last, finished with her recitation of her physical complaints, his mother announced, "Lord and Lady Damien's ball is tonight, John, and I insist you attend."

"Lady Camilla Harvey will be there, I suppose?"

"As it happens, yes," she trilled. He wished she wouldn't act coy. Such girlish behavior did not become her.

He was in no mood for games. "I note you're continuing your campaign to foist Lady Camilla upon me."

"Why, John." She clutched her heart and looked wounded. "You know my only thought is for your happiness. Lady Camilla is suitable in every way, as you very well know. Where else will you find a beautiful girl with such wealth, position, and lineage? She's the perfect mother for your children, and future children. You've only one son. What if, God forbid, something should happen to William? You know you need—"

"Yes, yes, yes." He could keep fighting his mother, but what was the point? She was right. He'd been single long enough. Obligation decreed he should marry again, and who would be more suitable than Lady Camilla? "All right, I shall go tonight."

His mother beamed. "Splendid."

He didn't think it splendid at all, but what was the use? In this particular matter, Mama was determined to win.

After breakfast, he escaped to his study with the *Morning Post*. He was still reading when, in the middle of the morning, Bosworth knocked and entered.

"A young woman to see you, sir. Didn't give me her name. I've left her standing in the entry hall."

"At this hour? Did she bring her maid?"

"If I may be perfectly frank, sir, she doesn't look as if she has a maid."

Who could it be? She could not be one of the *ton*, or Bosworth would have recognized her and directed her to the drawing room. Besides, no lady would dream of coming to call before noon, let alone unchaperoned. "Find out who it is."

When the butler returned, he said, "Miss Lucy Winthrop, sir. She said you would know why she's here."

He had to make a conscious effort not to let his mouth drop open. "Er . . . show her in."

A moment later she appeared in the study doorway. She was not dressed as she was yesterday. The fashionable white batiste that so suited her had been replaced by the governess gray. She still looked quite fetching, though, dreary gown and bonnet or no. Not that he cared if she looked fetching. He reminded himself of her previous rudeness, vowed to be barely polite, and if she showed any signs of yesterday's flippant attitude, out she'd go. "Won't you come in, Miss Winthrop," he said with near-unctuous smoothness. "I must admit, I am puzzled as to why you are here."

She entered the room, not eagerly, he noted, but with a reluctance resembling that of a prisoner being led to the gallows. She curtsied and said in a dead tone, "Good morning, Lord Granville. I have come to see you concerning the matter we discussed yesterday."

Really! Could it be she'd reconsidered accepting the position? He found such a speculation hard to believe as he gestured to the Louis XV giltwood *fauteuil* that sat directly across from his desk and politely invited her to sit down.

With dignified aplomb, she sat down stiffly, crossed her delicate ankles, and laid her small white-gloved hands neatly in her lap. He noted her face had lost its rosy glow, and her eyes no longer held yesterday's sparkle.

"Well?" he asked.

"I was wondering . . ."

He could see she was struggling to get the words out, but he wasn't inclined to help her in any way and sat in stony silence, drumming his fingertips.

She cleared her throat. "I was wondering . . . if the position of governess you offered yesterday is still open."

Aha! So she had changed her mind. For what reason, he could not fathom, but if she thought he would go easy on her, she was very much mistaken. He felt a surge of power, mixed with satisfaction, as, sounding entirely innocent, he inquired, "What do you mean, Miss Winthrop? I am thoroughly confused. Yesterday you made it clear you had no desire to be part of my household. You were adamant, as I recall, and although you were not exactly rude, I cannot say I was overwhelmed by your cordiality or, I might add, your gratefulness at my generous offer." There, that should get a rise out of her. All she did, though, was regard him solemnly with those big, resolute gray eyes.

"My circumstances have changed since yesterday," she said.

"In what way?"

"I'd . . . rather not say."

"I am indeed puzzled," he continued, still relishing the moment. "Yesterday I was, in essence, summarily dismissed. Today you expect to worm your way back into my good graces with nary an explanation? I must say, Miss Winthrop, you're asking a great deal." There. Let her grovel if she wanted the position. Come to think of it, should he now even consider giving her the position? His practical side said no, send her packing, but another part of him was relieved, if not downright delighted she had reconsidered.

She raised her chin. The small gloved hands that had rested so neatly in her lap now clutched the carved arms of the giltwood *fauteuil*. "If you must know, my financial situation has changed. Yesterday, I was planning to open a school for young ladies. I had the money, but . . . someone took it." She gulped. He could see she was on the verge of tears.

"But that's outrageous," he replied, forgetting his intended aloofness. "I am terribly sorry."

"My savings are gone, as well as my sister's." She seemed to realize she was close to falling apart and squared her shoulders. "I will tell you all the details but only if you wish."

"Er, no, that won't be necessary." He was beginning to feel like a cad for forcing her to discuss a subject that was obviously distressing. Still, there were other areas that needed discussion. "There's the matter of your sister," he ventured, noticing her ill-concealed flinch at his words. "If I recall correctly, you informed me yesterday you had vowed never again to hide your sister in the shadows. You said you would never again live in a house where your sister was reviled and ridiculed."

She studied him intently. "Would you revile and ridicule my sister?"

"Of course not, but you must understand, certain members of my family are ultra-conservative and do not hold with the revisionist views of your sister. If I did offer you the position, which, mind you, I am not saying I will, I would request you do indeed hide your sister in the shadows."

She bit her lip and visibly paled. A silence followed during which he could see she was doing battle with herself, her pride clearly struggling with her need for money. Would pride win? Doubtless she longed to fling a resounding "no" in his direction and march out of the study with her nose in the air. He must admit, he'd be sorry if she did, but would she? Or would she, out of sheer necessity, remain humble?

While he sat waiting, inadvertently his gaze fell upon the sweet swell of her bosom beneath the drab gray bodice. Out of nowhere the notion struck him that the diamond necklace Lady Camilla prized so highly would look absolutely smashing in that delicious space between Miss Lucy Winthrop's full breasts and her graceful, swanlike neck. Better, actually, than on Lady Camilla whose neck was rather short. The matching earrings, too, would look dazzling, swinging from those pearly white, perfectly shaped earlobes. Had a man ever kissed those earlobes? They cried for kissing . . .

Why is my mind wandering? he asked himself. *Now where was I?*

"I accept your conditions," she suddenly said.

"In that case, I am considering reconsidering," he announced, keeping his countenance stern.

To his immense satisfaction, she burst out, "Oh, thank you, sir," her voice catching with relief. "You won't be sorry."

"I hope not," he replied, and with those words knew he'd conceded, and whether for better or for worse he had most definitely hired Miss Lucy Winthrop. He remained stern, but the urge to make her grovel was fading fast. "I assume you can start right away."

"Immediately. Might I meet the children?"

"They're not here. Actually they seldom come to London."

"Then where are they?"

"At Penfield Manor, one of my country homes."

She slightly frowned. "Is it far? Do you see them often?"

"Not as much as I would like," he replied, feeling her silent criticism. He shouldn't have to defend himself, but he found himself adding, "Actually I'm so busy with my duties in Parliament, I haven't given much thought to how much time I spend with my children. It's not a problem, though. I have excellent servants who care for them well. Then, of course, my mother, Lady Granville, tends to their needs." *Oh, God, the Scottish woman,* he just remembered. *Mama.*

Speak of the devil. The door swung open and his mother swept in. Most annoying. She never knocked. In her mind, Cheltham House was still hers, not her son's. Until the day she died, she would come and go as she pleased.

"Oh, do pardon me, I had no idea you had company," Mama exclaimed, feigning surprise at the sight of his visitor even though Bosworth had no doubt filled her in on every minute detail. She made no attempt to leave, as politeness and good breeding would suggest, but stood there, obviously waiting to be introduced. *Damnation.* He devoutly wished he'd had the time to devise some tactful way to break the news, but too late.

"There has been a change in plans," he told his mother. He glanced toward Lucy who had politely stood, waiting to be introduced. "I would like you to meet our new governess, Miss Lucy Winthrop."

The silence following his introduction spoke volumes. Mama's mouth grew tight and grim. A muscle quivered in her jaw. Finally, glaring at Miss Winthrop, she asked, "*You* are going to be the children's new governess?"

"Yes she is," he quickly interjected.

Through gritted teeth, Lady Granville continued. "And I should now tell the Scottish woman we don't want her after all?"

His mother was never the sole of tact, but this rudeness was outrageous. He hardened his voice. "Tell the Scottish woman what you please. Miss Winthrop is the children's new governess."

"I see," Lady Granville said in the voice she usually reserved for railing at the servants. "Then—"

"You won't be sorry, your ladyship," Miss Winthrop interrupted. She dipped a curtsy and graciously continued, "I've had ten years experience as a governess. I don't look upon it as simply a position, I love to teach and find great satisfaction in shaping young minds."

Well put, thought Granville, pleased that his new governess had not taken offense but had placed herself on a more lofty plain. Still, he knew his mother would not be appeased.

Miss Winthrop smiled pleasantly. "I hope to meet the children soon."

"You'll meet them soon enough," snapped Lady Granville. With seeming relish, she continued. "And when you do, you will surely change your tune. They are quite unruly. I cannot tell you how many governesses have come and gone, some in no time at all. As a matter of fact, one stayed less than a day. Another one—"

"I am sure Miss Winthrop is not particularly interested in hearing about our past governesses," Granville interrupted.

"She'll soon find out for herself," retorted Lady Granville. She spun on her heel. Back stiff with anger, she stalked from the room.

Mama's behavior had been abominable. Granville was tempted to apologize, and he would have, only he'd been taught never to apologize to a servant. He would, however, give Miss Winthrop a chance to withdraw. "I shall be honest. My mother was . . . er, less than friendly because she favored someone else for the position. I trust in time she'll be pacified, but if you'd rather not take the position, I understand."

Not take the position? Lucy thought. How she would love not to take the position. How she would love to walk out of this palace dedicated to greed and waste without another word to the arrogant Lord Granville and his equally arrogant, as well as boorish, mother.

But could she?

She thought of Augusta's children and how they would soon have little to eat if she didn't humbly stand here, in full control of herself, and allow abuse to be heaped upon her head.

This was now her future, thanks to Montague. *I could wring his neck.* But what good would that do? Montague was Montague: weak, greedy, and he'd never change. Meanwhile, she would have to pay the price, and she would if it killed her. "Don't worry, Lord Granville. I perceived your mother was a trifle . . . shall we say, unprepared to meet me, but I have dealt with similar situations in my years as a governess. Doubtless all will work out."

"I trust you are correct," he said unconvincingly. "As for William, my mother is right, he is rather a handful. I know for a fact he has single-handedly driven off several governesses."

"He hasn't met me," Lucy said with a confident smile.

Chapter Five

*A*s the shiny black coach bearing the Granville family crest rolled up the tree-lined driveway, Lucy, alone inside, caught her breath at the first awe-inspiring glimpse of Penfield Manor, one of Lord Granville's country homes, and surely the most beautiful. She unabashedly stared out the window at vast lawns, colorful gardens, and the immense home itself, of Tudor design.

She was grateful she was alone. Both the annoying Lord Granville and his unpleasant mother had seen fit not to accompany her. Lord Granville's responsibilities in Parliament and Lady Granville's social obligations were far more important, it seemed, than escorting the new governess to Penfield Manor for her first meeting with the children. At least on their second meeting Lady Granville had remained civil. She showed little concern for the children's studies, though, other than to mention, "I trust, Miss Winthrop, that for Mary and Winifred you will give special attention to the use of globes."

"Of course, your ladyship." Silently Lucy lamented that for some strange reason, parents in the *ton* considered no well-bred girl's education complete without a full knowledge of the mysteries of the globes, both celestial and terrestrial. Well, no matter. Lucy planned a thorough education for Mary and Winifred, as well as William. It would go far beyond the superficial knowledge of the globes.

Lady Granville declared, "I shall give you complete authority to do as you think best for your charges."

"Thank you, your ladyship." Lucy tried to sound pleased. Actually, she wasn't flattered in the least that Lady Granville had displayed such trust in her. More likely, she simply didn't want to be bothered.

Despite Lucy's confidence in herself and her teaching ability, she felt a slight fluttering in her stomach at the thought of meeting Granville's children for the first time. It hadn't helped that Lady Granville had made a point of mentioning the many governesses who had come and gone. Nor had Lucy derived any comfort from Lord Granville's remarking that his son had single-handedly driven all previous governesses away.

The coach pulled to a jangling stop in front of the magnificent colonnaded entryway. Hastening down the marble steps came an elderly man in formal attire, no doubt the butler. Lucy was making ready to alight from the coach when she spied a slender boy of seven or eight speed down the steps past the butler. The coach door flung open. The boy poked his head inside. "Papa?" Seeing at once she was alone, a crestfallen look crossed his face, but only for a fleeting second. He stared at her coldly, then turned to the butler. "Look, Brooks, it's only another governess."

Lucy knew instantly this was William, Lord Granville's son. He had inherited the same dark eyes, stubborn chin, and straight, attractive nose. He even had that same unruly shock of dark hair hanging over his forehead. As further proof, his reedy voice held the same quality of arrogance she'd noticed in his father's.

The butler peered into the coach with faded, bleary eyes. He was at least seventy if he was a day, Lucy noted. Red veins bulged in his nose, leading her to wonder if he was a tippler. "You're the new governess, mum?" he inquired.

"I am indeed," she replied in her most confident voice. She smiled at the boy. "You must be William."

"'Tis Master William," the butler confirmed. He offered her a shaky hand as she stepped from the coach. Up close, she could see his face was a mass of wrinkles, and there were bags beneath his eyes. He was even older than she thought—at least seventy-five, perhaps more.

Lucy addressed the boy. "I'm delighted to meet you, William. I regret your father didn't come. I can see you're disappointed."

William stiffened with resentment. "I am no such thing. I don't in the least care what Papa does."

Lucy felt a pang of sympathy for the boy who obviously did care. "Well, I'm sure he'll be here soon."

"No he won't and you won't either." William regarded her with churlish, unconcealed resentment. "Our governesses never stay. You'll probably leave before the day is over."

Lucy answered firmly, "I shall be the judge of that. Brooks, can you see to my luggage and show me to my room? I shall want to freshen up before—" She smiled as she spied two little girls in white pinafores standing on the steps, regarding her curiously. "This must be Mary and Winifred."

They were both adorable: Mary with her pixie face, father's dark eyes, and long, dark, curly hair; round-faced little Winifred with her blond hair and blue eyes, thumb in mouth, clutching a doll. "Good afternoon, girls," she called pleasantly, "I'm Miss Winthrop, your new governess."

Mary screwed up her face with six-year-old disgust. "You won't be for long. William will see to that."

What a pity, thought Lucy. The poor child was obviously under the influence of her fractious older brother. Lucy kept her smile, climbed the steps, and bent down to face the smaller girl. "I am so pleased to meet you, Winifred." She took the little girl's hand. "We shall have great fun, you and I, as well as learn a great deal." She cast a pleasant glance at Mary, then glanced down the steps at William, who stood in a belligerent stance by the coach, fists clenched, openly scowling. "You, too, William, and you, Mary."

The ancient butler sadly shook his head. "I am reluctant to say it, Miss Winthrop, but the children's governesses come and go rather quickly around here. The way William's been acting, I doubt you'll last the week. I try, Becky tries, but there's no controlling him."

"Who is Becky?" she asked.

"The nursery maid. She takes a special interest in Master William, not like the rest of the servants who'll have nothing to do with him." His expression was one of faint amusement. "Mostly they run when they see him coming."

Unbelievable. Could it be true that between governesses,

the care of the children was left in the hands of a nursery maid
and an ancient butler who looked as if he tippled on the side?
"Don't worry, Brooks, just show me to my room." Lucy cast a
meaningful gaze at William, who stared back belligerently.
"Unlike your other, *most unfortunate* governesses, you may
rest assured I shall not be going anywhere soon."

"We'll see about that," William snapped back in the most
defiant, boorish manner he could muster.

Lucy felt sorry for the lad. What William didn't know was,
in her ten years as a governess, she had dealt with countless little lords and ladies just like him—defiant little ingrates who
believed that because of their family's exalted position they
were above obedience and good manners. Some acted like little savages because they were spoiled and pampered. Others
misbehaved because of their parents' sheer neglect. She suspected William was one of the latter. What a sad, but common
circumstance. In Lucy's opinion, one of the major tragedies of
modern England was that among the wealthy, and even the
semiwealthy, it was considered *de rigueur* for parents to ignore
their children. They were to be kept out of sight, left for nurse
maids, governesses, and tutors to raise. Lucy had just met
William, but judging from his disappointment at not seeing his
father, she would wager his atrocious behavior was a result of
neglect.

So they think they're going to get rid of me? Lucy could almost laugh. It wasn't a question of *if* their behavior would
change. She merely wondered how long it would take.

In a matter of hours, thanks to Becky, the nursery maid,
Lucy knew her assessment of William's behavior had been exactly correct.

"Master William's a 'andful," said the tiny, white-capped,
ruddy-faced maid as she helped Lucy unpack her things in the
lovely bedchamber that had been assigned. "If 'e ain't acting
all sullenlike, pouting in 'is room, then 'e's on a rampage, tear-
ing through the 'ouse like a 'urricane. 'E sits in class and re-
fuses to study. Says terrible, rude things to the governess. And
sassy! You should 'ear 'ow 'e treats the servants. I'm the only
one he'll listen to, and that's only because I've gone out of my

way to be friendly. The rest of the servants want nothing to do with 'im. Well, except old Brooks. 'E tries to help but he's old. Besides, 'e's in his cups a lot of the time." She realized what she'd said and quickly touched her finger across her lips. "Shh! No need for 'is lordship to know."

So she'd been right about the butler, Lucy thought as she glanced around her new bedchamber, delighted with the bright Axminster carpet, cherry wood furniture, damask draperies of blue. It was by far the nicest room she'd ever had. There was even a small writing desk in cedar, decorated in black and gold lacquer. Above the carved marble fireplace sat a beautiful mantle clock in bronze, ormolu, and dark red marble. She wondered who was responsible for providing such a lovely room and asked, "Becky, is this ordinarily the governess's room?"

"Not 'ardly." Becky suppressed a giggle. "This 'ere is one of the guest rooms. Her ladyship always puts the poor governesses in a tiny room next to the nursery. 'Twas Lord Granville 'imself sent word to Brooks to put you 'ere."

Really. There was a surprise. Judging from his lordship's less than cordial attitude last they met, Lucy would have guessed he'd assign her to the darkest, smallest room in the farthest corner of the attic.

"You must'a made quite an impression on him." Becky giggled again. "All the governesses Lady Granville hires are plain, some of 'em downright ugly, but you? Oh, la! You're a pretty one. I'd wager 'er ladyship didn't approve."

Lucy had learned long ago never to complain about her employer or engage in gossip with the help. "Approve or not, my main concern now is the children," she replied, leading the subject to safer ground. "Can I count on your help, Becky? I shall need advice on how to handle them, especially William."

"I'll do me best," Becky promised, "but mark my words, the young master's 'opeless. You'll *never* get 'im to behave."

As the weeks passed, Lucy often remembered Becky's words. There were times when she feared Becky was right: William was indeed " 'opeless." At first, he refused to take his meals with Lucy and his sisters in the cozy nursery next to the classroom on the fourth floor. "When I'm hungry I just go get something from Cook," he proclaimed.

To Lucy's dismay, she discovered he was right, and that Mrs. Wenders, the good-natured cook, would indeed supply him with food whenever he came to the kitchen and begged. "I know it isn't healthy," Mrs. Wenders told Lucy. "The child never bothers with anything hot. He takes mostly bread, cheese, and cold chicken legs." Where he took the food, she didn't know, except it most certainly wasn't properly eaten at the table.

"I would prefer that from now on he take his meals with his sisters and me," Lucy tactfully informed Mrs. Wenders. "So next time will you please tell him no?"

The cook complied. William sulked in his room for a whole day and went hungry, of his volition. Finally that night, when the enticing smell of roast beef wafted under his door, he surrendered and took his place at the table in the nursery.

"All right, I'll eat here, but you cannot make me study." His jaw jutted firmly.

"Really, William?" Lucy calmly replied. "Does this mean you wish to remain ignorant all your life?"

"May I remind you I'm the son and heir?" William tilted his nose haughtily high. "Someday I'll have the title and the money and it won't bloody matter if I'm ignorant or not. So why should I learn anything?" A defiant smile curved his lips. "I consider studying a complete waste of time."

"What a pity," Lucy equitably replied, choosing to ignore the boy's blatant use of a forbidden word. "And here I planned to start lessons tomorrow for all three of you."

"Not me." William set his firm little chin defiantly. "I shall go fishing tomorrow."

Winifred suddenly started to cry.

"What's wrong?" Lucy asked.

"Don't want William beat with the strap again," the little girl answered through her tears.

With careful questioning, Lucy soon ascertained that a leather strap hung in the classroom and that preceding governesses had put it to liberal use on William.

Lucy comforted the little girl, using her handkerchief to dab away the tears. "The strap will go." She concealed her anger. Even though her past employers had recommended beatings as an appropriate form of punishment, she considered the infliction of pain on children barbaric and had never so much as raised a hand to any of her charges. "You'll never see the strap again, not as long as I'm here."

"Then how will you punish William?" asked Winifred, her innocent blue eyes wide.

"You can't make me mind," William said with scorn. "I don't care what you do."

Lucy made a show of shrugging casually. "The choice is yours, William. I cannot force education down your throat. It appears I shall be concentrating my efforts on Mary and Winifred. It's a pity you'll be left behind."

"Why should you bother with Mary and Winifred?" asked William. "They're only girls."

"Girls need education, too." Lucy recognized that now was not the time to plunge into a detailed discussion of Mary Wollstonecraft's *Vindication of the Rights of Women*, although it most definitely would be included in later curriculum. "They'll be learning much more than watercolors and piano. I plan to teach them history, languages, mathematics, astronomy. By the time they're grown they'll be able to hold their own in the most brilliant company."

"I don't care." William was parroting his favorite phrase, only this time he didn't sound quite so sure.

Lucy felt a pang of anxiety for the troubled child. It was easy to see that beneath all the resentment and rebelliousness, a sensitive, motherless boy cried for attention from his father. What was wrong with Lord Granville? Why must he spend all his time in London when he was sorely needed here? Could the proceedings in Parliament be that important?

As the weeks went by, sometimes at night, when she'd fallen into bed after a hard day's work and couldn't sleep, she would stare into the darkness and think of Lord Granville. He ought to have traveled to Penfield Manor long before now. She wanted him to come, strictly for William's benefit, of course, although . . .

Many a night, despite herself, she felt a yearning deep

within her when she remembered the first time she'd ever seen him, that day in front of Westminster Palace, when he'd looked so devilishly handsome with those piercing dark eyes and that confident set of his broad shoulders. And his walk: so effortlessly graceful, proclaiming to the world how utterly sure of himself he was.

Those nights she would tell herself, such nonsense. Lord Granville was everything she despised in a man, and yet . . .

There were times when she wrapped her arms around her pillow that it wasn't a pillow at all but that impossible man, his arms around her, lips pressed hot against hers. Those were the times she had to remind herself what an absolute fool she was for even thinking that a lowly governess could capture the love of one of the most powerful men in England.

Gradually, as the days went by, William's attitude changed, due mostly to Lucy's infinite patience in talking reasonably to the boy, never raising her voice, and most certainly never using the strap, which had been banished from the classroom the first day. Instead of spending his time acting out his resentment, William began to listen, and to learn. Lucy grasped the opportunity with hidden glee. The girls were still too young to appreciate the delicate nuances of the issues before Parliament, but she made a point of ensuring that William was conversant with the struggles over Catholic emancipation, penal reform, votes for all, slavery, and other issues.

"Imagine, William, how pleased your father will be when he discovers how much you know about the issues of the day."

"I couldn't care in the least."

Oh, but he did care, and Lucy was delighted that like a sponge, William's sharp young mind was beginning to absorb her teachings. He showed an interest in all subjects, including natural history as demonstrated by his ever-changing collection of mice, lizards, tortoises, snakes, toads, and frogs.

Most of all, though, his keen inquisitiveness was directed toward the field of politics—anything that might involve his father. Although he never mentioned Lord Granville, Lucy was sure he planned to dazzle his father with his knowledge of the doings of Parliament.

If he ever saw his father.

Three months passed. During that time, the children had not received one single word from either their father or grandmother in London. Let alone a visit. *Disgusting man*, Lucy railed to herself, how could he treat his own son that way, let alone his daughters?

Finally one sunny September morning the Granvilles' crested coach came rumbling up the driveway, bearing none other than Lady Granville and her daughters, Ladies Regina and Florinda. Following behind, a commonplace coach carried several servants from the London mansion including Mrs. Berenson, the highly respected housekeeper. Via the servants' gossip, the reason for the visit spread like the wind throughout the house.

"Next weekend there's going to be a 'ouse party," said Becky, her face a dark cloud. "As if I didn't 'ave enough to do. Now me legs'll be killing me from 'auling 'ot water up the stairs for all the snobs."

"Lord Granville will be here?" Lucy asked.

Becky sniffed. "You think 'is mother would give a party without her precious son?"

He's coming. A hot joy filled Lucy's heart. She was shocked at herself. This was not at all the kind of joy she should properly be feeling because poor little William would be seeing his father again. This was a purely lustful joy, brought on by . . . she could hardly put the thought to words, even to herself . . . These past weeks, in the cold morning light, she had tried even harder to ignore those heated middle-of-the-night fantasies she'd had of Lord Granville holding her in his arms, telling herself she could not possibly be attracted to such an arrogant man. Now she recognized she'd been fooling herself. What folly to think she'd only wanted him here because of William. She'd wanted him for herself. Her heart lurched at the thought of seeing him again. Just to gaze upon him once more, that's all she wanted—that's all she could ever have, but it would be enough.

Becky leaned confidentially toward Lucy. "I got this straight from Mrs. Berenson, the London 'ousekeeper. Lady

Camilla Harvey will be coming and guess what? She's about to get 'erself betrothed to Lord Granville, if she ain't already."

Lucy's spirits plunged. "How nice," she managed, feeling even more idiotic. How everyone would laugh if they knew the dull, mousey governess, resigned to her lot in life, hid fiery dreams of a man so far out of her reach she may as well be crying for the moon.

"'Er ladyship thinks it's nice all right," replied Becky. "She's jumping for joy. Like usual, she got her way. Well, not entirely." A wicked giggle escaped her lips. "Mrs. Berenson tells me Lady Regina has 'erself a gentleman caller, Lord Kellems, and 'er ladyship is fit to be tied."

"But that's good news, is it not?" Lucy asked. "I have heard she's an invalid and leads rather a constricted life. Surely her mother would be happy if she's found a suitor."

"Not likely." Becky snorted with derision. "Lord Kellems is a fine gentleman, nothing to complain about there. From what I hear, Lady Regina likes 'im real well, but Mama throws a fit each time 'e comes to call." She leaned forward confidentially. "If you ask me, 'er ladyship don't want Lady Regina to have any friends. Keeps her daughter completely dependent on 'er, if you get my meaning."

Not wanting to sink into gossip, Lucy said no more. She had not yet met Lady Regina, had caught only a quick glimpse of her when she arrived and was carried to her room. She felt a pang of sympathy, though, for a woman who was all of thirty-five years old yet still living under her domineering mother's thumb.

Chapter Six

*H*ow interesting, Lucy noted, that the arrival of the demanding Lady Granville changed the slow, near-somnolent pace of country living into one of bustling activity. Before she even saw her grandchildren, her ladyship swept through the mansion, declared it filthy beyond belief, ordered a thorough cleaning, warned the servants that every detail of preparation for the coming festive weekend must be aimed at perfection. Finally in the late afternoon, Lucy received orders from her ladyship that she and the children were to present themselves for tea in the drawing room.

Greatly relieved, Lucy was delighted that at last she could report the children's progress. She was proud of all three, but especially William, who had come such a long way, in both his behavior and his scholarly achievements.

With Becky's help, Lucy saw to it that the children were well scrubbed, dressed in their best, and given a quick review of good manners. She watched with pride when, after arriving in the drawing room, the girls, dressed in starched white muslin dresses, dipped flawless curtsies, and William, all correct formality, bowed to his grandmother and said in a properly respectful tone, "Good afternoon, Grandmama, I trust you are well."

"I am never well, William," Lady Granville ungraciously replied. Dressed in black, she gave the appearance of someone quite unwell with her thin, bony figure and pinched, pale face. She glanced toward the settee where her older daughter half lay, covered by a light coverlet. "Nor is your aunt Regina."

Lucy curtsied. "Good afternoon, your ladyship, Lady Regina."

Lady Granville frowned. "I see you are still with us, Miss Winthrop. I should have thought you'd have left us long ere now."

Lucy ventured a slight smile. "I haven't given a thought to leaving." She cast a warm glance at the children. "I am most pleased with their deportment, as well as their academic achievements."

"William as well?" Lady Granville made no effort to keep a certain sneering skepticism from her voice.

"William as well. And if you'll permit, I should like to tell you—"

"You have no doubt heard we are having a number of guests for the weekend?" asked Lady Granville with obvious impatience.

"Yes, indeed, and I—"

"Very important people will be here, Miss Winthrop. Lord Morpeth for one, as well as Lord and Lady Holland, Lord and Lady Fitzwilliam, Lord Crewe—"

"Do not forget Lord Kellems is coming," Lady Regina interrupted from the settee.

Her ladyship frowned in exasperation. "Er, yes, of course. At any rate, Miss Winthrop, the guest list also includes—"

"Mama, that's quite enough," Lady Regina tartly interrupted again. "I am sure our governess is quite properly impressed, are you not, Miss Winthrop?"

"Quite properly." Lucy was at a loss what else to say to this rather blunt young woman.

"Too bad Prinny isn't coming," Regina continued with thinly veiled contempt. "Mama and my sister would shout it from the rooftops. Oh, what a coup. We'd be the talk of the *ton*, and a cut above the rest, which is what it's all about, isn't it, Mama?"

"Regina, that is quite enough," chastised her mother, at least having the grace to look uncomfortable. "You must forgive my daughter, Miss Winthrop. She is not at all well and tends to overstate matters at times." She eyed Regina. "Time for your tonic." She arose and headed for the bellpull, addressing Lucy. "So you can see how busy I shall be this week preparing for our guests. Actually, I summoned you here particularly to tell you to keep the children out of sight. You're familiar with the saying, children are to be seen and not heard? I want them neither seen nor heard, is that clear? I shall try to fit in some time for them each day when we take tea. Otherwise, they are to be, in essence, invisible." As an afterthought, she added, "And when Lord Granville arrives, he's not to be bothered. We have a busy weekend ahead. Keep the children entirely away from him unless summoned."

"Of course, your ladyship," Lucy answered with a sinking heart.

William asked, "But when will I see Papa?"

"He has much to do this weekend." Lady Granville's countenance suddenly lit, as if she'd been gifted with the crown jewels. "Your father is arriving sometime Friday, accompanied by Lady Camilla and her mother. I've rung for tea." She returned from the bellpull and bent confidentially toward William, as if imparting a delicious secret. "You have never met Lady Camilla, but high time you did. She's going to be your new mother." Lucy detected a derisive sniff from the direction of the settee where Regina lay, but Lady Granville chose to ignore it. "When you meet her, you and your sisters must be on your best behavior. Can you do that?"

When the children all nodded, she continued. "Well, sit down and we shall take our tea." She patted the cushion beside her. "Sit here, Winifred. Mary and William, sit on the settee across. Miss Winthrop, take that chair and tell me, not in any great detail, if you please, about the children's progress."

Lucy seated herself, mindful to keep her poise and not reveal that she was flabbergasted. How could this woman be so utterly unmindful of the children's feelings? To throw the earth-shaking news they would have a new mother into the middle of an ordinary conversation was unconscionable. William looked stricken, Winifred bewildered, Mary as if she was about to cry.

"Is it really true, Mama?" asked Regina as the butler and maid arrived with an elaborate tea. She had pulled herself straight on the settee. "I was not aware my brother had proposed."

"Merely a formality." With a Cheshire-cat grin, Lady Granville reached for the silver teapot. "The betrothal will take place this weekend. Winifred, you must take lots of milk with your tea . . . William . . . William? Whatever is wrong?"

The boy slid from his seat and stood, fists clenched, eyes blazing. "Nothing's wrong," he yelled. "My father isn't going to marry anybody." Without another word, he raced from the room.

Lucy started to rise from her chair, anxious to follow the poor child and comfort him.

"Stay where you are, Miss Winthrop," Lady Granville commanded. "William will soon get over his little snit. He must be punished for his rudeness, of course. See that he's sent to the attic without his supper tonight."

The very last thing William needed. Lucy quickly replied, "If you will permit me to offer an opinion, your ladyship, William doesn't need punishment as much as he needs time with his father. You see, he—"

"The attic. No supper."

Lady Granville's brusque words were so imperious, so uncompromising, that Lucy knew further argument would be a waste of time. She quickly decided not to say another word concerning William's punishment. Instead, she spent the rest of the time answering perfunctory questions concerning the classroom from a largely disinterested Lady Granville.

She sensed her ladyship's relief when tea was over and governess and children could safely be dispatched back to the distant fourth-floor environs of the house.

"William," Lucy whispered, "are you awake?" Napkin-covered plate in hand, she swung open the door to the remote attic room and stepped inside.

"Miss Winthrop?" came a small, miserable voice.

Only moonlight lit the small room. A narrow bed stood in the corner. She could barely make out William, huddled beneath the covers.

"Are you all right, William?"

"I'm hungry."

"Well, we shall take care of that."

Her heart pounding with unease, Lucy carefully made her way across the darkened room, knowing full well what the consequences would be if she was caught. She could not stay away, though. The thought of this thin little boy going without his supper was enough to make her take the chance. She reached the bed and sat on the side. "There's cheese, bread, an apple, and a chicken leg."

"Thank you, Miss Winthrop." William sat up with alacrity, took the plate, and began wolfing down the food. "I was so hungry."

Lucy watched in silence. When he finished, she said, "You were extremely rude to your grandmother. Just because I brought you food does not mean I condone your behavior."

"Papa is *not* going to get married," William answered fiercely. "He would have told me——" A choking sob halted the boy's next words.

Lucy put a comforting arm around him as he fought back tears. "Your father's been very busy. I'm sure he'll explain everything when he arrives this weekend. But you must understand, it's only natural he would wish to marry again. Even if he does, though, that doesn't mean he will love you one bit less."

William buried his head against her shoulder. "He doesn't love me at all," came his muffled voice. "Now he'll have other sons and he'll forget all about me."

"Oh, William, that's not true. He loves you very much, and don't forget *you* are the heir apparent, and that will never change. It's just . . . he's busy in Parliament, you see. I wager this weekend he's going to spend lots of time with you, and he's going to explain that just because he's getting married again doesn't mean he plans to ignore you and the girls. Look at the bright side. You're getting a new mother, and I'm sure she's . . . very nice."

William tipped his head back to look at her. "How do you know that?" Even in the moonlight she could see the tears glistening on his cheeks.

"Because if your father chose her, how could she not be

nice?" What convoluted reasoning was that? she asked herself. She had no idea why Lord Granville would want to marry Lady Camilla. Was it for love? She was supposed to be quite pretty. Or greed? Becky had mentioned Lady Camilla's considerable dowry. Or perhaps he was simply bending to his mother's wishes. If that was true, Lucy could no longer respect him. A man who could not stand up to his mother lost considerable stature in her eyes. She had thought he was his own man, but how did she know? *You don't know him at all.* Just because she held an insane attraction for the man, did not mean he was a saint. Far from it. Aside from the possibility he was a mama's boy, he could be the most selfish man on earth, not caring a fig for the well-being of his children.

I just don't know.

The one thing she knew for certain was, when Lord Granville came to visit this weekend, she would do everything within her power to see he spent time with his loving daughters and his troubled son.

A noise at the door made her gasp and clutch at her heart. Someone was entering the room. Fearsome thoughts flashed through her mind. She'd be caught, sacked, sent back to London in disgrace by morning's first light.

"William?" came a vaguely familiar voice.

"Aunt Regina!"

She stood in a patch of moonlight, her right hand resting on a cane, in her left hand—a plate. "Are you hungry, William?" she asked. Suddenly she spied Lucy and gasped. "Good grief. You startled me."

Lucy quickly gathered her thoughts. "Good evening, Lady Regina. I, too, did not want William to go hungry."

"Then it appears we are here for the same purpose." Regina stepped to the bed. "Well, William, I suppose you're not starving after all."

"Yes I am too." William quickly took the plate.

Regina laughed and ruffled William's hair. "You little pig," she said fondly. "Well, eat hearty. There's bread, ham, cake, and all sorts of good things." She addressed Lucy. "I trust this will be our little secret?"

"Of course."

Leaning heavily on her cane Regina made her way to the door. "My mother means well, you understand. However, her ideas on the subject of punishment are not mine."

"I most certainly concur. Good night, Lady Regina."

What a surprise, Lucy thought as she made her way down the dim staircase back to her bedchamber. She had just witnessed a perfect example of why it was foolish to make swift judgments. Without realizing, she had assumed Lady Regina was as rigid and uncharitable as her mother, as well as bitter and acid-tongued. Instead, risking her mother's ire, she had demonstrated love and compassion by sneaking food to William.

Lucy decided she liked Lady Regina after all.

"La," exclaimed Becky, "'ow splendidly handsome he is, 'ow dashing." She, Lucy, and the children were peering through one of the fourth-story windows that overlooked the portico and had just viewed the bustling arrival of the crested black coach from London that bore Lord Granville, Lady Camilla Harvey, and her mother.

"Mmm," came Lucy's noncommittal answer, although she heartily agreed. Lord Granville had just alighted. She couldn't keep her eyes off him, he looked so elegant in his woolen waistcoat, loosely tied cravat, nankeen breeches, leather Hessian boots, and kid gloves.

Carrying a walking stick and top hat, his demeanor was a study of grace and elegance as he turned and extended his hand to someone inside. Lucy caught her first glimpse of Lady Camilla as her blond head, bedecked in a blue, silk-covered bonnet with an ostrich plume and bow tie, poked through the doorway. Carefully she peered around. Taking her time, with queenlike poise, she took Lord Granville's hand and stepped from the coach. How beautiful she was in her simple, long-sleeved traveling gown of blue, her lovely blond curls poking from beneath her bonnet. Without thinking, Lucy looked down at her plain gray gown and fingered one of the few curls that poked beneath her simple cap. She caught herself and wondered, why was she even comparing her plain, ordinary self to the beautiful Lady Camilla? How ludicrous. She must remember her place.

"When can we go see Papa?" asked William.

"When we are invited."

Lucy made a point to smile, concealing her irritation that Lady Granville had ordered the children not to "come rushing down the stairs" when their father arrived but wait to be summoned, possibly at teatime. "But possibly not. The ball is tonight, and we are all quite busy."

As expected, William looked crestfallen. The children were only halfway through their lessons for the day, but after all, Lucy reasoned, because of the party it was a special day and they needed a distraction. "Come, children, let us return to the classroom and while we're waiting, I shall read you the story of . . . let's see—"

"Aladdin and his magical lamp," chirped Winifred. The story was her favorite that she never tired of hearing, even though she'd heard it dozens of times before.

William made a face. "Aladdin's for babies."

"And big children, too." Lucy led them back to the classroom, pulled a large volume titled in gold, *Arabian Nights*, from a shelf, and after the children settled in their seats again, started to read the story of Aladdin, the lazy son of a poor tailor. Once again she related the tale of how, after his father's death, Aladdin met a magician who posed as his uncle and persuaded Aladdin to retrieve a wonderful lamp from a hidden cave. When Aladdin failed to give the lamp to the magician before emerging from the cave, the magician became enraged and sealed the cave.

"Is Aladdin going to die?" asked round-eyed Winifred who knew full well that he would not.

"No, Aladdin's not going to die." Lucy noticed that despite his protests, William was engrossed in the story, too. She read on, telling how, in his misery, Aladdin wept and wrung his hands, thus releasing a genie from a ring given him by the magician. The genie freed Aladdin. Once out of the cave Aladdin discovered the lamp, like the ring, held magical powers. When he rubbed it, a genie appeared and granted him his every wish.

Because of the lamp, Aladdin eventually became immensely wealthy and married the daughter of the sultan.

"He could have anything he wished for?" asked Winifred. This was the part of the story she liked best.

"Anything."

"Then I wish I could have my own magic lamp," she cried with five-year-old excitement. "If I did, I should ask the genie for all the ginger cake and peppermint drops I could eat every day."

Mary spoke up. "I would ask the genie to let me stay up every night as late as I wished."

"And you, William?" Lucy asked, hoping to distract the boy.

A look of sadness covered William's face. "The genie cannot give me what I want."

Such a poignant answer from so young a child left Lucy speechless. She would no longer pretend that everything was fine when it was not. What was the point? William was too wise to believe her.

William's face grew even sadder as the afternoon progressed and they were not summoned. Finally, when Lucy and the children were having supper in the nursery next to the classroom, the door burst open and Lord Granville appeared, accompanied by Lady Camilla. They were an overwhelming presence and seemed strangely out of place as they stepped into the nursery crowded with dolls and dolls' houses, rocking horses and hobby horses, guns, tops, and toy soldiers. *They belong in a glittering ballroom*, Lucy thought: he, dashing in his formal evening attire; she, beautiful in a ball gown of white Italian crepe, trimmed with silver and bandeaux of lace. She carried a huge plumed fan of deep purple. A stunning diamond necklace glittered around her neck. Up close, Lucy saw that she was indeed beautiful, with her heart-shaped face, blue eyes, cupid bow lips, and slender figure.

"Papa," cried the two little girls. Quickly they slid from their chairs and ran to throw themselves in his arms.

Smiling, Lord Granville knelt to receive them. "Mary . . . Winifred, I swear you've both grown a foot since last I saw you, and you're as pretty as ever." After he gave his daughters a hug, he looked toward William who sat rigid at the table. "Well, William? Are you going to sit there or are you going to come hug your father?"

With seeming reluctance, William slowly slid from his chair, approached his father, and extended his hand. "Good evening, sir." He used the same voice he would use in addressing a stranger.

"William!" Lord Granville swept his son into his arms. Over the top of his son's head he locked gazes with Lucy. "Miss Winthrop," he said, smiling broadly, "I understand the children are doing quite well."

Lucy felt a warm glow flow through her. It was going to be all right. Lord Granville was not going to neglect his children. "I'm delighted to see you, sir."

Lord Granville proceeded to introduce Lucy and the children to Lady Camilla, whose greeting, Lucy noted, was not especially warm. Interesting that Lord Granville had introduced Lady Camilla as "his friend," not mentioning she was to be his future bride and mother of his children.

For a minute or two they chatted, the children excitedly chiming in as Lucy described their progress in the classroom.

"Do you teach them French?" asked Lady Camilla in a tone that Lucy found more challenging than warm and friendly.

"We speak French at teatime exclusively. Even Winifred, young as she is, is becoming quite fluent."

"Good." Lady Camilla raised her plumed fan and languidly began to fan herself. "There is nothing so inferior as a gentlewoman who has no French. And do you make use of globes?"

Lucy smoothly answered, "Both celestial and terrestrial," again wondering why there had to be such an emphasis on the learning of the globes for young ladies. But then, Lucy easily perceived from Lady Camilla's disinterested demeanor that her questions were just for show. Plain to see that underneath, she was not a whit interested in the children or their education. Lucy was about to relate in fond detail William's interest in natural history when Lady Camilla spoke again.

"We really must attend to your guests, m'lord. Everyone's waiting."

"Er . . . yes, of course," Lord Granville replied. "Time for us to go, children. Dinner awaits, and then the ball."

"When will you be back?" asked William.

"Not tonight I'm afraid, but tomorrow—"

"Don't forget we are all going riding in the morning," Lady Camilla reminded Granville. "And then we promised we'd go visiting. Then lunch, and after that, we shall be getting ready for our dinner party tomorrow night. Then early Sunday, we must get back to London." She smiled sweetly at the children. "It seems your father won't have any time at all, but perhaps next time." She looked toward Lord Granville for confirmation. "Is that not so, m'lord?"

"I'm afraid it is," Lord Granville answered. "It's a busy weekend. It appears we may have to wait until next time, children."

Lucy did not have to look at William to know how devastated he must be at his father's callous disregard. She swallowed hard, trying to check her emotions, but raw anger lashed through her. *You must stay in control,* she told herself. The man was her employer. His wish was her command, no matter how thoughtlessly he treated his children. She would be a fool to offer her opinion and most certainly would be immediately sacked if she did.

You must keep silent.

She could not. Reason and self-preservation were beyond her. She knew she must speak her mind no matter how devastating the consequences. "I must speak to you, Lord Granville."

Lord Granville and Lady Camilla exchanged glances. "Your guests await," Lady Camilla reminded him.

"Can it not wait?" he asked.

"No, it cannot." Lucy nodded toward the door that led to the classroom. "It will only take a moment. It's urgent I speak to you alone."

Lady Camilla appeared to bristle, but before she could speak, Lord Granville raised his hand. "Lady Camilla, will you go downstairs and tell the guests I shall be down directly?" He turned to Lucy. "Very well, Miss Winthrop, let us go to the classroom."

Lucy caught a quick glimpse of Lady Camilla's frown of exasperation before she led Lord Granville into the classroom and firmly closed the door.

"Well?" His hands were on his hips. Annoyance was written all over him.

Looking up at him, she felt uncertain and had to clear her throat. As she did so, she thought of William and anger stirred within her again. "I am concerned about William."

"In what way?"

She knew complete honesty was best so she plunged ahead. "You hardly ever see the child. He misses you dreadfully. He was so excited you were coming this weekend, but now, as it turns out, you're too busy to spend any time with him." She had tried to keep her voice firmly under control, not allow herself an accusatory tone, but she knew she hadn't quite succeeded.

"I lead a busy life." He didn't appear angry, nor did he look at all pleased.

"I'm sure you do, sir, but surely not so busy you couldn't arrange to spend some time with your son." She knew how blunt that sounded, but she didn't care.

He paced to the window and glanced out a few moments as if to collect his thoughts. Finally he turned. "You are the first governess ever to criticize me."

"I am not criticizing, I am only—"

"Ha!" His hands went to his hips again and he glared at her from across the room. "Why are you deviling me like this? You are indeed criticizing. I'll have you know, I have always hired the most competent of servants to look after my children." His lip curled into an ironic smile. "That includes you, Miss Winthrop."

She had no interest in flattery. "It's not a matter of hiring good servants," she sharply replied. "Can't you see, the best servants in the world cannot take the place of a parent. William needs to spend more time with you. He needs to visit you in London, instead of being cooped up here almost like a prisoner with no one to talk to but his sisters and the servants."

Granville paced back across the room again and stared down at her. "Let me tell you about parents." He spoke softly, but there was a silken thread of mockery in his voice. "I, too, was raised here in Penfield Manor, just like William. I grew up totally alone, with no companions except the servants. What affection I received came from the housekeeper who died when I was seven. I never went anywhere—never saw my parents for months at a time. Training was by way of punishment. Many's the time I was sent to bed for the rest of the day without my dinner, or I was whipped for the slightest infraction, or my ears were boxed, or I was dosed with bitter rhubarb powder put in my milk. I could go on and on—"

"You need not," she interrupted. "I can see you had a dreadful childhood."

"I don't want your sympathy. What I'm telling you is—"

"That you suffered, therefore William should suffer?" She knew, before the words left her mouth, that she had stepped far beyond the boundaries of proper behavior for a governess. It didn't matter. Let him sack her. Her blood was boiling and for once she would speak her mind.

He was infuriated. She could tell from the way the corner of his eye twitched and from a certain grim, white tightness that had appeared around his mouth. Pronouncing each word with exaggerated clarity, he said, "In no way is William having the childhood I had."

"Really?" She jammed her hand to her hip. "I grant you, he's not been dosed with bitter rhubarb powder, not that I know of anyway, but otherwise, the child is lonely and miserable. In fact, I would wager as miserable as you were on your worst day."

What are you doing? inquired the little voice within her, all aghast. She ignored it, finding herself as angry with Granville as he was with her. Angry not only about William, but other things, too, such as the impure thoughts of him that tormented her in the wee small hours, depriving her of sleep. Now, despite herself, she found his presence most troublesome, not only because of William, but because even in her rage she was acutely aware she was alone with, and only inches from, the only man in her life who had stoked a growing fire within her, a fire that, until she'd met him, she had been able to ignore.

She felt his icy stare. "You have no idea what the worst day

of my life was all about, Miss Winthrop." His voice was cold
and exact as he added, "This conversation is closed."

Reality struck. A flood of regrets assailed her. Not only had
she failed William, she had lost her position. No doubt his next
words would be, *Pack and leave immediately, Miss Winthrop,
you are dismissed.* Well, she would save a bit of her pride, if
that was possible. "I think it best I find another position."

He had been glaring down at her, but all at once a quizzical
look crossed his face. "Why do that? Doesn't William need
you?"

"Yes, of course, but I would have thought that under the circumstances you would want to be rid of me."

"Nonsense." He, too, was calming down and actually
smiled. "I don't want you to go. You're doing an excellent job.
I see no problem"—his mouth twisted with irony—"that is, if
we stay off the subject just discussed."

He was so close. Her own anger evaporated as she felt the
taut pull of him. She could almost taste the heady, tantalizing
musky-almond scent of his *eau de cologne* as it wafted beneath
her nose. Their eyes met. For the briefest of moments a silent
but intense awareness of mutual desire passed between them.
She felt a sudden urge to step forward, knowing if she did, his
arms would wrap around her and pull her tight against his
broad, muscled chest. The moment swiftly passed. Next he
was looking away and in a near-disinterested voice asking, "So
will you stay, Miss Winthrop?"

I belong in Bedlam, she thought as she steadied herself and
took a gulp of fresh air. Surely the scene that had just tran-
spired was a figment of her imagination. What folly to think
the lofty Lord Granville could have the slightest interest in a
mere governess. But aside from that, she desperately needed
this position and felt a vast relief he wasn't going to sack her.
"Very well, sir," she said, all correct politeness, "I shall stay.
And I apologize for—"

"Don't apologize," he cut in. "I appreciate your concern
over William, but rest assured, the boy is fine." He looked toward the door.

"You must attend to your guests," she told him.

"Yes, I must."

After he left, she found her knees felt watery and she had to sink into one of the tiny classroom chairs. As she sat, making a futile attempt to pull herself together, all her loneliness and confusion wedded together in one upsurge of devouring yearning. She shut her eyes, picturing John Weston, Lord Granville, as he had stood in all his splendor before her, so handsome in his elegant clothes, so charming, so utterly unobtainable. She thought she'd seen the mirror of her desire in his eyes. Had she been mistaken? Logic struck, and she realized it didn't matter if she was mistaken or not, the illustrious Lord Granville was far beyond the reach of a lowly governess.

As, slowly, she regained control of her emotions, she remembered William. Lord Granville had said he would be fine. Wrong. William would *not* be fine. Gradually she managed to put aside her lustful thoughts of her employer and replace them with her worry over his son.

Chapter Seven

"$\mathcal{A}$ fine morning, eh, Granville?"

"Quite," Granville tersely replied to his friend, Lord Darwood. Attired in their riding clothes, they were both mounted, waiting for the rest of the guests who milled about the driveway in front of the mansion, some mounted, some not yet. So far, the house party had been a rousing success. Mama, not prone ever to making positive statements, had surprisingly proclaimed the dinner and ball the previous night the best she had ever given. Now, as the morning sun drew up the dew from the vast expanse of lawns, Granville planned to take his guests for a ride through the lush woods that surrounded the estate. Their goal, the gamekeeper's lodge where the servants, loaded with baskets of food, linen tablecloths, and the best family silverware and china, had gone ahead to prepare breakfast.

"Why so glum this morning?" his friend called.

Curse the man. "It's a beautiful day, Darwood. Rest assured, I'm in the best of spirits." He wasn't. That unsettling scene with the governess last night had ruffled his usually imperturbable composure. He made it a point never to discuss his miserable childhood, yet the little governess had set him babbling, revealing dismal memories best forgotten. Even more unsettling, in the midst of all the wrangling, he had found himself absolutely enchanted with her, a circumstance he never experienced before. This unexpected feeling didn't suit him at all. Many, if not most, of his peers thought nothing of dallying with a servant, but he never had, nor did he ever intend to. He prided himself on being a man of honor. As such, he would not dream of taking advantage of a vulnerable female, no matter how willing she might be, or how tempting. Not to say he hadn't kept a few mistresses in the years since his wife's death, but they were women of a different breed, not in the least vulnerable, and extremely well paid. As for Miss Winthrop, he simply must put her out of his mind. The problem was, the harder he tried to ignore this almost giddy feeling of attraction, the more it persisted.

Lord Kellems rode up. He was a huge bear of a man with a ruddy face, blond curly hair, and thick shoulders. " 'Tis a pity Lady Regina cannot ride," he said.

"She never rides, I'm afraid."

Kellems looked quite dejected. "I missed her at the ball last night, as well as dinner."

"Unfortunately she's been in quite delicate health." *Poor Regina.* That was another thing that was adding to Granville's state of malaise this morning. In London, Kellems had taken to visiting often. It was obvious he was smitten with Regina, and though she tried to hide it, she with him. Mama was highly annoyed. Regina was far too ill to lead any sort of a normal life, she claimed, let alone marry. Granville was sadly aware she would never permit Regina such a union, not with Kellems, not with anybody.

And another thing . . . this weekend he was supposed to propose to Lady Camilla. He had planned it, his mother expected it. Both yesterday and last night he'd had plenty of opportunity. More than enough, he thought with a cynical sniff. In fact, last night Lady Camilla had hardly let him out of her sight. He'd had chances aplenty to ask for her hand, yet the words kept sticking in his throat, refusing to be voiced. Now he could see her across the drive, daintily seated on her mount, looking marvelous in her green velvet riding gown, jaunty plume rising from her matching green hat. At the moment, she was gazing at him with a quizzical look in her eye, as if she were asking, *Well, what's holding you back?*

What indeed was holding him back? He did not love Lady Camilla, but there was nothing new about that. It didn't matter. He hadn't loved his first wife either, but they'd become friends and after a time he'd developed a fondness for her. He

felt certain that in time he would feel the same about Lady
Camilla. Never could he love her, though. Never could he feel
the slightest spark of passion for her, not like . . .

His thoughts pulled him up short. *Not like he had felt for the
little governess last night*, there, in his old classroom, surrounded by the familiar jumble of books, papers, pens, and
globes, when he'd had the most intense desire to nibble her
soft, white neck, just there, above the prim collar of her un-
adorned gown, and to slide his lips up from there to the under-
side of her dainty little chin . . .

"Your lordship, I would like a word with you."

Blast, his mother. White lace cap perched atop her gray
head, dressed in her morning gown of mud brown, she stood
with regal bearing upon the marble steps and beckoned to him.
He knew she never rode. Had not, in fact, mounted a horse for
years, what with all her ailments. All the same, out of sheer
perversity he called, "What a delightful surprise, Mama. Do
you plan to ride with us this morning?"

"Don't be ridiculous. Come here, I wish to speak to you."

Concealing a sigh, Granville slid from his horse and went
up the steps to face his dour-faced mother. "What is it?" he
asked, slapping his riding crop impatiently against his thigh.

Lady Granville leaned close. "*When* are you going to ask
her?"

"Ask who what?" He knew her meaning full well, but could
not resist the urge to bait her.

Her brows flew together in a scowl, causing even more
wrinkles to seam the parchment-thin skin of her face. "This
weekend you were supposed to ask Lady Camilla to marry
you. You have not, have you? *Not* that you didn't have the opportunity. My word, you had all day yesterday to propose, as
well as last night at the ball."

He didn't care to answer, partly because he didn't have an
answer, mostly because he resented his mother's ubiquitous in-
terference. "Everything in its own good time, Mama. I must
go." Before she could respond, he was down the steps and
back on his horse, noticing as he took up the reins his heavy
gold signet ring was loose. It had slipped to his knuckle and
could easily be turned around. He must take it to the jeweler's

upon his return to London. He'd do it right away. He had inherited the ring from his father, whom he had deeply loved despite his neglect, and he wouldn't want to lose it.

Minutes later all the guests were mounted and ready. As the horses started their brisk trot down the curving drive, Granville spied his three children coming through the entrance of the manor. Behind, dressed in her usual prim gray, came Miss Lucy Winthrop. It appeared they, too, were headed for the woods, no doubt out for their morning walk.

His heart raced at the sight of her.

What idiocy, he told himself, and touched his heels to the flanks of his horse to catch up with Lady Camilla.

"Oh, look," Winifred called happily, "there goes Papa on his horse with all his friends. Can we go after them, Miss Winthrop?"

"I'm afraid not." Lucy looked after the retreating horses and for a brief moment thought how wonderful it must be to be rich and privileged. Not a care in the world, just constant rounds of dinners, balls, all sorts of parties, and riding your horse through thick woods with your friends where, at the end of the trail, solicitous servants would serve you a sumptuous breakfast.

"We shall follow their trail a little way," she told her charges as they started for the woods. She glanced at William, who was pale and listless this morning, not his usual talkative self. "We shall make this a nature walk and look for deer. Perhaps we shall even find some wild strawberries."

If she was expecting an enthusiastic response from William, she was doomed to disappointment. She most certainly could understand since she, herself, had hardly slept last night for thinking of her emotion-charged conversation with Lord Granville, not only because of her disconcerting feelings for him but also because of her concern over William.

Once in the woods, the boy perked up. There was much to do in the woods: hunting rats and rabbits, chasing a deer on foot, searching for frogs' eggs in a tiny stream.

It was while they were happily engaged in trying to trap a lizard that Lucy, catching a golden gleam out of the corner of her eye, caught sight of a ring, touched by sunshine, nearly hidden by a pinecone lying beside the trail.

When she picked it up, she immediately recognized Lord Granville's gold and ruby signet ring. She recalled how she had admired it on his hand last night, thinking how suited to him it was, with its stunning ruby setting and elegantly engraved crest and initials.

"That's Papa's ring," Mary exclaimed.

"He treasures that ring," said William. "It belonged to my grandfather. How splendid that you found it, Miss Winthrop. Papa wears it all the time."

"Then I'm sure he'll be happy when we tell him we found it." Lucy slid the ring onto her right thumb. It was slightly loose, but she didn't think it would slip off. "We shall return it as soon as he comes home."

Hours later, long after Lucy and the children had finished their walk, Lord Granville and his guests returned to the manor. Lucy waited a suitable time. Then, when Becky informed her they were all gathered in the drawing room, she said, "Come, children, we shall go downstairs. William, you can present your father with the ring. I'm sure he'll be most relieved you found it."

"But *you* found it, Miss Winthrop."

Lucy didn't care who found it. What mattered was, this was a fine opportunity for William to shine in his father's eyes. "Let's say we all found it, William, but you're the one who shall present it to your father."

"But we're not supposed to go down there," Mary protested.

Lucy recalled Lady Granville's adamant words concerning keeping the children out of her sight. Today, though, she would disregard them. "This is a special occasion. I'm sure we'll be forgiven."

The first thing Lucy noticed when she and the children stepped into the grand salon was the scowl that appeared on Lady Granville's face. Choosing to ignore it, Lucy herded the children toward their father, who stood chatting with Lady Camilla. As they made their way across the room, Lucy could not help but notice what a glittering scene it was: the guests, dressed in their finest wools, satins, and laces lounged about, some playing cards, some having tea, others simply chatting. Servants served scones and little sandwiches and sweets from sterling silver trays. Overhead, lighted tiers of the finest white wax candles, ensconced in two glittering crystal chandeliers, dispelled the shadows of late afternoon.

Seeing them approach, Lord Granville abruptly stilled his conversation with the beautiful Lady Camilla and turned to greet them. "Why, Miss Winthrop, children, what a pleasant surprise. I didn't know you were coming down for tea."

"We weren't." Lucy placed her hand on William's back and pressed him forward. "William has something to give you."

Smiling, William extended his palm. Upon it rested the gold signet ring. "I believe this belongs to you, Papa."

"My ring!" Lord Granville gasped with relief. "I knew I'd lost it in the woods somewhere. I searched everywhere for it. Had about decided it was gone for good."

Some of the guests, including Lords Darwood and Kellems, gathered around, exclaiming upon Lord Granville's good fortune in recovering one of his prized possessions. He took the ring and slipped it back on his finger. "Where did you find it, William?"

"I didn't find it, sir, Miss Winthrop did."

Darwood smiled and applauded. "Bravo, Miss Winthrop. His lordship was quite distraught at losing it. I was afraid we'd all be compelled to go back to the woods and peek under every rock and leaf."

"How nice you found it," commented Lady Camilla with somewhat less than unrestrained enthusiasm.

"You must give her a reward," said Lord Darwood.

"Indeed you must," came a chorus of enthusiastic voices.

Lord Granville's eye caught Lucy's. Instantly she perceived this was more than a casual, disinterested glance. Even in the midst of the grand salon with people all around, somehow she felt as if she were alone with him as a nebulously sensuous perception passed between them. He said softly, and with deep sincerity, "This was my father's ring and I'm deeply grateful you found it."

"Then so am I," she said simply.

"What would you like? A monetary reward, perhaps?"

"Nothing. I have no need of a reward."

Winifred tugged at her skirt. "Yes you do, Miss Winthrop. Papa ought to give you some wishes, just like the genie gave Aladdin."

A titter of laughter, accompanied by a murmur of approval, swept the room.

"How quaint."

"What a clever little girl."

"Splendid idea," Darwood exclaimed. Noticing the dubious expression on Granville's face, he elaborated. "Well, not unlimited wishes, of course. Three wishes should do it, don't you agree, Miss Winthrop? And anything within reason, of course. A wish that he grant you the family fortune might be a bit too much."

"I don't think—" Lucy began, but William interrupted.

"You should do it, Papa. Three wishes for Miss Winthrop. She deserves them."

"Yes, Papa, give her three wishes," Mary chimed in, eyes bright with excitement.

Granville had appeared unsure but now burst into laughter. "It would appear I'm outnumbered and have no choice. Well, I think it's a splendid idea, Miss Winthrop. I do not pretend to be a genie, but in gratitude for your finding my ring, I grant you three wishes. Anything within reason, of course."

Lucy's first impulse was to state in no uncertain terms she thought the whole idea quite absurd, most unnecessary, and would have nothing to do with it. Then an audacious thought struck her. For a moment she mulled it over and concluded she would indeed express a wish. What she planned to ask for was undoubtedly unwise, but worth a try nonetheless. She dipped a brief curtsy and replied, "Very well, sir. I accept your offer. Three wishes it shall be."

"Just like Aladdin." Winifred clasped her hands together in delight. The sprinkling of laughter and applause that swept the room indicated everyone was pleased.

So I've amused them, thought Lucy. But she had not accepted Granville's offer for amusement. She had a definite plan.

Lady Camilla offered a condescending smile. "So what shall you wish for, Miss Winthrop? A new gown? A bauble of some sort?"

Lucy was gratified when Lord Granville threw the beautiful blond a decided look of displeasure. "Perhaps Miss Winthrop needs time to decide."

"That won't be necessary," Lucy spoke up briskly. "I know what my first wish will be."

Again, a titter ran through the gathering of guests. Someone declared, "We are all ears, do tell us, please."

Lord Darwood jabbed Granville's ribs with his elbow. "You're in for it now, old man. Better get your money out." He addressed Lucy. "Don't ask for just a bauble, my dear. At the very least, make him bring you something inordinately expensive from Rundell and Bridges."

Lucy ignored the guests' comments and Lord Darwood's farcical suggestion. Instead, she gazed deep into Granville's attentive eyes. "Rest assured, my lord, I have no desire for costly jewels. My first wish is this. I request the honor of your presence at dinner tonight in the nursery with your children and me."

A surprised silence was closely followed by a few guffaws as well as amused comments.

"Well, Granville?"

"What do you say, will you do it?"

"Pity poor Granville. He'll be dining on milk and porridge tonight while the rest of us enjoy our *Magrets de Canard* and buttered lobster."

Lady Granville appeared. Obviously she'd overheard the conversation because her face was suffused with ill-concealed exasperation. She glared at her son. "We have guests," she snapped. "You cannot possibly run off to the nursery for dinner tonight."

Lucy's spirits fell. She had only wanted to make William's father pay him some attention, but she should have realized Lady Granville would object. Not only that, now she wondered what insane notion had led her to believe the lofty Lord Granville would take time away from his guests for a simple meal in the nursery.

She felt a crushing disappointment, sure his mother's wishes would prevail.

Until that moment Granville had remained expressionless. Now a slow smile spread across his face. Ignoring his mother, he bowed to Lucy. "Your first wish is my command, Miss Winthrop. You may expect me in the nursery for dinner tonight."

Chapter Eight

*T*wo hours later, attired in formal evening clothes, Granville started up the main staircase from the entry hall to the fourth-floor nursery.

"Enjoy your dinner with the children." Darwood's goading voice came from below.

"Indeed I shall," Granville replied over his shoulder. He knew he would not and had resigned himself to a dull evening. Still, he'd rip his tongue out before he let Darwood know how much he'd sorely miss the fine food and brilliant conversation in the dining room.

Darwood wasn't through. "Now do you see why I got rid of the governess? She's trouble. Her silly wish has ruined your evening."

Irritated, Granville paused on the steps and turned to regard his friend. "What blatant hypocrisy. It was you who urged her on. I would not have granted her those idiotic three wishes if it were not for you."

Darwood grinned. "Well, you're stuck with them now." It was plain he was enjoying Granville's discomfit immensely.

Granville answered smoothly, "Thank you for your concern, but I don't need it. It won't be the end of the world if I dine with my children."

"We shall miss you at dinner," said Darwood, dropping the sarcasm and sounding sincere. "Say, old man, here's a thought. Try not to eat too much. Perhaps you can slip away early and join us."

Granville issued a noncommittal "Perhaps," and made his way upstairs, reminding himself he must make the best of an inescapable situation. Naturally he could see right through the governess's little ploy. She wanted him to spend more time with the children, especially William. What she didn't realize, or if she did realize she failed to accept, was that parents did not involve themselves in the rearing of their children. It simply wasn't done, not among the *ton* anyway. Children were to be seen and not heard. Let the servants raise them. According to his mother, he must devote his efforts toward becoming a leader in Parliament with the likely goal that someday he would become prime minister. As for ignoring his children, that's how he was raised, and if he'd been terribly lonely, well, that was simply one of the unavoidable drawbacks of childhood. He did draw the line at physical punishment, though. No whippings, or boxing of ears, and most certainly no being sent to bed without supper. He had made all that very clear to his mother when he'd turned the rearing of the children over to her.

At least there was one bright edge to the evening. If the truth be known, although he dreaded eating in the nursery, a small part of him was bursting with eagerness. *She* would be there. Despite his best intentions, he looked forward to seeing her again.

Even so, Darwood's suggestion had merit. He would eat lightly and leave early, in time to join his guests in the dining room.

Also, he would propose to Lady Camilla this very night. Tomorrow at the latest.

As he approached the nursery door, he heartily wished the evening ahead would reveal some sort of imperfection in his governess. Perhaps she would talk too much: babble on and interrupt everyone. Perhaps she would spill crumbs all over herself, or slurp her tea.

He heartily hoped she would. Then, when he saw her imperfections, this deuced fascination he felt for her would disappear.

Entering the nursery, Granville noticed immediately she wasn't wearing gray. In place of the dowdy governess garb, Miss Lucy Winthrop wore a lovely gown of blue—a chemise he thought the ladies called it—trimmed at neckline and wrists with some sort of white lace flounce. Compared to the ladies' latest fashions, the bosom was modestly cut, but compared to her customary high-necked gray, she was practically indecently exposed. The gown had a matching Paisley shawl, edged with satin ribbon, hanging in graceful folds from her shapely shoulders. What a difference. Her gown and shawl, combined with the high color in her cheeks, the sparkle in her clear gray eyes, the warmth of her welcoming smile, made her quite lovely to behold.

Actually he'd seen the gown before and recognized it immediately. It had once belonged to Lady Darwood, doubtless a hand-me-down, a common occurrence between mistress and servant. An irrational resentment swept through him. This lovely girl should not have to wear hand-me-downs. Not, of course, that he'd ever indicate he knew.

The children, too, were dressed in their best. Even the room had been miraculously transformed into the semblance of an elegant dining room. A small fire burned in the cozy fireplace. The clutter of toys had been put away. The old mahogany table he knew so well—his initials were carved upon it still—had been covered by a damask cloth and set with fine silver and china.

"Do sit down," Miss Winthrop said, indicating a chair at the head of the table. "Morris, kindly light the candles."

The servant stepped forward. What the deuce? How on earth had she managed to purloin his mother's favorite footman? But however she'd done it, here was Morris, dressed in all his liveried splendor, lighting candles ensconced in what Granville recognized as his mother's favorite silver candelabra.

"How did you manage?" he asked as he seated himself.

The governess returned an inscrutable smile. "Morris will be serving us, but he'll leave directly after dessert. That should give him time to serve your elegant friends downstairs." She made a sweeping gesture over the table. "To be perfectly candid, I was hoping all this would impress you."

"It has."

A spark of humor lit her eye. "You will note we are *not* having milk and porridge?"

Granville's gaze swept over the table loaded with *Magrets de Canard*, vegetable pudding, buttered lobster, and so many other dishes he could not name them all. "I see you've borrowed the food as well as the footman."

"Cook was generous."

"Sorry you heard the remark about the porridge. Can you forgive my guests their thoughtlessness? They were trying to be amusing but plainly were not."

"Quite all right," she easily replied.

"Papa, we are *all* trying to impress you," Mary said earnestly as they began the meal. "Isn't that right, Winifred?"

Little Winifred nodded and stood. Her little face frowning with purpose, she picked up a large platter. Shakily, but successfully, she passed it to her father. "Do have some *Magrets de Canard*, Papa," she said in a practiced, perfect imitation of a well-mannered grown-up. "It is quite delicious."

It *was* delicious. As the meal wore on, Granville found that in the warm and friendly ambiance of the cozy nursery-turned-dining room, he was enjoying himself immensely. What perfectly mannered children he had. He had never realized they could be so civilized. The conversation was delightful, too, consisting of light chatter, led by Miss Winthrop, who with her bubbling laugh appeared the essence of charm and wit.

But toward the middle of the meal, the conversation unexpectedly turned toward the serious.

"Papa, why are you a Whig?" William suddenly asked.

Granville was so taken aback he stopped his forkful of *Magrets de Canard* midway to his mouth. "Why am I a Whig?" he repeated.

Miss Winthrop nodded. "It's a simple request. Explain to your son why you are not a Tory."

After a pause, in which he was compelled to put his thoughts in order, Granville replied, "The Tories are the party of the King. 'The King's friends' they're often called."

The expression on William's small face turned deadly serious. "But the King can't lead the party. He's blind, deaf, and insane."

"All the better for the Tories. You see, son, in reality, the Tories want only a puppet king. The insanity of George III has made not the slightest change in the governing of the country. The same cabinet, supported by the same majority, remains in office, just as before."

"But we have the Regent, and all the King's other sons."

"Ha! Not fit to govern, the lot of them."

"But did they not inherit their father's virtues?" prompted Miss Winthrop in an obvious ploy to urge him on.

"Granted, the Dukes of Cambridge and Sussex are tolerable," Granville replied, "but they're insignificant. It's the Dukes of Clarence, Kent, York, and Cumberland who have made their father's virtues odious. They've inherited their father's fondness for discipline, which in itself is admirable. However, their fetish for discipline is tyrannical, narrow, and stupid."

"Yet Prinny rules," commented William.

"Yes, but he's vastly unpopular now. When he drives out in his carriage, the mob either stays silent or boos. If he isn't in fear of his life, he should be."

"So that's why you're a Whig?" William asked. "Because you don't like the King and the Regent?"

"Something like that, yes." Granville smiled, pleased with the sharp questions asked by his son. He'd had no idea the boy took an interest in politics. "Also, reforms are desperately needed in England, and the Whigs are the party of reform."

William looked perplexed. "Well, if the Whigs are the party of reform, why is slavery still legal?"

"You're missing something, son. May I point out that in 1806, Parliament, led by the Whigs, passed the Abolition of the Slave Trade Bill?"

"That's all very well and good, sir, but it doesn't go far enough. Slavery should be abolished, too, not just the slave trade. And another thing—" William's clear, young eyes glowed with zeal. "If the Whigs are the party of reform, why haven't they done more about the abom . . . abom . . ."

"Abominable," prompted Lucy.

"That's right, the abominable conditions in the prisons? In 1791 Thomas Paine wrote, 'What is government more than the management of the affairs of a Nation? It is not, and from its nature cannot be, the property of any particular man or family, but the whole community.'" William sat back and folded his arms. "So, Papa? I strongly feel the government, run by the people, should be making the rules, not your privileged few, and if the people are allowed to make the rules, they would reform the prisons and do away altogether with slavery."

What a brilliant child! Lord Granville was so astounded at the erudite words pouring from his son's lips, he had to collect himself and was compelled to put down his fork and take a long sip of water. Good thing the child's grandmother wasn't here. Without doubt she'd have one of her attacks if she heard her one and only grandson spouting the *Rights of Man*. Raising an eyebrow, Granville addressed the governess. "You're letting them read Thomas Paine?"

She smiled brightly. "Only William. Mary and Winifred are a bit young. Perhaps next year."

"And slavery? I see you've not been lax in teaching my son the issues of the day, at least one side of the issue."

"I do hope I haven't gone too far, sir." Although her words expressed doubt, she seemed not in the least concerned.

Actually she *had* gone too far. Granville knew his mother would be livid if she suspected her grandson was well on his way to becoming a flaming reformer. But as far as he was concerned, his mother's feelings were not of the greatest import. What mattered was, his son showed a sharp mind he'd not fully been aware of before. He admired William's plucky attitude, too, the way he didn't hesitate but spoke right up, expressing his views.

But the lad needed to be corrected on a few things.

"The Whigs are the party of reform. But, you see, son, it's all very complicated and when you are older—"

"I'm old enough now, sir. Please explain."

Granville had to concede the lad was right. With his bright demeanor and intelligent questions, the boy was indeed old enough. "You understand there's been a war on."

William spoke up. "Just ended, sir, with Napoleon's defeat at the Battle of Waterloo."

"Exactly right, son. Because of it, Lord Liverpool, who's a Tory, has been a popular prime minister. However, as I'm sure you know, he disagrees with those who advocate reform."

"But Napoleon is gone now," William earnestly continued. "What are you waiting for? For instance, there's the matter of the Luddites. Do you really think it's fair a person should be put to death just for breaking a machine?"

"Well, William, you can blame Lord Sidmouth . . ."

The lively conversation continued. Not only was Granville pleased with his son, he noted little Mary chimed in from time to time with bits of knowledge. He was deeply touched, not only by William's grasp of politics and issues, but also by his son's eagerness to impress him. In fact, Granville became so engrossed in his give-and-take with William, before he knew it the meal was over. As Morris cleared the last dessert plate, Granville belatedly remembered his plan to eat sparingly and leave early so that he could join the merriment downstairs. He had failed on both counts.

Too late now, he thought, feeling not a modicum of regret. "I've enjoyed myself immensely," he said, rising from the table.

"I'm so glad you came, Papa," William replied.

"So am I," he said with heartfelt sincerity. "I enjoyed our conversation, William."

Becky entered the room. "Time for bed, children."

Miss Winthrop also arose from the table. "Would you care to stay a few moments longer and tuck them in?" she asked Granville.

"Why . . . yes." He had hesitated, not because he was in a rush to get downstairs, he was not. It was just that the notion of putting his children to bed was completely foreign to him. Never in all his childhood could he remember his father tucking him in. Nor his mother. That task had always fallen to the series of nursery maids who came and went, most of them too fatigued from a long day's work to give more than a perfunctory peck on the cheek, followed by a hasty withdrawal.

Morris hastened downstairs. Becky took the children to their bedchambers to ready them for bed. Granville found himself alone with the governess in the nursery, dim now, since a lamp had not been lit and most of the candles had melted. He could not help but notice she looked beautiful in the dwindling light of the candles remaining, their glow casting flickering planes of musk-rose light across her delicate face. The success of the evening had buoyed him up, and he found himself searching for words to express the pleasurable experience he'd just had.

"I cannot tell you what a delightful time I had tonight," he began. "So much, in fact, I would like to come again."

Her lips curved into a charming smile. "Why don't you? You're more than welcome anytime."

"Then I shall," he answered, wondering when, in his busy schedule, he could comply. Soon, he hoped. It wasn't only William and the girls who had made his evening pleasurable. It was also this modest governess, glowing with wit and charm, and so knowledgeable. "I had no idea William had such a vast knowledge of the doings of Parliament. Although . . ." He paused to carefully frame his words. "My mother would not be overly pleased if she were to discover William in agreement with Thomas Paine."

She tipped her chin to a lofty angle. "Be honest. You know very well your mother would have a fit if she were to discover some of the reformist views I've taught him. I would doubtless be dismissed again."

"Then why do you—?"

"Why do I?" she interrupted with fervor. "Because I am only a small part of William's life and have only a short time in which to make some sort of impression upon his keen young mind. Soon he'll be off to Eton, or wherever you intend to send him, and become steeped in the antiquated views of the aristocracy."

"I suppose that's true," he answered equitably. "Tell me, with your . . . er, somewhat radical views, are you not afraid *I* might sack you, let alone my mother?"

"You could." She tilted her chin higher. "Why don't you? Heaven forbid, your children should be caught spouting such radical views as prison reform and the end of slavery."

He was enjoying the sparring, despite her fanatical views. And despite—it had just occurred to him—the fact that this conversation had rapidly evolved into not the kind of conversation that should properly occur between employer and governess. She was conversing with him like an equal. "It occurs to me that you, Miss Winthrop, are far more like your sister than I thought you were."

"And you, sir, are just like every other egotistical, selfish, thoughtless member of the aristocracy." She spoke the words lightly, as if she, too, was enjoying their bantering.

He ought to be affronted, he thought as he framed his reply. No servant had ever talked to him that way before. But instead of taking offense, all he was aware of was how her auburn hair caught rich glints from the candlelight, and how he would like to run his fingers over the ivory white skin of her throat down to the soft swell of her bosom.

He repeated, "Egotistical, selfish, thoughtless member of the aristocracy?" He gave her a mocking bow. "Guilty as charged."

She burst into laughter. "Please don't take my condemnation personally. Actually I find you quite ... quite ..." She stopped in confusion and glanced down, her long, dark lashes resting enticingly on her pinkish rose cheeks. It occurred to him that except for that day she'd come begging for a position, he'd never seen her when she was not totally sure of herself.

He searched for a suitable *bon mot* to put her down, but couldn't find one. He didn't want one. His usually cool demeanor was fleeing fast. To his surprise and chagrin, his heart was pumping madly. Damme. In the cozy quiet of this room, in the glow of the seductive candlelight, all he wanted was to sweep the little governess into his arms.

He fought for control, sternly informing himself such a course of action was preposterous, as well as against his principles. Before he knew it, though, he found himself actually voicing words that should have remained forever unuttered. "You're very beautiful," he said, acutely aware but not caring he'd lost his battle and crossed over the line.

For a moment Lucy's thoughts were in such a jumble she could not think what to say. She had been in a high state of suspense all evening, starting with her intrepid decision to wear the daring blue chemise instead of the proper gray. Early on, she determined she'd made the right decision, telling herself she must be bold for William's sake. In the short time available before dinner, she'd frantically schemed to make the evening as pleasant an experience as possible for the lofty lord who hardly knew his children. To her great satisfaction she succeeded, what with the delicious meal and Morris to serve it, the children dressed in their best and behaving remarkably well, the cozy, relaxed ambiance of the nursery-turned-dining room, and, yes, her own daring gown and self-possessed demeanor. Success! To say his lordship had been enchanted would not be far off the mark. And what a miracle. He had paid attention to his son and at long last perceived William's brilliance.

She had planned the evening carefully, but not this part. This dangerously intimate scene was not what she had bargained for. Or had she? Were her efforts all for William, or had there been at the back of her mind a hazy, secret hope that her impersonal relationship with Granville would blossom into something more? Now, completely alone with him in the nursery, she felt tongue-tied, torn by conflicting emotions. He was so close she could smell his cologne; so close that had she wished, she could reach up and brush that errant lock of dark hair that fell across his forehead. So close that just now, after he'd told her she was beautiful, she was having trouble maintaining her regular breathing pattern. She desperately needed to draw a deep breath but knew if she did, it would sound trembling and shaky, thus revealing the inner turmoil that was all his fault.

She must not let him know. She must maintain her dignity at all costs. She should back away this very moment.

As he stood intimately close, looking down at her, his ragged breathing gave him away. She wasn't sure before, but now she knew it wasn't her imagination: he wanted her. She noticed how an uncommon quiet had filled the room. But was it quiet, or just that for this moment they were in their own little world, so acutely aware of each other no other sounds or sights could penetrate?

Suddenly his hands clasped her shoulders, causing her flesh to tingle beneath the blue chemise gown. Even in the semi-darkness she could see a bright flare of desire in his eyes. He was hers, she knew it. She had only to give the slightest hint of her own desire and she'd be tight in his arms. But what a mistake that would be. Many times, during her years as a governess, she'd witnessed the tragic results when the master or sons of the household dallied with a susceptible female servant.

I cannot, she thought despairingly. With all the strength within her, she placed her hand flat on his chest, gave a little push, and backed away.

"We mustn't do this," she said.

His hands quickly dropped to his sides. "My apologies," he managed in a voice still trembling.

"I have seen too many servant girls seduced by their masters, dismissed in disgrace," she said, the words tumbling out. "Sent to the countryside where they gave birth to their byblows in some miserable peasant's hovel." The words that burst from her had given her strength and she drew herself up. "Not I, m'lord."

"But I did not mean to—"

"You *did* mean. I'm your children's governess and that's all. Promise me this won't happen again."

He opened his mouth to speak, but before he could, Becky opened the door and bustled in. "The children are ready to be tucked in, Miss Winthrop." If she noticed the tension in the room, she gave no sign.

"Thank you, Becky." In a voice that could not have been more formal, or impersonal, Lucy addressed her employer. "Would you care to do the honors, Lord Granville? Your children will be so thrilled to have you tuck them in."

Minutes later Granville found himself in his daughters' bedchamber, sitting on Winifred's bed, placing the doll she requested in her arms. He smiled down at her. "Good night, sleep tight." He had remembered the comforting rhyme one of his nursery maids used to recite.

"Good night, Papa." Winifred reached her dimpled little arms up. "Come give me a kiss."

He bent to kiss her, engulfed in the fresh smell of soap and faint peppermint. How he loved his children. Words he had never spoken sprang to his lips. "You're my darling little girl," he said, stroking her fine blond hair, "and I love you very much."

Marveling at himself, he repeated his affectionate good night at Mary's bed, then on to William's bedchamber where he proceeded to tuck in his son.

"Good night, Papa," William said. "It was great fun having you here tonight."

"Then I shall come again tomorrow night." *What did I just say?* Granville marveled. He had just made a decision that not only was poorly thought out, it was downright reckless. He was obligated to return to London tomorrow. Parliament was no longer in session, but his mother had scheduled numerous social events that she deemed imperative he attend. He had better propose to Lady Camilla tomorrow. Too late for it tonight.

Damme, that wasn't all. If he had any sense, tomorrow he had thought to pacify his mother. He had, after all, immensely displeased her by daring to dine in the nursery. That had been his plan, but now, if he chose to dine in the nursery tomorrow night, too, she would be less than pleased. He laughed to himself. "Less than pleased" hardly described what he knew would be his mother's reaction. He was not, however, going to live his life for his mother. She simply would have to understand.

As for that unsettling scene in the nursery with the governess, he had given Miss Winthrop his word and the matter was settled. No need to think about it further. His decision to stay, have dinner with his children tomorrow night, most certainly had nothing to do with his attraction to Miss Lucy Winthrop.

He had granted her three wishes, though. Two remained. He wondered what the little governess would wish for next.

Chapter Nine

*T*he children were tucked in. It was time for bed. Still shaken by her encounter with Lord Granville, Lucy walked down the fourth-floor hallway toward the staircase. The faint sounds of guests chattering drifted up from below, melded with the strains of Mozart's *Sonata in A* that someone was playing on the piano.

"Miss Winthrop?"

Turning, Lucy was surprised to see the hulking figure of Lord Kellems. He seemed unsure of himself, as if he were lost and had found himself on the fourth floor by mistake. He held a small book in his hand. She asked, "Are you lost, sir?"

He returned a rueful smile. "Apparently I am. I was looking for Lady Regina."

"You're on the fourth floor, not the third. Come with me and I'll show you—"

"No, no," Kellems demurred. "Damnation, it's too late. I wanted to give Lady Regina this book of poems, but when I spoke earlier to Lady Granville she told me her daughter was much too ill to receive company. I dislike being told no. Being the stubborn fool that I am, I set out on my own to find her."

"It's true she's been quite ill," Lucy replied. "She's not been out of her room for days."

"I wanted to find her myself, just to give her this book, you understand, but now . . ."

"It is rather late."

Kellems scowled. "Curse society's rules. All right, then. I can see I shouldn't trouble her. Her mother would be quite furious, wouldn't she?"

"I'm afraid so." Lucy smiled at the troubled man. "But if you'd like me to give her the book of poems, I would be glad to."

His face lit. "Would you? I would be most grateful. And while you're at it"—he slid a piece of sealed parchment from between the pages of the book—"will you give her this? It's a poem I wrote that I . . . well, I'd like her to have."

"Ah, so you're a poet."

He laughed. "Poetry is not my forte, Miss Winthrop. I am no Byron or Shelley, not even close. However, since she sets such great store by poetry, I would do anything . . . This"—he indicated the parchment—"is meant to convey my feelings for Lady Regina." His already ruddy cheeks flushed even more so. "I hold her in the highest esteem. I cannot understand why her mother . . . well, some things are best left unsaid."

"I shall see she gets both the book and the poem." Lucy was at a loss what else to say. Obviously the man was love struck with Lady Regina, but what a hopeless cause.

"I am most grateful."

Lucy watched with sympathy as Lord Kellems left to rejoin his fellow guests in the drawing room, then went directly to Lady Regina's bedchamber.

"Are you awake, ma'am?" Lucy knocked lightly on the door, waiting for the maid to open it. To her surprise, Lady Regina's grim-faced maid, Matilda, was nowhere to be seen. Wearing a white satin dressing gown, Lady Regina answered the door herself.

"Sorry to trouble you, but Lord Kellems asked me to give you this book and a poem he wrote."

"Really?" Regina made no attempt to disguise her delight. "I cannot imagine why he's wasting his time. But still . . ." She swung the door wide. "Won't you come in?"

Surprised at Regina's invitation, Lucy's first impulse was to decline. The events of the evening had left her exhausted. All she wanted was to go straight to bed. "Thank you, but I—"

"Oh, balderdash, come in." Regina took Lucy's arm and guided her into the room. "I should very much welcome your company if you don't mind. It's torture for me, hearing all the merriment down below, and knowing I'm too ill to join in. I was going to try, but Mama thought not." She waved Lucy to a seat by the chaise where she usually reclined. "Do sit down. I shall order up some tea."

Lucy seated herself, watching with interest as Lady Regina, who was supposed to be the complete invalid, made her way across the room to tug the bellpull. True, she walked with a slow, careful gait, but she did not appear to be nearly as fragile and debilitated as Lucy had been led to believe. No wonder Lord Kellems was attracted to her. What man would not be intrigued by her large, green-flecked, luminous eyes that peered out of her small, intelligent face, and red-hued curls that made such a startling contrast to the pure whiteness of her skin.

"It's good to see you up and around," Lucy remarked.

"Oh, I have my good days." Regina seated herself on the chaise and regarded the cover of the book of poetry. "Keats, I see. Lord Kellems doesn't know much about poetry, but at least he made a good choice. Do you like poetry, Miss Winthrop?"

"I adore poetry and read it constantly."

"Good." Regina handed Kellems's poem to Lucy. "Then you can read me his poem and tell me what you think."

"But it's something personal, and I really don't think—"

"Read!" Regina commanded. Softening her voice, she added, "I shall value your opinion."

Without further protest, Lucy broke the seal and began to read Lord Kellems's poem.

> "My lovely Lady Regina has a countenance divine
> In every way she is perfectly fine
> Ah, Regina! Ah, love! You are like a dewdrop,
> Purer than the purest,
> I prithee send back my heart,
> Since I cannot have thine . . ."

As she continued to read, Lucy heard the sound of laughter, muted at first, then growing so loud she ceased her recitation, peered over the parchment, and saw Lady Regina nearly doubled over with laughter.

"But that is just dreadful," Regina exclaimed. "I am like a dewdrop? Oh, hilarious!"

"It does need a bit of polishing."

Lucy's comment sent Regina into increased gales of laughter. "Polishing? God himself couldn't save that poem." Suddenly her laughter subsided. She reached for the parchment, and to Lucy's surprise clutched it to her bosom. "To think that a man who detests poetry thought enough of me to write this . . . this atrocious, wonderful poem." She clutched the poem tighter. "Do forgive me, Miss Winthrop. It's just . . . I am so touched that he would think to . . ."

Regina dropped the parchment to her lap. "I so admire Lord Kellems. I know he's blunt, and ignores the social graces, but beneath his rough exterior lies a compassionate heart."

"You are extremely fond of him, aren't you?"

"I find him quite . . . stimulating, if I may use the word."

Lucy thought of her passionate attraction to Lord Granville. "I know exactly what you mean."

"Silly, isn't it? But I find everything about him is perfection. If only I wasn't so ill." Regina heaved a wistful sigh and said nothing more.

Lucy perceived Lady Regina's misery and decided to distract her. There was a burning question she had to ask and now seemed a good time. "If you don't mind my asking, what exactly is your illness?"

"It started at birth," Regina replied. "I was born premature, seven months, Mama says, and according to her, barely lived. In fact, she says it's a miracle I survived. As Mama says, I should be grateful for every day I have on this earth, and if I am not as fit as some and must live as an invalid, then so be it. At least I am here to enjoy each day, which, believe me, I do."

"But what exactly is wrong?" Lucy persisted.

"It's my lungs, accompanied by a monumental weariness. Today is a good day, as you can see, but there are days when I am so fatigued I can hardly climb from my bed."

"Do you suppose it would help if you walked more? They say there's great merit in exercise."

"Oh, no. Mama is adamant that I not move around more

than is necessary. She would never permit me to walk anywhere."

The subject was dropped. When tea was served, they chatted of inconsequential matters. When Lucy left, she realized she'd enjoyed herself immensely, conversing with a woman who was not only bright but had been reading all her life and was marvelously self-educated.

As to what ailed Lady Regina, Lucy still didn't quite understand. She had seemed so well tonight, Lucy couldn't help wondering if she was really that much of an invalid. None of Lucy's business, of course, but early on she'd recognized Lady Granville's obsession with illnesses. It was horrifying even to contemplate, yet Lucy wondered what part Lady Granville might have played in making her daughter an invalid for life.

Back in her room, Lucy's thoughts turned to Lord Granville. She remembered the three wishes, and despite the tumult of the evening, had to laugh to herself. She had used up only one wish. Doubtless he'd be wondering what her other two wishes would be.

He needn't worry. One wish was enough. She would never ask Lord Granville for anything again.

The following morning many of the guests had already left or were sleeping late when Granville came downstairs. He found his mother and youngest sister in the grand salon, working on their needlework, fortunately alone.

His mother raised her eyes from her embroidery. "Ah, there you are, John. Have you told your valet you're to be packed and ready to leave by two o'clock? I am most anxious to return to London."

"Mama—"

"Next week is going to be tremendously busy. There's a ball Tuesday night you simply must attend. Lord Sidmouth will be there, and many of his cronies."

"I don't really think—"

"I trust you have not forgotten you stand for reelection next year?"

"Not with you to remind me every other moment."

Florinda had the perceptiveness to giggle, but Mama was

not amused. "Don't be flippant. With that kind of attitude, you'll never be prime minister."

Ah, the perfect opening, thought Granville. "If I cannot be prime minister without toadying to those in power, then I would just as soon remain where I am." His mother opened her mouth to speak, but he continued on. "And furthermore, I have no intention of dedicating my every waking moment to my future in politics."

"And what does that mean?" his mother asked, her voice full of foreboding.

"That means I shall not accompany you back to London today. In fact, I plan to stay several days, possibly all week, possibly longer."

She slammed her embroidery into her lap and glared. "Are you daft?"

"I plan to become acquainted with my children, who, in case you were not aware, have been grossly neglected of late. William in particular. I plan to spend much of my time with him, as well as Mary and Winifred."

Her eyes narrowed. "Does that governess have anything to do with this?"

"Of course not," he answered, aware he'd answered a tad too quickly.

His mother leveled the kind of gaze that meant a diatribe lay ahead. "Whatever has gotten into you? It has not escaped my notice that you have not proposed to Lady Camilla, which, I might add, is an absolutely lamentable lapse on your part. Now, to make matters worse, you're saying you'd rather wallow with the peasants in the countryside than return to the city."

"Wallow is hardly the word."

"Then go, John, just go"—for dramatic effect she waved her hanky at him—"do as you please. I'm a sick woman. I do not need the aggravation."

From past experience he knew he should do just that. Go. Wait until she'd calmed herself and come to accept whatever proclamation of defiance he had issued.

He had started for the door of the salon when Florinda uttered a startled, "Mama!" Turning, he saw his mother, pale, fallen back on the settee, clutching at her chest.

He rushed to her side and knelt beside her. "Mama, are you all right?"

She gasped, "It's my heart, John, but don't give it a thought, I shall be all right."

"Florinda, tell Brooks to send for the doctor." Granville's voice remained icy calm, but inside fear clutched his own heart. For all her faults, he loved his mother very much.

Hours later the doctor from the village had come and gone. He had dosed Lady Granville with foxglove to slow her heart, given her a generous spoonful of laudanum to make her sleep. The chest pains had ceased.

"This was all your fault," Florinda petulantly told her brother as they tiptoed from their mother's bedchamber. "You know how upset she becomes when you defy her."

Once outside, with the door to their sleeping mother's bedchamber firmly shut, Granville spoke. "Don't you see the pattern? Haven't you noticed she suffers some sort of attack whenever I dare challenge her?"

Florinda bristled. "Are you saying our mother feigned her attack?"

"Yes."

Florinda angrily shoved her fists to her hips. "I don't believe for a moment Mama's pretending. It's beastly of you to even think such a thing. Do you realize Mama could *die*? And if she does, you with your rotten, selfish attitude will be solely responsible."

Dear God. He knew he was right, and yet . . . What if his mother's attack truly was genuine, brought on by his callous indifference to her illness? William . . . Mary and Winifred . . . He had wanted very much to remain here at Penfield Manor, become better acquainted with his children. He'd looked forward to more occasions such as the lively dinner last night that was such a smashing success, thanks to Miss Winthrop. What an outstanding woman. Not a mere ornament like Lady Camilla, or his younger sister, or, come to think of it, most of the women he knew, but a woman of charm, wit, and keen intelligence who, he very well knew, had been the driving force last night in reacquainting him with his children.

Most definitely, he wanted to become closer to his children. He could not deny, though, that despite her rejection of him last night—and most proper it was—he very much wanted to see Miss Lucy Winthrop again.

Honor came first, though, and honor decreed he must set his personal desires aside.

With an inexplicable feeling of emptiness he told Florinda, "Very well, I shall return with you to London."

"Splendid. Mama will be most pleased."

"I suspect she will," he answered with an ironic smile.

London

A few weeks later Lords Granville and Darwood were in the middle of dinner at The Clarendon, where Jacquiers, the famous chef from Paris, had prepared them a sumptuous meal. "I'm sure I don't know what ails you," said Darwood. He popped a forkful of *fricandeau à l'oseille* into his mouth. "Hmm, delicious. You've been moody for weeks. Distracted. Is something on your mind?"

"Nothing, I'm fine," Lord Granville responded, aware of his lie. Since he'd returned to London, it seemed the world had turned sour. Precious little had been to his liking.

"I trust your mother continues to improve?"

"She does."

"Children?"

"All of them fine. Now what was so pressing you had to see me tonight?"

Darwood grinned. "Wait 'til you hear this. I have it on good authority that you, my good man, have definitely been pegged for a spot in the cabinet. Home secretary, I think. But no matter. You know what this means. You're being groomed for prime minister."

Granville waited for elation to strike. It did not. He wasn't sure why, considering he'd been working toward this moment for years. "Are you sure?"

"As sure as I know the Thames will ebb and flow tomorrow.

Lord Grenville is behind you, as well as Charles Fox. It's clear sailing, now that Napoleon's been defeated. All you need do is let them know you intend to retain the status quo."

"Meaning?"

"See to it there's no more of this wild reformist talk of abolishing slavery. Not for the near future anyway. As for prison reform, I hardly need mention any effort to improve the lives of those wretched prisoners is doomed to defeat. Anyone who supports such nonsense might as well kiss his political career good-bye."

"I see." Under the guise of cutting his *fricandeau,* Granville mused about how he'd always wanted to be prime minister. That was the goal his father had set for him, as well as his mother. While he did not feel quite the elation he thought he'd feel at such news, it would come in time, he was sure. He recalled his recent foolhardy proclamation to his mother: *If I cannot be prime minister without toadying to those in power, then I would just as soon remain where I am.* Courageous words, but hardly practical. If he wanted to be the leader of England, he would be compelled to compromise. "That's splendid news, Darwood," he told his friend. "They needn't worry. I'm no more a flaming reformist than I am a rock-hard conservative. Moderation is the key."

"Well said." Darwood raised his wineglass. "To the next home secretary. Soon to be prime minister."

They clinked glasses. As the claret burned a delicious path down his throat, Granville discovered that his principal emotion centered around how grateful he was Miss Lucy Winthrop had not heard that weak-minded, self-serving little speech he'd just made.

Later, when Granville returned home, he went to his sister Regina's room. As usual she was on the settee by the fireplace, reading a book, a coverlet over her legs.

Regina lowered her book. "Couldn't sleep." The glow from the fire lent a rosy hue to her pale cheeks.

"I received good news tonight." He proceeded to relate his conversation with Darwood. ". . . so it would appear I am being groomed for prime minister."

"Bravo!" Regina applauded. "Mama will be thrilled. But I must say, you don't appear all that excited."

"I'm not, oddly enough. You would think I'd be overjoyed, about to reach the pinnacle of success and all that rot, yet . . ." He shrugged. "Is this really what I want?"

"It's what Mama wants."

"But do I?" He sat pondering a few moments. "Nothing's ever perfect, is it? I find myself wanting to spend more time at Penfield Manor. I love the land. Making it produce gives me infinite satisfaction. Then, too, if I become prime minister, I shall be obliged to compromise my principles."

"Like what, for instance?"

"Prison reform for one thing. You know I'm in favor of it, but too many of my colleagues feel it's wrong to coddle criminals."

"But can't you stick to your position and make it clear how you feel? Perhaps if you're eloquent enough, you could win over those traditionalist friends of yours."

"Don't think I haven't thought of it, but it wouldn't work. They would never in a million years change their minds. Much as I detest the thought, if I want to be prime minister, I shall be obliged to forgo any effort toward prison reform."

"Our Miss Winthrop would not think much of that."

Startled, he asked, "How did you know?"

"I know her sister is the reformist, Mrs. Augusta Winthrop-Scott." Regina reached to give her brother a reassuring pat on his arm. "Oh, don't worry, Mama doesn't know and I shan't tell."

"Lord, I hope not." He remembered his and Miss Winthrop's agreement when he hired her, that she would never reveal her connections with the reformist. He hoped the governess had not betrayed their agreement. "How did you know?"

"Miss Winthrop didn't tell me, if that's what you're worried about. It was Lord Kellems."

"Ah, Lord Kellems again. I would have thought he'd given up, after you were too ill to see him at our house party." Granville raised a teasing eyebrow. "But I notice he's come calling quite frequently of late. Not, I'd wager, to hear

Florinda's prattle." To his surprise, a blush spread over his sister's cheeks. She looked discomfited, to say the least. "What? Do I detect a romance?" He would have kept teasing, but the look of misery that crossed her face made him instantly serious. Quietly he asked, "Do you care for him, Regina?"

"I adore him. Oh, John, we have so much in common. He disdains poetry and the classics, but all the same, we sit and talk for hours and hours, and still have more to say when he must leave. He's kind, and gentle, and he loves me, too. Only it's hopeless." She bit her lip and looked away. "I am thirty-five years old. Life is passing me by. Oh, why must I be an invalid?"

"Why didn't you tell me?" Heart full of compassion, Granville sat on the edge of the settee and took Regina's hand in his. "My sweet, patient Regina, someday you'll get better, I know you will."

"I am not sweet, and thank you but I don't delude myself. I shall be lying on this sofa until the day I die, long after Lord Kellems gives up and finds a woman who's not a sickly, weak creature such as I. One who's younger, too."

How it pained him to hear his dearly beloved sister talk this way. "You've always been so brave. I've never heard you express such thoughts before."

"I've never been in love before." She clasped his hand tight and gazed at him with her luminous eyes. Lowering her voice, she confided, "He wants me to run away with him."

"What? You and Kellems marry?" Although Granville considered himself so worldly-wise nothing would surprise him, he found Regina's revelation astounding. In truth, he had never thought of Regina as anything but an invalid, had never even pictured her with a man. "I . . . don't know what to say."

"You needn't say anything." Regina managed to muster her usual scornful smile. "I shan't run off with Kellems, much as I'd like to. I've thought about it, you know. Being in his arms. Being close in bed together, all warm, no clothes between us."

"He hasn't—?"

"No, of course not." Regina laughed at the thought. "The closest he comes to licentious behavior is a quick peck on my forehead. He also writes me the most atrocious poetry you ever heard. Other than that, our relationship has been circumspect. Most tediously, regrettably circumspect." At his amazed silence, she added, "I can see you're surprised your sainted sister has such feelings."

"I suppose I am," he admitted thoughtfully. "And that's thoroughly wrongheaded on my part. You're a woman, so of course you have feelings. I only wish . . . why don't you marry him? I mean, Kellems loves you just the way you are, does he not? If he's willing to take you as you are—"

"Never." Regina's fingers gripped the coverlet with resolve. "He needs sons. In my present condition, I'd never be able to give him sons. Therefore, I shall come to him a whole, well woman, or not at all. Besides, he's thirty, I'm thirty-five."

"A mere nothing when you consider our earthly lives are infinitesimally small blips in the vast eons of time."

"But think of the uproar my eloping would create. Can you imagine how Mama would react?"

Regina's question made him smile. "Doubtless she'd have an attack and fall dead on the spot, thus burdening you with overwhelming guilt for the rest of your life."

"There you are." Regina returned his smile with a rueful one of her own. "Lately Mama's been suspicious. Now, when Lord Kellems comes calling, she hardly ever leaves us alone. She'll make any excuse to come bursting in." Regina made a face. "Last time it was to dose me some evil-tasting elixir which she implied I must have or I would expire before sunset."

"But must you always worry about what Mama says?"

"Look who's talking."

Regina's turn-the-tables remark reminded him all too clearly of his own problems with his mother. He didn't care to discuss them. It was time to change course. "All these years you've been a tower of strength despite your illness—a model of bravery for us all. You're so deserving of a little happiness. I say, you should follow your heart and damn the consequences."

"You've been a tower of strength, too, John, but I don't see you following *your* heart."

"Whatever do you mean?" he asked, perplexed. He was not following her at all.

"I mean, Miss Lucy Winthrop." He started to protest, but she raised her hand. "Did you know you talk about her all the time? And when you do, there's a certain wishful gleam in your eyes."

Her words so disturbed him he rushed to protest. "For God's sake, she's only a governess."

"Shame. You sound like our mother. Are you saying you could only love someone of your own status and class?"

"You know I'm not like that."

"Oh, really?" Her voice was loaded with skepticism. "Would you marry the woman?" She waited for him to speak, but he did not have an answer. "Of course you wouldn't marry her. Chaos would result. Mama aside, think how your career would collapse in shambles if you decided to marry a lowly governess. You'd never be prime minister. And so, dear brother"—she wagged her finger at him to make her point—"much as we might protest, we must conform to society's rules. As a consequence, I shall remain lonely, sickly, and un-fulfilled, and you, poor man, shall marry the empty-headed Lady Camilla who will no doubt make you miserable for the rest of your life. You will no more follow your heart than I will follow mine."

Regina was right. A sudden rebellion raged within him. Without consciously realizing it, he was still allowing his mother to rule his life. True, she'd been ill . . . or had she? Either way, she was better now. He should be free to do as he pleased. "Society's rules be damned. For once I'm going to do what I want to do."

"And that is?"

"I shall leave for Penfield Manor first thing in the morning. For weeks now, I've been most desirous of seeing my children. I have allowed insignificant social functions to get in the way, but no more."

Regina clapped her hands. "Bully for you."

A fine idea struck him. "Why don't you come with me?"

"I cannot. You know I've never been away from Mama. She would never allow—"

"Forget what our mother would or would not allow. The woman smothers you. You've been under her thumb all your life. Don't you think it's time you got away from her for a while?"

"I never thought . . ."

"Do it, Regina," he earnestly replied. "If you do, I shall personally carry you anyplace you wish to go."

"But Christmas is coming. You know how Mama dotes on all the London Christmas parties."

He had another fine idea. "We haven't celebrated Christmas at Penfield Manor since Father died. Don't you think it's high time we did? We'll have presents, a Yule log, the children will be delighted. We shall have a grand party and invite the tenants, as well as neighbors. Friends from London, too, including Kellems."

"I told you it was hopeless between us."

"All right, it's hopeless. But wouldn't you like to have him there anyway? He could read you poetry, and"—in jest he gently nudged her arm—"haul you around when I'm not available."

Regina's eyes were beginning to light. "Oh, do you think we really could? It sounds too wonderful to be true. Let's do it."

"We'll leave first thing in the morning."

"Mama—"

"You think she'd give up the London Christmas season for rustic festivities in the country? I think not. She will definitely stay in London."

Regina looked enraptured. "And you and I shall have a glorious holiday from our dear mother, whom we love very much, but—"

"But who drives us to distraction and we need to get away from her," Granville finished, smiling.

Out of the blue, she asked, "And what will you do about Miss Winthrop?"

He didn't know. His sister's mere mention of the governess's name caused his heart to swell with anticipation. But anticipation of what? He didn't have an answer. All he knew was, now that he'd made up his mind to return to Penfield Manor, he could hardly wait to see Miss Lucy Winthrop again.

Chapter Ten

During the weeks following Lord Granville's and his family's return to London, Lucy made a point to keep herself extremely busy. If she was busy, she didn't have time to think. If she didn't have time to think, then tantalizing thoughts of Lord Granville would not creep into her head. And keeping busy wasn't at all difficult, what with three active, inquisitive children to care for.

But despite her best efforts, the errant thoughts pursued her. Each morning when she awoke, she envisioned that intimate moment in the nursery when, had she but given the slightest indication, she would have been in his arms. Then she would assure herself she'd made the right decision, the only proper decision she could possibly make. Why, then, could she not stop thinking about him? No matter how busy she was, she could not suppress those unguarded moments when a vision of his lean, sinewy body would slip into her thoughts and taunt her. Or she'd think of that jaunty smile, or those warm, brown eyes that held the light of desire when he looked at her. Or had they? Had she seen only what she wanted to see? Regardless, there were times her knees went weak, just thinking about him. Times when, to her hidden embarrassment and chagrin, one or another of the children would comment, "Miss Winthrop, you're not listening to me. You seem so far away."

She was thus engaged in daydreaming one morning when Becky, hearing a noise, peered out the fourth-floor front window of the nursery and exclaimed, "Oh, la! 'ere comes 'er ladyship."

Lucy went to the window and witnessed the Granville coach rolling up the driveway. "Is her ladyship expected?"

"Not that I know of," Becky answered. "That's strange. She usually sends word ahead so we can work our fingers to the bone getting ready for her."

Lucy watched as the coach door opened, expecting Lady Granville to emerge. Instead, her heart lurched as she saw Lord Granville step to the ground. He turned, leaned back inside, and lifted Lady Regina from the coach. Lucy couldn't hear what they were saying, but they appeared to be bantering, and both were smiling. Carrying his sister as he would a feather, he veritably sprang up the marble steps and out of sight.

Becky raised herself on tiptoe to get a better view. "So where's 'er ladyship?" The coachman slammed the door. Obviously no one else was getting out. "Oh, la, I guess she ain't coming after all. 'Tis me lucky day."

Lucy murmured a compromising "Hmm," as she tried to conceal the wild thoughts that suddenly tumbled through her head. He was here! Why had he come? She had been hard put to conceal her errant feelings before, but now that he was here . . . ? *Lord give me the strength.*

"Is it Papa?" William, who had been diligently working on his arithmetic, joined her at the window.

"It is indeed, William. Come, let's wash our hands and faces, then we'll go down to greet him."

Going downstairs wasn't necessary. Before the children had finished washing, Lord Granville appeared at the nursery door.

"Papa!" The children flew into his arms, even William who this time had no hesitation. With a whoop of pleasure, Granville knelt and hugged them all. Over the tops of their heads, he regarded Lucy with an expression that at first seemed but a casual acknowledgment between master and servant, yet for one singular moment Lucy stood powerless to move, inwardly shaken by the storm of sentiments, unspoken, unseen, but indisputably tangible, that surged back and forth between them. Without question, his eyes told her he remembered that night in the nursery.

It was Granville who broke the spell. "Good afternoon,

Miss Winthrop." His tone was a model of reserved politeness. "I trust both you and the children are well?"

Lucy managed to curtsy and reply in a stilted voice, "It's a pleasure to see you, your lordship. We are indeed well." Listening to herself, she could hardly believe she sounded so normal when her insides were jangling with excitement.

Becky asked, "Is there going to be a 'ouse party?"

Granville laughed indulgently. "No, Becky, although I'm not surprised you asked. That's usually the reason for my return to Penfield Manor, isn't it? But there's no party planned this time. Later we might have a few guests, but for the time being Lady Regina needs seclusion and rest, whereas"—he reached to ruffle William's hair—"I have come home to get better acquainted with you, and Mary and Winifred."

Thank God. Lucy rejoiced that at last Lord Granville recognized his neglect of his children.

"I've brought presents," Granville announced. "Shall we go downstairs and open them, children? You, too, Miss Winthrop, and you, Becky."

The presents had been piled on a table in the drawing room. Mary and Winifred squealed with delight when given dolls. William was pleased to receive a pair of binoculars. Becky, all in a dither, opened a box that contained lace handkerchiefs.

"Oh, la, your lordship, I ain't never seen such fancy lace."

"In appreciation of your diligence, Becky. They're straight from a little shop in Bond Street." Granville turned to Lucy, a book in hand. His voice held an odd but gentle tone as he said, "This is for you, Miss Winthrop. I remembered your love of poetry, so I stopped by Hatchards, thinking you might like this book of poems by Sir Walter Scott."

"How kind of you," Lucy answered quickly over her choking, beating heart.

William held up his new binoculars. "Now I can go bird watching. Will you come, Papa? Perhaps we could go tomorrow."

Lord Granville addressed Lucy. "You take the children for a walk each morning, do you not?"

"Indeed, sir, if the weather is not too inclement. I firmly believe children should have fresh air and exercise every day."

"Then I shall come along and we shall watch for birds."

"Splendid," William cried.

"We leave promptly at eight," Lucy remarked. That she had managed to sound prim, and quite proper, was no small achievement. Obviously Lord Granville was bent on forming a closer relationship with his children. On that score, her delight knew no bounds. On the other hand, the thought of taking a walk through the woods with him threw her brain into a complete dither. She would have to watch herself every moment. No matter how much she was tempted, never again, by as much as a word, glance, or gesture, would she ever reveal her inappropriate feelings for her employer.

The next morning Lord Granville looked his usual dashing self in a dark green hunting jacket, buckskin breeches, and top boots. As they started onto the path through the woods, he dropped back to walk alongside Lucy as the children scrambled ahead. "Ah, a chance to be alone," he said. "I must talk to you."

Lucy had dressed as plainly as possible in her governess gown, bonnet, and a voluminous wool cloak to guard against the chill November day. Thanks to Lady Darwood, she owned several more attractive gowns, but she'd pledged never again to wear any of them around Lord Granville. To her shame and regret, she had consciously been a temptress that night in the nursery. It would not happen again. "Talk to me?" She wondered what he meant.

"I wanted to thank you for the wonderful work you've done with my children and for opening my eyes to . . . well, I see clearly now how I was neglecting them."

"That's most pleasant to hear." No need to reveal how utterly overjoyed she'd been when she saw him step from the coach.

"Another thing." They were strolling at a slow pace. As they passed a baneberry bush, he broke off a twig and stripped it bare.

"Yes?" she prompted when he didn't speak.

"It won't happen again, I give you my word."

She wasn't going to play coy. "You mean, that night in the nursery."

"My behavior was less than correct and for that I apologize."

"Apology accepted. We won't think of it ever again."

"It's done." Granville shot Lucy a quick glance, thinking how he would very much like to tweak a certain shiny curl that poked from beneath her bonnet and bobbed on her forehead. From there, he would run his finger down her pretty nose, across those rosy, luscious lips, trail it down over her fine, stubborn chin. And from there . . .

Her cloak covered all, but no matter. From memory he could easily draw a vision of the sweet curve of her full breasts, her slender waist, the alluring flare of her hips. Of course, he could only imagine her legs, but he'd wager they were as shapely as the rest of her . . .

"I have a question," she said.

"Ask away, Miss Winthrop."

Feeling awkward and self-conscious, Lucy had groped madly for a change in subject. "I have been meaning to ask if you have given any consideration to giving Mary her own horse."

"You think she's outgrown her pony?"

"Why not give the pony to Winifred? She's old enough to ride now. Then we could go riding every day . . ."

As they strolled, chatting, along the path, Lucy caught the occasional glance of Lord Granville's signet ring as he swung his arm. It brought her attention to his strong, square hands, which in turn caused her to recall her secret musings in the dark of night when she could almost feel the stroke of his exploring fingers sending jolts of passion through her as he held her tight, and . . .

"Do you ride, Miss Winthrop?"

"I have, on occasion. With Lord Darwood's children." She must get a grip on herself. If he could read her thoughts, she would expire of embarrassment.

"Splendid." Granville advised himself this foolishness must stop. If she could read his thoughts, she would know his facade as a lofty lord was but a sham and he was all too human. "Then we shall go riding tomorrow. Mary and William shall ride horses, Winifred the pony."

"That's excellent." As they continued on in silence, Lucy felt a curious disappointment. She recognized she was being utterly irrational, but the fact was, a heaviness had centered in her chest when he assured her he would never make advances again. *Foolish girl, what do you want?* Now she felt even more self-conscious and awkward. She'd been happy he'd returned, but knowing she would never be able to relax around him, she almost wished he would leave.

"Look, Papa," William called from up the path. He was pointing to a pinecone-covered area beneath an evergreen. "This is where Miss Winthrop found your ring."

"For which I shall be eternally grateful." Granville addressed Lucy, "That reminds me. I granted you three wishes. What of the other two?"

"Is there a time limit?"

"Did the genie set a time limit?"

She laughed. "Um, I don't think so."

"Then no."

She had decided never to ask anything of him again. She hadn't changed her mind, but he needn't know that. "I haven't decided yet. When I do you will be the first to know."

"Fine. I shall be here at least two weeks, possibly longer. Perhaps you'll have thought of another wish by then."

So he was staying for a while. How could she feel both overjoyed and full of trepidation at the same time? In the coolest voice she could summon, she replied, "The children will be delighted you're staying."

"And you?" He looked at her sideways. There went that jauntily raised eyebrow again.

"I'm happy for the children, of course."

A long moment of silence slipped by.

"God's blood," he suddenly exclaimed.

His sudden oath made her jump. "What's wrong?"

"Must you sound so . . . so servantlike?"

"I *am* a servant."

"You didn't sound like a servant that night in the nursery."

"My mistake. I forgot my station in life."

"Don't be absurd."

"I am not being absurd. Besides, didn't you just say you weren't going to talk about it?" Suddenly amused, she shot him a determined glance. "From now on, I plan to be the epit- . ome of a perfect governess." Mockingly she continued. "Yes sir, no sir, thank you sir. I am your humble servant, sir." As she spoke, she held out her cloak and dipped in an exaggerated curtsy along the path.

He burst out laughing. "You could never be humble."

She, too, had to laugh. "Try me. It's for the best, you know." Suddenly all the tension, all the awkwardness, vanished between them. She felt relaxed, could see no good reason why they could not be friends, despite the currents of never-to-be-fulfilled desire that flowed between them. "I must confess, that night in the nursery I did everything I could to entice you. I was determined you should enjoy dinner with your children, no matter what the cost."

"You succeeded. You looked beautiful that night. I was indeed enticed."

"Thank you, but rest assured, I shall never let it happen again. I'm a governess. I know my station in life. The greatest joy of my life is teaching, which I shall do until I become a withered old ape leader, when, as my sister predicts, I shall simply dry up and blow away."

His mouth quirked into a lopsided grin. "Somehow, I doubt it, Miss Winthrop." He looked at her, and the double meaning of his gaze was quite obvious. "You were meant for better things."

She let his comment lie, knowing they were again close to where danger lay.

Later, when they were returning, Lucy thought to ask about Lady Regina. "Is she any better at all?"

Granville heaved a discouraged sigh. "I was hoping a change of scene might perk her up, but I guess not. For years I've been hoping she'd improve, but she stays the same."

"Such a pity. Tell me, do you suppose . . . ?" She hesitated, aware she was about to go where she had no business going. Still, it wouldn't hurt to try. "Do you recall when I was talking about the merits of fresh air and exercise? I firmly believe in it, you know. I noticed Lady Regina hardly leaves her room. She never goes outside. And the windows in her room are always shut, and the curtains drawn to keep out the sun."

"Those are my mother's orders. Her perception of how best to care for an invalid is, I fear, in juxtaposition to yours. She finds no merit whatever in fresh air. In fact, considers it quite harmful. As for exercise—" Granville chuckled at the thought, then grew serious. "I fear poor Regina will be spending the rest of her life lying on the sofa."

"But if she could walk outside in the sunshine a little each day—just a few steps—"

"Never," Granville adamantly replied. "Mama would never allow it. Besides, Regina's so weak, I doubt she could."

"I see." Lucy knew it was useless to say more. She should not have brought the subject up in the first place. It was just that it was hard, seeing a beautiful woman like Lady Regina wasting her life away.

When they returned to the manor, Lucy was surprised when Lord Granville announced, "I shall see you and the children at dinner tonight."

"You're coming to the nursery?"

"No. You are all to dine with me in the dining room."

Mightily pleased, she replied, "It might be a bit late for Winifred."

"Then I shall notify Cook we're moving dinner up an hour. How does seven o'clock sound?"

She had to suppress delighted laughter. She had hoped he'd get to know his children better but never in her wildest dreams expected such a turnaround. "Sounds quite satisfactory, m'lord." She remembered his invalid sister. "I hope Lady Regina will be there."

"I doubt it. As you know, she generally isn't up to dining with the family and takes her meals in her room."

"Will you ask her?"

"Of course, but don't be disappointed if she says no."

The curtains were drawn in Regina's bedchamber when Granville entered. He was so accustomed to her existing in a darkened room, he hardly noticed, but remembering Lucy's remark, he commented, "Why not pull back the curtains? It's a sunny day outside, even if it is November."

His sister met his remark with a disdainful sniff. "And risk Mama's wrath? I think not. You know how she feels about the harmful rays of the sun."

Granville seated himself in a chair beside the chaise where Regina lay. "What happened to that fine mood you were in?"

Regina held up a letter. "Apparently Lord Kellems must have found out you and I left London. This is from him, brought posthaste by his footman. He wanted to come visiting."

"But that's splendid. Isn't that what you want?"

"Of course it's what I want, but what's the use? I'm feeling worse, John. Right now I'm so fatigued I want nothing but to go straight to bed. I have already written and told him no."

Her despairing voice cast a pall over his heart. "But you'll feel better tomorrow."

"No, I won't, I shall never feel better. It would have been a waste of time to have Kellems come down from London, and for what? A visit with a pathetic invalid who will never be well?"

Granville knew better than to pursue the subject. "At least come down to dinner tonight. It should be lively. The children will be there, as well as Miss Winthrop."

"Ah, the ubiquitous Miss Winthrop." Regina appeared to bestir herself slightly from the fit of the dismals she was in. "Perhaps I shall come down. It might be interesting to gauge your degree of finesse in handling your flimsy pretense of *not* being attracted to her."

"That's nonsense. She's only the children's gov—"

"Spare me."

Granville was pleased to see his sister was amused, even if it was at his expense. "Granted, I find Miss Winthrop quite charming, but do you seriously think I could be interested in a governess?"

"Yes."

He didn't argue. Regina was too perceptive to deceive. *Especially now*, he thought resentfully. Since his walk in the woods today, he had stoked a slowly growing fire within himself, unable to think of anything or anybody except Lucy Winthrop. He recalled how he used to taunt his lovesick friends, so arrogant in his belief that he, himself, would never act the fool over a woman. How the mighty had fallen. Now, each beat of his heart seemed to intensify his longing, turning his normally composed, well-organized brain into a seething cauldron of desire. How he ached to hold her, kiss her, take her to his bed . . . *Oh, God, why do I want what I can never have?*

With great casualness he got up to leave. "Oh, by the way, we're dining an hour early tonight. We don't want little Winifred staying up past her bedtime."

Which gown?

After bathing, Lucy stood in her soft batiste chemise in the middle of her bedchamber, gripped in the throes of a dilemma. In her wardrobe hung the plain gray, without doubt the gown she should befittingly wear to dinner. On her bed, spread out in all its glory, lay a dazzling white bombazine dinner gown, another of Lady Darwood's generous gifts. Although it was her favorite, Lucy had never found the occasion to wear it. She had, however, spent considerable time admiring the gorgeous gown with its daringly low-cut bodice and lush trim of bands of satin ribbon. She adored, too, the dainty puffed sleeves, edged with lace ruffles, which appeared under the capped sleeves. With loving care, Lucy had laid the matching accessories in their proper place around the gown: below, slippers covered in the same fabric; above, a pearl comb for her hair and dangling pearl ear bobs; on the side, long white gloves and a sandalwood fan.

Becky entered. Regarding the bed, she declared, "La, Miss Winthrop, what a beautiful gown. Is that what you're wearing tonight?"

"I'm afraid not," came Lucy's rueful reply. "In fact, I shouldn't be entertaining even the slightest notion of wearing anything other than the gray."

"But why not?"

Lucy replied with vehemence, "Because a governess is never supposed to bedeck herself in anything other than some colorless, no-style, high-necked atrocity."

"But you wore the blue chemise with the white flounce the other time."

"That night in the nursery was an exception." Lucy did not care to elaborate. No need mentioning how Lord Granville's eyes had lit at the sight of her in the beautiful blue gown. In fact, Lucy sternly reminded herself, his ardent reaction was all the more reason why tonight she should dress conservatively.

"Will you help me with my hair, Becky?" She reached for the loathsome gray.

Becky clicked sympathetically. "Such a waste. If you don't mind me saying so, Lord Granville's eyes would bug out for sure if he saw you in the white. An' what with your manners an' the witty way you talk, I'd wager you could trap him"— Becky snapped her fingers—"just like that."

"To what purpose would I trap him, Becky?" Lucy could not keep the bitterness from her voice. "He most certainly wouldn't marry me, and I have no desire to be his mistress, or any man's."

"I s'pose you're right," Becky answered reluctantly.

"I know I'm right. It would be sheer folly for me to wear anything else. I might be miserable wearing this ugly thing"— distastefully she held up the gray—"but at least I shall be doing the proper thing and cannot be accused of enticing the lord and master of the manor."

With great purpose of mind, Lucy donned the gray. Becky helped her with her hair. When Lucy was ready, she regarded her somber self in her small mirror, recalling Becky's words that Lord Granville's eyes would indeed bug out if he saw her in the lovely white dinner gown. And indeed they would. How thrilled she would be if . . . but, no. She must put temptation behind her.

It was time to go downstairs. Although Lucy hadn't meant to, when she reached her door she turned, assuring herself there would be no harm in taking just one more look at the gorgeous but totally inappropriate ensemble she'd spread on the bed.

Just one more little peek . . .

*   *   *

Dinner that night was a sparkling, jovial affair. Granville could not remember when he'd more thoroughly enjoyed himself. Not only did his children behave with impeccable manners, his pride knew no bounds when both Mary and William were able to contribute bits of wisdom to a lively discussion of politics. Thanks to Miss Winthrop, of course. Little Winifred didn't have to speak. Her childish peels of laughter were a delight to hear. Perched on a pillow, she looked adorable with her dimples and blond curls.

Even the servants were in a jocular mood. Although they tried to keep their customary stony expressions, Granville caught an occasional surreptitious smile. They were enjoying the rare spectacle of children enlivening the usually sedate evening meal.

Regina had consented to let him carry her to the dining room. Her dismal mood seemed to have lightened somewhat as she joined in the lively conversation.

But most of all . . .

Miss Lucy Winthrop sat across from him. He had assumed, if he thought of it at all, she would be dressed as a governess. Instead, she was such a vision of loveliness in white he was hard put to take his eyes off her. He liked what she'd done with her hair piled atop her head in soft, shiny curls, adorned with a lustrous pearl comb. Frequently, to his delight, she threw back her head and laughed, thus causing her pearl ear bobs to swing jauntily, and most enticingly, from her pretty earlobes. She wore no necklace, which was just as well, considering no adornment in the world could enhance the graceful curve of her long, lily white neck. It led, when his gaze dropped ever so slightly, not so it would show, to the velvety soft, flawless expanse of skin revealed by the low cut of her gown. If he allowed his gaze to drop lower still, he could trace that soft expanse of skin to the bodice of her gown where the teasing swell of her breasts disappeared beneath a confection of lace and white satin . . .

"John . . . ? Brother, dear, you're not listening."

Granville jerked his thoughts back to the matter at hand, grateful that despite his near-overwhelming, and quite disgusting, desire to ogle his governess all evening, he'd managed to conceal his lust and maintain an expression of indifference. The dinner was nearing an end. Regina was speaking. "I fear I'm tiring and must go to bed." When Granville started to rise, she told him, "Don't get up. I'll have one of the footmen carry me upstairs." She addressed Lucy. "I understand you're all going riding tomorrow. Do have fun. The evening has been grand, by the way. I had a lovely time."

Lucy, too, could not remember a dinner where she'd enjoyed herself more, yet she'd secretly been in a fret all evening over her reckless decision to change to the daring dinner gown. Whatever had possessed her? It was as if some uncontrollable force had commanded the last-minute change of gowns, causing her to forget all common sense and reason. Worse, Lord Granville had been pleasant enough, but judging from the inscrutable expression with which he'd regarded her all evening, she was sure she'd provoked his displeasure. She knew she must pull herself together, and she would, as soon as this wonderful dinner was over.

Now, in response to Regina's question about their ride tomorrow, Lucy's heart went out to the thin, pale woman who had so little enjoyment in her life. She supposed she shouldn't, yet spurred by the friendly repartee of the evening, the next words out of her mouth were, "Why don't you come riding with us?"

"I?" Regina laughed in surprise. "One can only imagine the horror on my mother's face if she saw me on a horse."

"But you wouldn't have to walk a step," Lucy persisted. "His lordship could carry you to the entryway. There, you could mount the horse directly. We'd only go a little way, and just think, you'd be out in the fresh air and sunshine."

Lady Regina sighed. "I've been an invalid all my life, Miss Winthrop. I cannot conceive of doing something normal, like riding a horse."

And why not? Lucy silently asked. She wasn't getting anywhere and decided to let the subject drop, at least for the time being.

After Regina left and the children finished dessert, Lucy arose from the table. "It's their bedtime," she told Lord

Granville. Actually, judging from his indifferent attitude at dinner, she was anxious, herself, to get away.

"We shall do this again tomorrow," he answered.

"That . . . would be lovely." She wasn't sure if she really thought it was lovely or not. She only knew that she'd had her little fling and tomorrow night most definitely would be back in the gray. The children gathered around her. "Say good night to your father," she said. "I'm sure it's time for his brandy and cigar."

Lord Granville shook his head decisively. "I don't want any brandy and I despise cigars. I shall be up to tuck them in shortly, just as I did before."

Just as I did before. The words rang repeatedly in Lucy's ears all the way upstairs.

Just as before, after a few minutes Lucy was in the dimly lit nursery when Lord Granville entered. "They're all tucked in?" she asked.

"All tucked in." With more force than necessary, Granville shut the nursery door. Hands on hips, he stood regarding her. She could not make out the strange expression on his face, but it did not bode well. "Why did you wear that gown?" he asked.

"Because I was foolish," she answered promptly, taken aback by his abrupt manner.

"Then might I suggest you start using your head?"

His vehemence made her back a step away. She thought to explain why, in a moment of weakness, she'd decided to act the temptress again, but on second thought, even if she could explain, why should she? Why give him the satisfaction? She would give him a quick apology and be done with it. "I overstepped my bounds. I apologize. From now on, I shall wear nothing but my servant's uniform. There, is that humble enough?"

"Not humble enough by half. You really do make a very poor servant, you know," he said. "It's your attitude."

"Are you going to sack me?"

"If you wear that gown again I might."

"You cannot mean that."

His mouth twisted into an ironic grin. "I am beginning to think I would be far better off if I did sack you."

"I told you, from now on—"

"It won't help." With a suddenness that caused her to gasp, he gripped her shoulders and gazed deep into her eyes with fiery intensity. "You are beautiful no matter what you wear. And I am . . ."

"You are what, m'lord?" she asked, bewildered by his sudden change of mood.

"I am smitten with you, Miss Winthrop." He paused to consider. His lips twisted into a cynical smile, almost as if he was amused at himself. "No, smitten is hardly the word. Besotted. So transfixed with thoughts of you, I can barely function. That's what you've done to me. It's got to stop." He thrust her at arm's length and shook her slightly. "It will stop. I gave you my word I wouldn't bother you, and I intend to honor my word—even if . . ."

With a self-deprecating laugh, he continued. "A dip in the icy river might help."

Her thoughts were spinning. "I don't know what to say, other than—"

"My behavior is most inappropriate?" He laughed again. "Indeed, that would be the word you'd use. Inappropriate indeed. But at any rate"—he dropped his hands from her shoulders—"from now on, I guarantee you are safe from my . . . er, shall we say, lecherous advances. I shall continue to tuck the children in, but in future I shall refrain from coming to your door afterward to further annoy you with a scene such as this."

He started to back away. For a moment she stood immobilized, acutely aware of the tingling spots on her shoulders where his hands had gripped. Every sensible fiber within her told her, let him go, he was nothing but trouble. Too late. No way in the world could she fight the hot desire that coursed through her veins. *Don't throw caution to the winds,* cried the little voice within her—a faint, fading voice that she ignored. Her heart taking a perilous leap, she reached out her arms. "Don't go yet."

Chapter Eleven

*I*n an instant, he pulled her to him roughly, almost violently. An inarticulate cry came from deep within her throat as his mouth hungrily covered hers. She wrapped her arms around his neck, pulled him tighter still, and responded with an eagerness that unmasked her own aching hunger. She had no idea of time, no idea how long they remained locked in their tight, swaying embrace.

He raised his mouth and looked at her, a glint of wonder, mixed with desire in his eyes. "God, how I've wanted you," he whispered. Not waiting for a response, he started trailing ardent kisses down her neck until, to her exquisite pleasure, she felt the moistness of his tongue and mouth as he explored the pulsing hollow at the base of her throat.

She threw her head back and managed to gasp, "And I've wanted you. I knew I shouldn't—"

"*I* shouldn't."

"*We* shouldn't, and I—"

Before she could say more, his lips crushed hers again in a kiss so wildly passionate it made her knees go weak. She clung to him, in a fog of wonderment that after all the months of fruitless, hopeless daydreaming she was actually in his arms. But this was no daydream. She had only to hear the pulsing excitement in his urgent, rapid breathing, feel his manhood pressed in near-bruising hardness against her pelvis, to know that here, in the mundane confines of the children's nursery, she was miraculously, incredibly, in a torrid embrace with the esteemed member of Parliament, likely-to-be-next-prime-minister, and frighteningly desirable Lord Granville.

When he lifted his lips again, he planted quick kisses on her forehead, nose, cheeks, and chin, causing little rivulets of passion to surge through her veins. Through it all, she was very much aware of his hand, first at her waist, then slowly burning an increasingly pleasurable path as it slid up the side of her gown. Though locked in a haze of passion, she informed herself that if it got much higher she would push it away, end this madness. The trouble was, her arms, still wrapped firmly around his neck, not only refused to cooperate, a power quite beyond herself caused her to slide her hand up the back of his neck, bury it in the luxurious thickness of his hair, and press him even closer.

But this unacceptable conduct could not continue. She must stop immediately . . .

Well, in a minute . . .

She had not stopped his hand. She could feel its warmth through her bodice. It started spreading such pleasure she felt transported to a soft, wispy cloud. His mouth covering hers made it impossible for her to speak, but she expressed her feelings with a muted "Mmm."

He pulled his mouth away. "This won't do," he said, fitting his words between long pulls of ragged breath. He broke from her arms. Two steps took him to the door that led to the small, now unused governess's bedchamber beyond. He yanked it open, returned, and without warning, scooped her into his arms.

"Where are we going?" she asked. Silly question. If he had answered, "To hell," she would not have protested.

He made no reply but silently carried her into the bedchamber where, next she knew, she was lying on her back on the small bed in a state of sweet surrender, her whole warm, throbbing body attuned to him, awaiting with exquisite anticipation for the touch of his hands, his mouth.

"Oh, Lucy," he groaned, and buried his head into the hollow of her shoulder. Shortly he raised up. Even in the midst of the passionate moment, she saw his eyebrow quirked mischievously. "I *may* call you Lucy," he inquired, "considering the circumstances?"

She returned a soft laugh, enraptured with his closeness and the intimacy of his dialogue. "Call me anything you please, your lordship."

Your lordship? thought Granville. Lucy's amusingly odd formality came as a jarring, most unwelcome intrusion into his hot, single-minded pursuit. *What am I doing?* he asked himself. His conscience answered, *You cad, you're seducing your governess,* and further inquired, *Where have your brains gone?* He knew the answer to that. His brains had sunk to that near-uncontrollable area of his anatomy that demanded fulfillment.

He wanted this woman, burned for this woman—

Still, she was a servant, for God's sake, he the master. However much he wanted her, however much she wanted him, the cruel truth was, she would be ruined if he got her with child whereas he would suffer not one wit. How totally unfair life was for a woman. He, the aggressor, would glean nothing but pleasure from their impassioned union, whereas she would be in complete disgrace. If she were some wanton doxy, he would have no qualms about taking advantage of her. But she wasn't a doxy, she was a woman of substance and character, the trusted teacher of his children who not only adored her but held her in the highest esteem.

He ought to stop but how could he? A man wasn't meant to stop when he was so far gone in his passion that all he could think of was the driving need to plunge himself into her.

"No," she suddenly cried, planting one hand firmly on his chest and pushing him back.

"You want me to stop?" he asked.

"We must."

"Of course." With a supreme effort he wrenched himself away from the beautiful woman who lay beneath him. Realizing he would have to put himself completely away from her or go mad, he strode to the window and stared, unseeing, into the moonless night.

"Are you angry, m'lord?" She sat up, swung her feet to the floor, smoothed her dress.

"My name is John," he replied with suppressed vehemence.

He strode back to the bed, knelt in front of her, and grasped her shoulders in a viselike grip. "*John,* do you hear me? Not *your lordship*, not *m'lord*, not *sir*, but if we ever make love again, you will call me *John*."

"It won't happen again," she declared, regarding him steadfastly. "I am so sorry, but I—"

"Hush," he replied, touching a finger to her lips. "You have no need to apologize. I, too, was having doubts."

"You were?" she asked, surprised.

"I was," he answered with a laugh. Strange, how he could almost cry with frustration at the same time. "At the risk of sounding like a self-righteous idiot"—his fingers reached to stroke her cheek—"I don't know if I could have gone through with it. It would not have been fair."

Leaning down, she twisted her fingers in his hair. "You are indeed right, my lord. No, for the moment it's John." With a wistful sigh she continued. "I shall call you John tonight, but only tonight and never again."

"Hell and damnation." He bit his lip in frustration. "If only—"

"Let's forget *if only*s. You are the lord, I am the servant. That's one thing all the *if only*s in the world cannot change."

"Let me hold you one more time." Still kneeling before her, he slid his arms around her waist. She bent, pulled his head to her breast, wrapped her arms around him, nuzzled her face against his hair. Passion subsided, he had no idea of the passage of time or how long they clung to each other thus; he only knew he wanted to hold this enchanting woman forever, here, in this small servant's bedchamber, feeling the warmth of her, grateful she had stopped him and that he had readily agreed, protecting her from the folly of his own weaknesses.

A noise, no doubt from a servant in the hallway, brought him to his senses. "I must go."

"I know." They broke apart and rose to face each other, clutching hands. "There's nothing more to say, is there?" she asked. "Good night, John." She gave him a gentle smile. "Tomorrow I promise you will be *your lordship* again."

"And I promise"—it was hard to get the words out over the unexpected lump that had formed in his throat—"the other morning I told you this would never happen again. This time I give you my word, it will not."

"You're right, this is utter foolishness and most inappropriate on both our parts."

"Absolutely."

"You have Parliament to think about, and being the next prime minister, and marrying Lady Camilla Harvey, as your mother wants."

The mention of his mother triggered an angry leap of his pulse. "If I marry Lady Camilla it will be because it's what I want, not my mother. Trust me, she doesn't rule my life."

"Of course not, but your mother loves you and wants what's best for you. She's not a fool. You should listen to her."

Not caring to hear another word about his mother, Granville held his tongue and looked down at the woman who had just drawn him to heights of desire he'd never known before. "I had best be going." He raised her hand to his lips and kissed it tenderly. "Good night, my dearest Lucy, I do apologize."

"Tonight never happened," she firmly replied.

He left, appearing calm and collected on the outside, but within, his senses were churning. *Tonight never happened? Good God!* He dreaded going to bed, knowing memories of their smoldering moments of passion would keep him from sleep this night. Other troubling thoughts ran like wildfire through his mind. Just what was the nature of love? It was a question he'd never had cause to dwell upon before. What was happening to him? He needed to know because if love meant wanting to hold a woman in his arms forever and never let her go, then he loved Lucy Winthrop.

But reflection upon such a question was a waste of time. The plain truth was, they had been born to different worlds. Fate had decreed their paths were not meant to cross. Love or not, he would keep his vow and never touch her again. A feeling of hopelessness descended upon him. All his life he'd been satisfied, indeed proud, to live by his code of honor. Up to now, he had played out his contented existence in a sort of smug, self-satisfied cocoon. He had deluded himself into thinking whatever honor decreed was always the correct and proper thing, whereas those forbidden desires to which every man was subject were to be fought, conquered, and set aside. Now he could no longer deny the bitter truth: selfish, demanding Honor had become his cruel mistress. It forbade him from having the one woman in all the world he had ever really wanted.

Yet Honor ruled. It would always rule. He would not break his word.

Tonight never happened.

The next morning dawn was barely breaking when Lucy awoke. Or had she really been asleep? The astonishing events of the previous night had set her mind in a chaotic whirl of thoughts as she recalled those intimate moments with Lord Granville. Clearly he wanted her. Despite all her guilt and agonized soul-searching, part of her rejoiced in the wondrous knowledge that the overpowering attraction she felt for him was mutual.

But last night never happened. That's what she'd told Lord Granville, and he'd agreed. If she were halfway smart, she would listen to her own declaration.

Oh, but it had happened. Last night was an awakening experience that left her reeling, shocked at her own driving need. Now she knew why good girls did bad things. Over the years, she had witnessed a sad, never-ending procession of servant girls, compelled to leave their master's employ in disgrace, their swollen bellies concealed beneath their cloaks. She had always felt nothing but sympathy for the pitiful outcasts. In no way had she ever condemned them. Still, she recalled how deeply perplexed she'd been, wondering how a girl could risk the monumental shame of bearing a child out of wedlock, all for the sake of a few intimate moments with a man.

Now she knew. She'd had to gather all her strength to halt their lovemaking before the ultimate end. Thank heaven Granville had the presence of mind to contain himself immediately. That he had, told her a great deal. He had not wanted to hurt her. Assuredly she had his respect, if nothing more. A wry smile curved her lips. *For whatever respect is worth.* That she loved Lord Granville there could be no doubt, especially after last night. But she must face the fact that such a love was hopeless and never to be. *He is the love of my life and I shall never find another*, she thought with resigned despair. The dis-

mal years stretched ahead. She could see herself growing old,
always a governess, never a bride. Doubtless she would teach
until the day she died, dried-up, unfulfilled, and full of regrets
for what might have been but never was.

That's enough, she told herself, knowing she must not suc-
cumb to misery and self-pity. She had only one honorable
course to follow, and that was to ignore her tormented heart
and carry on. There was much to keep her busy, what with her
governess duties.

There was even something new to worry about.

Only yesterday she had received a letter from Augusta. She
and the children were doing fine, thanks to Lucy's generosity,
and now Montague's. He had finally secured a position as a
clerk at Edgemont-Percival & Company, a prestigious London
bank. The only problem was, lately Montague had taken to
bringing home expensive gifts. Elegant clothes for the children—a dinner set from Josiah Wedgwood—a brise fan of
mother-of-pearl for Augusta that she would never, ever use.
Augusta surmised these gifts cost far more than he could afford on a bank clerk's salary. She was appreciative, yet wondered if—oh, what a horrifying thought!—could he be stealing
from the bank?

Lucy most wholeheartedly hoped he was not, considering
the penalty for fraud and forgery was death by hanging.

After the tumultuous scene of the night before, Lucy
dreaded seeing Granville again, fearing their meeting would be
horribly awkward. She needn't have worried. Following his
usual routine, Granville appeared in the entry hall, just as Lucy
and the children were leaving for their daily ride. He greeted
the children warmly and looked at Lucy with precisely the
proper amount of detachment. "Good morning, Miss
Winthrop," he said with great aplomb. "I trust the weather is
not too inclement for a ride through the woods."

"Indeed not, m'lord." She was grateful her voice was
steady and she was able to return a matching dispassionate
gaze of her own. During the ride, Lucy was vastly relieved it
was uneventful, marked by the formalness between them.

In the days that followed, Granville was true to his word.

Lucy was surprised that under the circumstances, he did not return to London but instead continued to enjoy spending time with his children. Toward her, his attitude was the soul of discretion: polite, yet not too formal. In fact, he seemed to value her opinion highly, since he would occasionally seek her out to discuss the events of the day, or some concern about his family.

One day, while they and the children were riding through the woods, Granville brought his horse parallel to hers. "I am worried about Regina."

She immediately caught the slight nuance of address. If he regarded her as strictly a servant, he would have said "Lady Regina." That he used the more familiar name warmed her heart. *But what of it?* Was she looking for crumbs tossed from his lordship's table? In her most impersonal voice she replied, "I notice your sister has not dined with us since that very first night."

"Unfortunately you're right," Lord Granville replied. "I had hoped . . . well, lately she's been blue-deviled, for some reason. Won't leave her room, hardly touches her food. I had thought to invite Lord Kellems, in hopes he would cheer her up. She says she'll refuse to see him, so I was wondering . . ."

"If I would speak to her?"

"Yes," he replied, grateful she'd immediately understood. "My sister likes you very much. I know she's listened to you in the past. If you could just speak with her. I doubt she'll leave her room, but if you could persuade her to at least receive Lord Kellems, I would be most grateful."

"Of course, I would be happy to." *I would do anything in the world for you*.

She could hardly keep her eyes off him as he rode by her side, devilishly handsome, moving with graceful ease atop Thunder, his Irish thoroughbred. "I shall visit Lady Regina this afternoon."

A stern-faced Matilda answered Lucy's knock on Lady Regina's door. "She's not up to seeing visitors," whispered the elderly servant.

In the background, Regina's querulous voice called, "Whoever it is, tell them to go away."

Lucy called, "It's only I, and I'll only stay a minute."

"Miss Winthrop? Well, that's different. Come in."

Lucy exchanged commiserating smiles with Matilda and stepped into the bedchamber. The air was stuffy. The curtains were closed tight. Through the dimness, she saw Lady Regina lying listlessly in her bed. "I'm so sorry you're not well." She seated herself in a chair next to the bed.

"I am never well." Quite unexpectedly Regina smote herself on the forehead. "Dear Lord, I sound just like my mother."

"A little perhaps," Lucy tactfully replied. "But you are not your mother."

"A small consolation, considering my miserable lot in life." Regina's lower lip curled disdainfully. Staring at the ceiling, she bitterly declared, "So I am not my mother. God has thrown me a crumb."

Lucy took her time to answer. Clearly Regina was feeling extremely sorry for herself, and not without good reason. A shallow answer, such as "You'll soon be feeling better," would be totally inadequate and surely do nothing except elicit Regina's scorn. At the risk of stepping beyond her bounds again, Lucy formed her reply. "It must be terrible, being sick all the time."

"My brother sent you, didn't he?" Jaw set, Regina still gazed fixedly at the ceiling. When an answer from Lucy was not immediately forthcoming, Regina finally turned her head and gave Lucy a long, intense gaze. "Is that not so, Miss Winthrop?"

No sense denying it, Lucy thought uncomfortably. So far, she was getting nowhere. "You are most perceptive. His lordship is indeed concerned about you. It would please him no end if you would at least come down to dinner tonight."

Regina stared at the ceiling again. "Well, I would *not* be pleased. What would be the purpose?"

"Better to ask, what would be the alternative?"

"The alternative is to lie here until I die, which, as you can see, is just what I plan to do."

"But you mustn't give up," Lucy cried, forgetting all the

careful words she'd planned to say. "You're still a young woman. You could still have a wonderful, fulfilling life, if you'd allow it. It seems to me—" Just in time, she recalled she was only a servant and had no right to speak her mind.

"It seems to you what? Finish your sentence."

"It's not my place—"

"I admire you tremendously, Miss Winthrop." For the first time, Regina managed a faint smile. She hitched herself up on the bed, plumped a pillow, leaned against it, and regarded Lucy quizzically. "Go ahead. Say what you please. I shan't hold it against you."

Lucy did not hesitate. "I know you've suffered from poor health all your life."

Regina sniffed with amusement. "Hardly an understatement."

"You've suffered greatly. But now . . ."

"Now what, Miss Winthrop? Out with it. I give you leave to say whatever it is you wish to say."

If Regina wanted the truth, she would get the truth. "It strikes me you're not trying."

"What do you mean?"

"I mean just what you think I mean. True, I know you are weak, but by just . . . just lying there"—Lucy gestured widely across the bed—"you're not doing one single thing to improve your condition."

"That's not so. The doctors tell me I am supposed to rest, so that's what I do. And God knows, I've choked down enough cod liver oil, and turnip juice, and snail tea, and other abominations—"

"All simply to please your mother. From what I've seen, you've given up. Now you're doing nothing to help yourself."

In a voice heavy with sarcasm, Regina inquired, "So what would you suggest I do? Get up and dance around the room?"

"Come down to dinner tonight." Listening to herself, Lucy was astounded. She had never dreamed she could speak so frankly to someone whose station in life was far above her own, but now that she'd started, she would stay the course and speak her mind. "Also, I think you should invite Lord Kellems for a visit. I know he'd raise your spirits tremendously. And another thing—"

"There's more?" Regina asked with ill-concealed skepticism.

Lucy took the plunge. "You ought to come riding with us tomorrow."

Regina exploded in false mirth. "Have you lost your mind? I told you before, I have never been on a horse. I would not have the slightest—"

"And I told you before, through no effort on your part, you could ride with us. It's easy. Your brother would carry you down and place you on your mount, which will be gentle, I assure you. You'd have nothing to fear. From then on, all you'd be required to do is hang on. Lord Granville, or I, or a groom will walk along beside you and guide the horse."

"And all this is to what purpose?" Regina's mouth was set in a grim, stubborn line.

"To what purpose?" Eyes alight, Lucy leaned forward in her chair. "To exercise your limbs. To soak in some sunshine. To put clean, pure air in your lungs instead of the foul and fetid substance you're breathing in this dark, stuffy, airless room. Why not give it a try?" Surprised at her own vehemence, Lucy sat back to await Regina's response, which could well be sheer fury at her audacity.

Lady Regina appeared to have no response at all. She lay staring at the ceiling until finally she turned toward Lucy and listlessly replied, "I appreciate your efforts. However, you need not waste any more of your time."

"I trust I have not offended you?"

"You mean well, Miss Winthrop. You just don't see, as I do, that my situation is quite hopeless. I shall never regain my health, not that I ever had it in the first place. Quite frankly, I have reached the point where I am not going to try."

"So you won't be coming down to dinner tonight?"

"No, nor shall I go riding tomorrow, nor shall I ever see Lord Kellems again."

Lucy rose to leave. Clearly she had met defeat, but even so, she would try one more time. "Do give some thought to what

I said." At the door, she softly added, "I could be right, you know. And besides, what have you got to lose?"

Lucy hurried to her own bedchamber where, her heart racing, she threw herself on the bed and contemplated her audacity. She knew she would not be dismissed. After all, Lady Regina had given her leave to speak her mind. Even so, never, in all her years of service, had she spoken to an employer's family member in such a bold manner.

The sad part was, her little lecture had all been for naught. Lady Regina was adamant, she could tell. Lucy hated disappointing Lord Granville, but she'd done her best, more than should have been required, actually. Nothing could help now.

Unless . . . Could Regina possibly change her mind? Perhaps as she lay in the semidarkness of her gloomy bedchamber, hour after hour, she would hear Lucy's words ringing in her ears: *What have you got to lose?*

Not much chance of it, Lucy realized, but she could always hope.

True to her word, Lady Regina did not appear at dinner that night. "You spoke to her?" Lord Granville inquired of Lucy.

"Yes, but you know how stubborn she is. I was even bold enough to ask her to come riding with us tomorrow, but there's no chance she will."

"Had my sister said yes, you would surely have performed a miracle. As it is, you've done your best. We cannot force others to do what they do not wish to do."

But my best was not good enough. Lucy sat silent and defeated. She had disappointed Lord Granville. Not only that, a beautiful young woman who might not be as ill as she supposed lay in her bed upstairs wasting her life away, and there was nothing anyone could do.

Although winter was coming, the following morning was a perfect day for riding, with a clear blue sky and the early rays of the sun fast dispersing the slight chill in the air.

When Lucy led her charges outside, she noted Lord Granville, who was usually early, was not there to greet them.

The groom had already brought the horses around . . . strange, was there an extra? She counted. Six, when there should have been five. Was someone joining them? An impossible thought struck her. *Could it be?*

"Good morning, Miss Winthrop."

It was Lord Granville, coming out the entrance, smiling, and in his arms, Lady Regina.

Lucy dropped a quick curtsy. Hardly able to contain herself, she managed to maintain her calm as she answered, "Good morning, your lordship." She greeted Lady Regina, fighting an urge to clap her hands with delight. But the prickly Regina would most certainly not appreciate such a display of emotion. In an offhand fashion Lucy remarked, "I see you've decided to join us."

Unsmiling, Regina tilted her nose in her oft-used saucy fashion. "You win, Miss Winthrop. You were so adamant yesterday, I decided to risk the ride. Once only, though. Then I shall return to my bed, which I should not have left in the first place."

"Well, I am delighted you're here." Lucy smiled benignly as she thought, *We shall see about that.* She beckoned to the children. "Come, let's mount up. Isn't it grand your aunt Regina is riding with us today?"

It was a rather strange procession that headed at the slowest speed possible into the woods, everyone riding except Lord Granville. On foot, he led his own horse, Thunder, as well as Buttercup, the oldest and most gentle horse in the stable. Atop Buttercup perched his sister, riding sidesaddle, gripping the saddle with both hands.

At first, Regina's pale face was pinched with stress, her forehead furrowed, lines of tension deep around her mouth. "I do not wish to go very far," she declared. She had spoken in her usual imperious manner, but the slight quaking in her voice gave her away.

"Only a little way," Lord Granville jovially replied. Lucy could tell from his grin how pleased he was, despite Regina's lack of enthusiasm for her first ride.

They made a happy, amiable group as they entered the woods, the children with their carefree laughter, Lord

Granville in fine fettle, making jokes as he carefully led his
sister's horse. The wildflowers of summer had faded, yet Lucy
thought how fortunate it was that despite its being late November, the woods were still a pleasant place. As the riders followed the sandy, winding path, they could still find beauty in
the thick growths of evergreen pines, their branches inter-
twined above forming a sheltered citadel. Most of the birds
had gone, but there were still magpies, chaffinches, and red-
wings that chose to remain behind. The little brook still gur-
gled as it wound its way between tall grasses and shrubs of
bird cherry, baneberry, and hazel.

"Isn't this a pretty spot?" asked Lucy.

"It is, rather," Regina replied. Coming from her, that was a
giant concession indeed.

By the time they halted by the brook to let the horses drink,
the lines of tension on Regina's face had eased. "Get on your
horse, John," she commanded.

"You don't want me to lead you?"

"Certainly not." Regina tossed her head. "If this is all there
is to riding, I can manage Buttercup myself."

Lucy's spirits rose. Regina was enjoying herself. Should
she dare hope she might try riding again?

When the ride was over and Lord Granville was helping his
sister dismount at the front portico, he inquired, "So did you
enjoy your ride?"

"It was all right I suppose." Regina's lukewarm answer was
belied by the sparkle in her eyes, the touch of color in her
cheeks.

"Then we shall ride again tomorrow," Granville declared.

Lucy held her breath. Was this Regina's first and last ride?

"I should like that," Regina replied, to Lucy's relief and delight. She scowled at her brother. "And next time, you needn't
lead Buttercup. If you'll just help me on, I daresay I can manage her myself."

Chapter Twelve

My Dearest Augusta,

   I trust this letter finds you and the children in good spirits and excellent health.

   Do you recall my mentioning in my last letter my concern over Lady Regina? She had become a recluse, lying in her bed most of the time, well on her way to becoming the complete invalid.

   I have wonderful news. Lady Regina's health is greatly improved. She is riding with us every day that the weather is not too inclement. Not only has she been taking breakfast and dinner with the family downstairs, just last night she declined to have his lordship or one of the footmen carry her down to the dining room. Instead, she descended by herself. Later, although it took some time, she climbed back up a half flight. Breathless but triumphant, she vowed that someday soon she would climb clear to her bedchamber on the third floor.

   If you are wondering what brought about this miraculous transformation, I am not a physician and cannot say. I must admit, though, I was more than pleased when Lady Regina heeded my advice concerning sunshine, fresh air, and exercise. The turnabout in her health appears to have begun from the first day she went riding. At the same time, I persuaded *her to allow some sunshine into her bedchamber by opening the heavy curtains that previously had remained closed. Soon after, she didn't need much persuasion to allow the window to be opened, just a crack because of the cold. She was pleased, despite the chill. Now she breathes clean, fresh air instead of living in a room that was unbearably close to stifling.*

Needless to say, Lord Granville is delighted, as are we all. As yet, Lady Regina has chosen not to write her mother concerning the improvement in her health. Although she grows stronger every day, she is still weak and feels she needs a few weeks more to further improve. Actually Lady Granville is not due here from London until after Christmas. One can only imagine the delightful surprise she will receive when she finally arrives and finds her daughter with rosy cheeks, a sparkle in her eyes, and a new outlook on life.

So, my dear sister, as you can well imagine, merriment abounds at Penfield Manor. The children are in a happy frame of mind, not only because Christmas is coming but because Lord Granville remains, even though his mother is most anxious he return to London. Why he has chosen to remain here, I cannot say, except he seems to delight in spending time with his children. He has, in fact, become a loving father, most generous with his time and attention. He even spends time in the classroom. He calls himself my fourth pupil, claims he learns from me, yet I cannot tell you the number of times he has shared his vast knowledge of politics, history, the classics—so many things—with his children and me. He is indeed a remarkable man whom I admire more each day. I consider myself extremely lucky to be in his employ.

Meanwhile, we prepare for what portends to be a joyous Christmas. We shall have a Yule log, of course. Also, a Christmas fair on Christmas afternoon. All the servants and many of the local children are invited to see the decorations and all the Christmas gifts piled up, and then they'll receive their share of gifts.

I do ramble on, don't I? But before closing, I shall touch upon a subject that daily causes me concern. I do hope Montague is behaving himself and that your suspicions concerning his nefarious activities at the bank have been proven false. My blood runs cold when I think of the penalty for fraud. I tell myself Montague is too smart ever to risk such a punishment, but, silly me, I still worry.

Do write soon, dear Augusta. I am anxious to hear that all is well.

Your loving sister,
Lucy

London
December 14, 1815

My Dearest Lucy,
I was pleased to receive your letter and know that all is well. That is indeed good news concerning Lady Regina. I must make one comment, though (you know that annoying habit I have of speaking my mind). Though you expect Lady Granville to be delighted at her daughter's improvement, her reaction may well be otherwise. Bear in mind, her past overpossessiveness, coupled with her obsession with her daughter's various illnesses, as well as her own, may well be what turned Lady Regina into an invalid in the first place. If such is the case, Lady Granville may not be as delighted with Regina's improvement as you anticipate. I have met Lady Granville's kind before. She may well be hard put to relinquish the total control she's had over her daughter.
Just a warning. I do hope I'm wrong.
I wish I had better news concerning Montague, but alas, he continues to bring us lavish gifts, as well as spend what seems like momentous sums of money upon

*himself. Just this past week he purchased a new suit for
himself from Westons of Bond Street and boots from
Hoby's of St. James Street. All the height of fashion and
quite costly. This, mind you, in addition to the amount
(unknown by me of course) he tosses away each night
at the gaming tables. Incidentally, he has come up in
the world. No longer does he gamble in the gambling
hells of Jermyn and St. James's Streets. Somehow he
finessed a membership at both White's and Brook's.
That means he's gambling with some of the richest men
in England, men who think nothing of throwing obscene
amounts of money away on the tables every night. He
denies everything, of course. Insists he is living within
his means, so what can I say? I do wish that you could
come home. He listens to you. Perhaps you could talk
some sense into his head.*

*Before I close, one word of caution (here I go again,
speaking my mind). Reading between the lines of your
last few letters, I perceive how fond you have become of
Lord Granville. I do hope your admiration for the high-
and-mighty lord is of an impersonal nature. Otherwise,
beware. We all know what happens when a servant
forgets her place and becomes entangled in a starry-
eyed relationship with her employer. In the end, she is
bound to lose, and sometimes suffer dire consequences.*

*Do write soon, dear sister. Your Christmas packages
have arrived safely. May you have a wonderful
Christmas.*

*With deep affection,
Augusta*

Finishing her sister's letter, Lucy, with a small chuckle, let
it fall to her lap. She had thought her letters to Augusta contained nothing except the most innocent, carefully crafted remarks concerning Lord Granville. She should have
remembered Augusta's keen perceptiveness. Her sister needn't
worry, though. Since that night in the nursery, Lucy's conduct
had been above reproach, as was Lord Granville's. Their behavior toward each other was totally circumspect. No one

would ever guess they'd ever been other than employer and governess. And yet, how she'd agonized. What sweet torture it was, having the man she madly loved so near, yet constantly having to restrain herself from touching him, from hiding the adoration in her eyes when she looked at him.

As for Lord Granville, he seemed to have no problem in regarding her simply as the children's governess. There were times when her heart ached at his remoteness and she wondered if he had forgotten that incredible night. Then she'd remind herself, what did it matter if he had or had not forgotten? All was hopeless between them. The sooner she resigned herself to that fact, the sooner she could stop this endless self-torture.

You have other things to worry about, Lucy informed herself. Augusta had provided food for thought, but surely she was wrong about Lady Granville. Was she not a mother? How could she be less than delighted when she discovered her daughter in vastly improved health?

But Lucy's main concern was over Montague. How she hoped hers and Augusta's suspicions were groundless. Much as Lucy enjoyed living at Penfield Manor, she wished she could return to London to question Montague herself.

"Be gone," playfully declared Lady Regina to Lord Granville.

It was two days before Christmas. Unassisted, Regina had come downstairs and for the past hour had been directing the decoration of the dining room, halls, and grand salon with mistletoe and garlands of yuletide greenery. Despite a slight fever she'd contracted the day before when they'd slogged through the snow to collect the Yule log, there was a spring in her step. To Lucy's hidden amusement, she was charmingly impertinent as she bossed the servants about as well as the children and her brother.

Minutes earlier, Lord Granville, handsome as always in casual riding clothes, had returned from a ride around his estate and, quite innocently, was offering his comments concerning the decorations until his sister ordered him out. His lordship didn't appear to mind, though. With an amused exchange of glances with Lucy, he declared to Regina, "Am I not the lord of the manor? You cannot order me out."

"Oh, yes I can," Regina tartly replied. "Go tend to your horses, or whatever it is you do."

"Can we stay, Aunt Regina?" Winifred asked.

Regina fondly patted her young niece's cheek. "Of course you can stay, darling, and Mary and William, too. It's only your father who's in the way." She pointed dramatically at the door. "Out! Leave the decorating to those who know how to do it."

As Lucy watched Lord Granville take his reluctant but grinning departure, she reflected that never had she had so much fun before or, for that matter, never had she felt so happy. All seemed right with the world: the children in a merry mood, Lady Regina in better health than Lucy had ever seen her. Perhaps best of all, Lucy had been treated with such respect and consideration these past few weeks she felt less like a servant and more like a member of the family.

Then, of course, there was Lord Granville . . .

She felt the usual empty, aching tug at her heart as she thought of him. At least she could be close to him. How privileged she was to share with him this joyous Christmas season. He would be leaving for London soon and she would miss him terribly, but for now, she would savor the precious moments he was here.

"You've done a beautiful job," Lucy remarked.

Regina smiled. "Thanks to you, Miss Winthrop, this will be my happiest Christmas ever."

"Then perhaps . . ." Lucy's hesitation lasted only a moment. Lately she'd been speaking her mind to Lady Regina who so far had accepted her remarks with good grace. In fact, they chatted frequently, and she had begun to treat Lucy more like a friend than a servant. "Since you're feeling so much better, perhaps you should revisit your decision not to see Lord Kellems again."

To Lucy's surprise, Regina nodded in agreement. "I have been thinking of Lord Kellems quite frequently of late. Perhaps upon my return to London after Christmas, I shall have a discussion with Mama. When she sees the improvement in my health, I am sure she'll be more amenable to my seeing him."

But you're a grown woman, Lucy silently protested. *Why do you crave your mother's approval?* How strange that a willful woman like Regina could seem so independent, yet in the presence of her mother her determination crumbled like a castle of sand. This was going to be a wonderful Christmas. *Without Lady Granville*. Lucy did not wish to think uncharitable thoughts, but thank heavens that vexatious woman would not be at Penfield Manor for the holidays.

Not an hour later, just as Regina and Lucy were completing the decorations, Lord Granville entered the dining room. Never, in all the months she'd known him, had he ever appeared unsure of himself, but now was the exception. Frowning slightly he addressed his sister. "I did something you might not approve of."

Regina cocked her head. "And what is that?"

"You were so much better, I invited Lord Kellems to come for a visit. He's come down from London for the night."

"You mean he's here?"

"He's here."

"That was most presumptuous of you," came Regina's cutting reply. But Lucy had seen her eyes light at Granville's news. "Where is he?"

"In the drawing room."

"Then I suppose I am obliged to go greet him." Regina feigned an annoyed sigh that was so transparent it made Lucy want to laugh. "Really, John, you shouldn't have."

"I am so glad you did," Lucy told Lord Granville after his sister left in pretended high dudgeon.

Granville's gaze swept the dining room. All day family and servants had been bustling in and out, but for the moment they had it to themselves. He drew close. "I've been wanting to talk to you. It's difficult, finding you alone."

What did he want? Lucy's heart started pounding. *Be strong,* she warned herself. "That's the way we both wanted it, m'lord."

He drew closer still, exposing deep contemplation in his gaze. "I wanted to thank you."

"What for?" Now her heart was positively hammering in her chest.

"For your kindness to my sister. Without you, she would be lying upstairs in her bed right now, feeling sorry for herself. You've given her new life, and I am extremely grateful."

Is that all? So all he wanted to do was thank her? She felt a keen disappointment. But what did she expect? She was being completely irrational in wanting him to break the agreement they had made that unforgettable night. "I am pleased for whatever part I played in Lady Regina's recovery." How stiff that sounded. How fortunate he couldn't read her thoughts. If he could, he would find her mind full of turmoil and discover that the stern resolve she'd managed to maintain since the night in the nursery was so fragile it could easily break down. A good thing he didn't know she was so besotted with him that she would swoon with pleasure if he so much as touched her.

She could hardly breathe as, for a long, disturbing moment, he looked down at her. His arms moved slightly. Was he reaching for her? They tightened, remained at his side. Surely she must be mistaken, but was he trembling? Oh, surely not, yet she could have sworn he was. Not only that, when she looked deep into those warm brown eyes, she saw unspoken pain alive and glowing.

"Ah, Lucy," he said in a strange, choked voice, "I have not forgotten."

Before she could answer, he shook his head and quickly left the dining room, leaving her confused, shaken, and all alone.

Don't be a fool, Granville told himself as he hastened away. He recalled the vows he'd made that night in the governess's bedchamber next to the nursery. Nothing had changed. He hated to admit his mother was right, but as she'd pointed out, he could forget about becoming prime minister if he took up with a governess. His career, as well as his reputation, would be ruined.

But would he really care?

He was beginning to wonder.

He should have departed for London long before now. Mama was clamoring for his return, and rightly so. *Stay in the country much longer and they'll forget your name,* she had warned in the last of a series of letters that were becoming increasingly irate.

The trouble was, despite his better judgment he could not bring himself to leave Lucy Winthrop. Thanks to her, these weeks he'd spent at Penfield Manor had been the happiest of his life. For one thing, she had reintroduced him to his children who now gave him hours of newfound enjoyment. For another, he had discovered he drew great satisfaction from managing his own estate instead of leaving it in the hands of an overseer. But mostly his happiness came from his fascination with the little governess. So much, in fact, that every time he thought to leave, he could not bear to tear himself away. Her wit, charm, and beauty—that tinkling little laugh she had—held him like a vise. But it was not only her visible qualities that kept him prisoner. Unlike most of the airheaded London belles he'd known, Lucy was a woman with honor, depth of character, a caring heart, as well as keen intelligence. In every way she was so entrancing he had even, God help him, taken to visiting the classroom, pretending he was there for the sake of the children when in reality he relished any excuse to jam his knees beneath a child's small desk, listen to her melodious voice, watch her every graceful move to his heart's content.

Because of her, he wasn't sleeping well at night. With a self-deprecating laugh, he had to admit it wasn't thoughts of the depth of Miss Lucy Winthrop's character or her keen intelligence that kept him awake or made him tremble just now, simply because she was near. Engraved in his mind was an image of how she looked that heated night when she'd lain beneath him on the narrow bed and they had kissed with such passion he'd thought his heart would pound its way right through his chest . . .

Dear God, here it came again, that driving, hot desire for Lucy Winthrop that for the life of him he could not prevent from sweeping through his body, coursing through his veins. It caused him to forget he was the esteemed Lord Granville, respected member of Parliament, future prime minister; it turned him into a quivering mass of frustration, aching to hold her again.

This must stop. Directly after Christmas, he would return to

London. He was loath to go, but it was time he got on with his life and forgot this nonsense.

"Well, upon my word, could this be Lord Kellems? The man I said I never wanted to see again?"

In the doorway of the grand salon, Regina regarded Lord Kellems with her head to one side in her usual cocky fashion. She had not come directly, but had gone to her bedchamber to change to an elaborate afternoon gown of green striped silk, trimmed with two solid green satin rouleaux around the hem. It immensely flattered her fair skin and red hair that Matilda, exhorted to make haste, had lifted into soft curls atop her head.

Kellems rose to his impressive height. "I knew you didn't mean it when you said you'd not see me again. You must have been temporarily deranged at the time."

"I did so mean it."

"Did you receive my latest poem? You never said."

"Oh, I got it all right."

"Well?"

"I've told you before, your poetry is absolutely dreadful. I shall never forget that first one you wrote where you compared me to a dewdrop. Oh, please. Your poems are the worst I ever read." With a firm step Regina crossed the room, yanked the bellpull, then sat across from Kellems on the settee. "Now that you're here, I suppose you'll want some tea."

Kellems appeared not hurt in the least that she'd insulted his poems. Instead, a delighted expression lit his face. "You're looking marvelous. Last time I saw you—"

"The last time you saw me I was an invalid. I am much better now, thank you, as you can see."

Scratching his head, Kellems let his large bulk sink back into his chair. "This changes everything."

Regina tilted her chin. "Whatever do you mean?"

He glared. "You know what I mean, you obstinate girl. It means we can get married. You have no excuse now. Even your mother would have to give us her blessing."

"I never said I'd marry you."

"Oh, you'll marry me all right," Kellems replied with the utmost confidence. "Who else would have you?"

Regina raised her nose in the air. "If ever I were to marry, which I won't, it would be to a man who is refined, and genteel, and doesn't have the gall to order me around."

"You want a milksop?" Kellems roared with laughter. "No you don't. You want me."

"Why?"

Kellems abruptly stopped his laughter and grew serious. "Because I love you, Regina, and you love me, I don't care what you say. You would be bored to tears with some pudding-hearted simpleton. You need a man like me, who isn't cowed by that damnable impertinence of yours." With one swift move, he sat next to her on the settee and took her hand. "You don't know how delighted I am that I don't have to treat you like a fragile flower anymore. It's time we kissed."

"The butler . . . I don't think—" Regina began, but Kellems seized her roughly and cut off her words with a brief but ardent kiss.

"Since when do you worry what the servants think?" he asked as he pulled away. Suddenly gentle, he brushed the back of his hand down her cheek. "Ah, Regina, how dear you are to me. Marriage aside, you have no idea how indescribably happy I am your health is restored."

Regina frowned. "I grant you I have improved, but I shall always be in delicate health. I doubt I could ever bear you children. It isn't fair to you—"

"You let me worry about what's fair and what's not."

"I'm older than you."

"What's five years?"

"My mother—"

"Forget Mama."

"*Your* parents—"

A slight frown crossed his face. "You let me worry about them." His hands slid up her arms, bringing her closer. "You talk too much. I see I shall have to kiss you again."

In answer to the bellpull, Brooks quietly opened the grand salon door. He started to enter but stopped short at the unexpected sight on the settee that greeted his ancient eyes. At first all he could see were the hulking, broad shoulders of Lord Kellems. He was holding somebody tight in his arms and kissing . . . Lady Regina! Brooks stood in astonishment. Surely a woman as independent as she would not have given her consent to such tomfoolery and he, Brooks, might be compelled to summon help at any moment. But no. Not only had her fingers crept around Lord Kellems's neck, Brooks heard a distinct, pleasured, female "Mmm."

With a little smile, Brooks tiptoed from the room and shut the door. Good for her, he thought. After years of illness, Lady Regina deserved a little happiness. Thank heaven, Lady Granville was in London. He devoutly hoped she stayed there. In his many years on earth, Brooks had learned a thing or two about human frailties, enough to know that when her ladyship discovered the nature of this new relationship between her daughter and Lord Kellems she would not be pleased.

Christmas eve arrived. Lord Kellems had returned to London. Unfortunately Lady Regina's illness had gotten worse. She had a high fever and had taken to her bed.

Downstairs in the dining room, Lord Granville, the children, and Lucy were in the midst of a merry dinner when, without warning, Lady Granville burst through the door, Florinda close behind.

Lucy had a spoonful of turtle soup halfway to her mouth when, spying her ladyship standing in the doorway, she almost spilled it before returning it quickly to her plate.

"Mama." Lord Granville tossed his napkin aside and rose quickly. "I had no idea. Were you and Florinda not planning on spending Christmas in London?"

"Obviously we are not." Lady Granville stood like a statue, pinched nose high in the air. Lucy noticed her chest was heaving. She appeared to be regarding the merry diners with repressed rage.

"Come join us," said Granville. "Brooks, set another place for her ladyship and Lady Florinda."

"No thank you," his mother rejoined. "I have lost my appetite." Her gaze swept over the dining table. "You dine with the children now?" She stared at Lucy. "As well as the servants?"

"Grandmama," little Winifred called in a delighted voice.

She slid from her chair, came around the table, and wrapped her chubby arms around her grandmother's stiff, black bombazine skirt. "We don't have to eat in the nursery anymore. Papa allows us to eat in the dining room, and Miss Winthrop, too. Isn't that grand?"

Lady Granville ignored the child. In clipped words she said to her son, "When you finish your dinner, I would like to see you in the library. Where is Regina?"

"She's not feeling well."

"Oh, really?" she asked with great skepticism. "And here I had been informed she had turned into the picture of health." None too gently she disengaged herself from her granddaughter's arms. "I shall be waiting in the library," she said, and marched off.

A sudden pall replaced the noisy merriment that had filled the room. Except for the oblivious chatter of the children, and Florinda's prattle, Lord Granville ate in silence, as did Lucy. Or tried to eat. Lady Granville wasn't the only one who had lost her appetite. Lucy had, too, just thinking of what her ladyship's sudden arrival might portend.

"You were rude, Mama." Granville stepped into the library and firmly shut the door.

She stood waiting for him, all stiff and bristling. "I am appalled," she said.

With a deep sigh, Granville slung himself into an armchair, stretched out his legs, and folded his arms across his chest. "Sit down, Mama, and if you must, kindly tell me why you are appalled."

Lady Granville seated herself, her posture so rigid her back didn't touch the back of the chair. Her nose twitched with distaste. "There is so much wrong I hardly know where to begin."

"Begin somewhere." Granville's impatience was ill-concealed.

"Well, then . . ." Lady Granville began her litany of complaints, none of which surprised Granville in the slightest. She was shocked that the children, as well as that brazen governess, were now allowed to take their meals in the dining room. What was he thinking of? And worse, word had reached her ears that despite her extremely delicate health, Regina had been allowed to ride a horse, not once, but many times, and in the worst sort of weather. Now Regina was sick and it was all his fault, as well as that Winthrop woman's.

"We didn't go out if it rained," Granville commented. "Besides, the riding did Regina a tremendous amount of good. A little exercise, fresh air, sunshine, that's what she needed. You should have seen the improvement. She was much better until that deuced 'flu'—"

"Are you daft?" Obviously Granville's remarks had added fuel to her ladyship's increasingly smoldering fire. "She's an invalid. She'll never get better. It's cruel to let her get her hopes up."

Granville calmly asked, "How did you hear all this?"

"Dear Dr. Fraley had the consideration and the courtesy to write me," Lady Granville snapped. "He was most concerned, especially when he discovered she's no longer taking any of her medicines."

"Calm down, Mama. She doesn't need them anymore."

His remark so enraged his mother she leaped to her feet. "How could you? You know how delicate she is. If she's so much better, why is she now sick in bed?"

"It's only a mild case of the 'flu,' I believe. I assure you—"

"Only the 'flu'? I just went up to see her. She's burning with fever. She's seriously ill, thanks to you and that hussy of a governess."

Granville sat straight, his casual pose forgotten. "You are mistaken. Miss Winthrop is not a hussy. She's the best—"

"I don't want to hear it." Lady Granville began pacing the room. "What if Regina dies? I shall hold you directly responsible."

"She's not going to die." Granville's patience was wearing very, very thin.

Lady Granville's eyes became stony with anger. "You have no conception of the sacrifices I made to be here. You *know* how I dote on the London Christmas Season. It wasn't easy for me to break all Florinda's and my social engagements, but of course I was obliged to when I heard about Regina." Her eyes turned stonier still. "And it's all thanks to you and that governess. I want her dismissed."

"Miss Winthrop?" This time it was Granville who leaped from his chair. "Don't be absurd. She's the best governess the children ever had. Why don't you go back to London then, if you feel you're missing so much? I assure you, Regina will improve. She is in the best of hands."

"I am not going anywhere." As if to emphasize her point, Lady Granville seated herself again, quite firmly in the chair, and crossed her arms. "I shall stay right here, to administer to Regina and see she receives the proper care. That's not all. Since you won't get rid of Miss Winthrop, I feel it's my duty to look after the children."

Not until that moment did Granville realize how truly much he had enjoyed these past weeks at Penfield Manor without his mother. Now the thought of her continued presence caused his spirits to plunge.

"And another thing," his mother went on.

What now?

"You had the gall to invite Lord Kellems here when you knew Regina did not wish to see him."

"Good grief, Mama."

"Which only strengthens my resolve to stay on at Penfield Manor indefinitely, to care for Regina as well as protect the children from that dreadful woman."

He had tried to keep his temper, but this last was too much. His voice was cold and lashing as he replied, "Need I remind you, this is my home, not yours? Since that is the case, while you are under my roof, you will not speak of Miss Winthrop in that tone, or insult her in any way."

She jerked back as if he had physically assaulted her. Automatically her hand covered her heart. "Why, John, how could you talk to your poor, sick mother that way?"

"Don't play the sick game, Mama, it's not working."

She gasped and went on, "It's that governess, isn't it? Don't think for a moment I have not heard how she has wormed her way into your affections, how she eats all her meals with you in the dining room, how you attend her classroom as if you were one of her adoring pupils."

Considering he had just had a fleeting but nonetheless real urge to strangle his own mother, Granville decided the best course to follow was to leave. Fast. He strode to the door and turned. "You heard what I said. Stay as long as you like, but you must be civil to Miss Winthrop."

Her upper right lip pulled into an ugly sneer. "And you are staying, too, aren't you? You have completely forgotten they are grooming you for prime minister. You have let that . . . that—" She caught herself, obviously fearing his wrath, then plunged ahead. "You have let that governess lead you around by the nose."

He spoke softly to conceal his wrath. "I would leave to-morrow if it weren't Christmas. The day after will do. Yes, I am returning to London, and no, I have not forgotten I shall be prime minister someday. I'm no fool."

Later, after Granville had calmed down and was sitting at his desk in his study, he thought of the argument with his mother, groaned, and put his head in his hands. What a mud-dle. Christmas wasn't exactly ruined. The children would still enjoy the day, but otherwise, his mother had managed to put a damper on what was to be a festive occasion.

Then, too, lately he had learned some things that were un-settling. William had let it slip that his grandmother had once sent him to the attic to spend the night without his supper. This, after Granville had made it quite clear to her he would not con-done such a punishment. Also, he had heard about the strap that hung in the classroom until Miss Winthrop had ordered it removed. His mother was in charge. She must have known. What he ought to have done long before now was move her to Brighton where he owned a perfectly fine townhouse. She could be happy there—be the queen of Brighton society if she so desired—and at long last be out of his hair. And yet, he had already told her she could stay. God's blood! He shuddered to think of what would happen after Christmas, when he would be in London, and Regina, Lucy, and the children would be at her mercy . . .

Or would they? A thought struck him. Of course. The per-fect solution. Why hadn't he thought of it sooner?

Chapter Thirteen

*I*t was Christmas night. Lucy had just tucked the children into their beds and was on her way to her room. It had not been easy, calming them down after all the excitement of the Christmas celebration, the house swarming with neighbors and tenants, the lighting of the Yule log, the feast, and, of course, the presents. But the day had been most satisfying. The children had enjoyed every minute despite the long-faced presence of their grandmother. No wonder Lord Granville had made himself scarce most of the day. Florinda was pleasant enough, but to Lucy's knowledge, her ladyship had not smiled one single time. But despite Lady Granville's complaints about missing her London Christmas Season, she had made it clear she planned to remain at Penfield Manor for an indefinite time, not only to care for Regina but to "make sure the children are cared for properly." Lucy sighed with grim awareness. From now on, life at Penfield Manor would not be the same.

"Miss Winthrop?" Lord Granville's voice, behind her. *John.* What could he want? As often happened when he was near, her pulse started to race. She turned, trying to compose herself.

"Good evening, m'lord."

"I wanted a word with you."

In the dim light of the hallway, she could hardly see his face, yet she could tell from the rigid intonation in his voice he intended to remain impersonal. "What did you wish to say, sir?" She matched his clipped words with those of her own.

"I am leaving for London tomorrow."

Her heart sank, even though she'd known he'd soon be leaving. "The children will miss you."

"No they won't, they're coming with me, as are you."

His sudden announcement was so startling she just barely managed to stifle a gasp. "To . . . to London?"

"Have you any objection?"

"No, none." She was hard put to keep a straight face since she could hardly contain her joy. "Of course I don't mind. As you know, I have a sister in London."

"Ah, yes, the inestimable Mrs. Augusta Winthrop-Scott."

"And a brother, too, whom I am anxious . . . to see again." She had never mentioned her concerns about Montague. No need to start now.

"Then I am pleased you're pleased," replied Granville. "We shall leave first thing tomorrow. Have a footman help you pack up the classroom. I should imagine the children will need their books and whatever else you deem necessary for their studies in London."

"Will Lady Regina be traveling with us?"

"She's too ill. Lady Granville will remain here to care for her, along with Florinda."

She was suddenly curious. So much so, in fact, that despite his detached attitude, she plunged ahead. "I thought you wanted the children raised in the country, as you were raised. Might I ask why you've changed your mind?"

"Many reasons, Miss Winthrop. Let us just say it's the best solution all around."

Of course, his mother. She was struck by the happy realization that Lord Granville was no milksop, knuckling under to his mother's every wish. What a relief to know he thought enough of her and the children to remove them from her ladyship's smothering influence.

"Then good night, sir. Rest assured, the children and I shall be ready first thing in the morning."

Lucy continued on toward her room. After determining the hallway was deserted, she clasped her hands to her heart, did a little skip, and whispered softly, "London." How good it would be to return.

Then a disturbing thought struck her.

These past weeks at Penfield Manor she had made it a point to assiduously avoid his lordship whenever she could. Aside from their rides, and the time he spent in the classroom, it was not a difficult task, considering the huge size of the mansion and surrounding grounds. There were, in fact, days when she hardly saw him at all. But the London mansion wasn't nearly as large as Penfield Manor. Inevitably, in smaller confines she would be seeing him more often, and that, she knew, would put even more strain on her already troubled heart.

In the dimness of Regina's bedchamber, Granville seated himself beside her bed and took her hand. How pale and drawn she was. She was wheezing, and seemed to be having difficulty drawing a breath. "Perhaps I shouldn't leave," he said.

She scowled at him. "Nonsense. You've remained here far too long. You absolutely must get back to London."

"But you're sick and I am worried. I should never have let you come outdoors with us to get the Yule log. I shall postpone my return—"

"Don't you dare. Imagine how bad I shall feel if you lose the next election on my account. I shall be fine." With a touch of irony, she added, "Mama's here. You know how she'll smother me with care."

Her remark drew a laugh from him, although a brief one. "Oh, by the way, speaking of Mama, she doesn't know it yet, but I'm taking the children back to London."

"I'm glad. I never approved of your children being buried in the country. They'll love London . . . uh-oh." A look of realization crossed her face. "You'll be taking Miss Winthrop along, won't you?"

"Anything wrong with that?"

"I shall miss her dreadfully, of course. We've had some lovely conversations. Aside from you, she's the only adult around here who makes any sense. However"—she gazed at him with observant eyes—"there's something between you two, isn't there?" He opened his mouth to answer, but she continued on. "You cannot fool me, so don't even try."

"How can you be so sure?"

"It's strange. You and Miss Winthrop don't exchange fond

glances. I am almost certain you're not having secret trysts in the woods. It's just . . . whenever you two are close to each other, it's as if waves of . . . it's hard to describe . . . desire? awareness? flow through the air in both directions."

"Do tell," he smoothly replied, "and what else do you think you've gleaned from these supposedly perspicacious observations?"

"In my humble estimation, you've had some sort of encounter. Of course, you both know it wouldn't work, so that's why you are now carefully staying apart. But the reality is, the both of you can hardly restrain yourselves from leaping into the nearest bed and making mad, passionate love." Regina ended by tilting her chin and awarding him one of her smirks.

Granville could see there was no use denying his sister's accusations. He did not, however, give her the satisfaction of knowing how close she'd come to the truth. "It's true, there's a certain, shall we say, warm feeling between us. Nothing I cannot handle, though." Keenly desirous of changing the subject, Granville asked, "What of Lord Kellems? I trust this illness won't cause you to give him up."

"Mama's always told me I would never be able to lead a normal life, and yet . . ." Regina's face lit with optimism. "I've been feeling so much better. Dare I hope, John?"

"But of course."

"Then I shall. And once I get past this latest illness, I'll start making plans."

"Plans that include Lord Kellems?"

"Oh, yes," Regina answered, her voice full of purpose.

London

When Lucy was a child, her family was too poor to afford the many dazzling amusements London had to offer. Later, when she became a governess, her free time was so limited that her rare off days were spent visiting her family. Never had she attended the theater, strolled through the lavish Vauxhall

Gardens, or Covent Garden, or gazed upon the sawdust ring at Astley's Royal Amphitheater where various astounding feats of horsemanship were performed. She accepted her situation with equanimity. Let the members of the "Polite World" wallow in the unrestrained pursuit of London's pleasures. Such delights were not for her. It had been her choice to become a governess, a positive step toward opening her school for girls.

All that changed when Lucy returned to the city, and Lord Granville introduced her to a London she had never seen.

They had been back only a day when he announced, "I am taking the children to the Egyptian Hall this afternoon."

"They'll love it," she replied. "I hear it's full of curiosities and has a well-preserved assortment of small animals and insects from all over the world."

"The children will find it of great interest," he went on, "especially William."

"I'm sure he'll tell me all about it when he returns."

Granville looked at her strangely and cocked an eyebrow. "But didn't I make it clear? You're coming with us."

That was the beginning. In the days that followed, Lord Granville, Lucy, and the children embarked on special outings nearly every day. Covent Garden wasn't yet open for the season, nor Vauxhall Gardens, but Granville managed to find an endless number of attractions of interest to the children, and Lucy, too. On consecutive afternoons, after lessons were done, they visited the British Museum, Cadiz Memorial, Madame Tussaud's. Especially exciting was the day they visited Lord Elgin's exhibit of the marvelous Elgin Marbles, kept in a shed attached to his home. Lucy enjoyed each outing immensely. Not only were the children expanding their education, and loving it as well, she, herself, was fascinated by everything she saw, grateful that at long last she'd seen something of the sights of London.

And, most of all . . .

For long periods of time, she could be near the only man she knew she would ever love. Not that she ever forgot her position. Dressed primly in her uniform, she performed her governess duties with the utmost propriety, never once uttering an improper word or overstepping her bounds. Still, there were times when she came perilously close to allowing her real feelings to show. It would happen when one or the other of the children said or did something funny, and they all laughed, and for a magical moment she could believe this was her husband, these were her children, and they were all enjoying a merry family outing. At such times she always scolded herself, holding herself to blame for such idiocy. Not entirely, though. Lord Granville offered scant support in maintaining their impersonal relationship. Instead, he appeared to take great delight in showing the sights to her as much as to the children. There were times when he, relaxed and enjoying himself, treated her more like a beloved wife than a governess. He never actually touched her, yet on more than one occasion he seemed to want to reach out to her, then quickly caught himself. At those moments, her heart swelled with longing and she desperately wanted to capture his gaze and signal with her own eyes all the love she felt for him, all her joy that he had allowed her into his life, if only for a little while.

She did no such thing, though, and forced her gaze modestly down when occasion required.

One afternoon they were driving through Hyde Park in Granville's smart, open landau. Granville was driving, Lucy by his side, the children tucked in back. The Duchess of Richmond passed by, viewed the occupants of the landau, and delivered a hostile stare.

"Oh, dear," said Lucy, the words inadvertently popping from her mouth.

Granville slanted a glance at her, lifting an eyebrow in the quirky way he had. "You're concerned?"

So far it had been a forbidden subject, but she had known sooner or later she would be compelled to speak. "People do talk, you know. Perhaps your reputation would be better served if you were not seen so often in public with your governess."

Granville's jaw tensed. His hands tightened on the reins. "You fancy I give a groat what the Duchess of Richmond thinks?"

"Your career—"

"A pox on my career."

They drove in silence until Granville, calmer now, spoke

again. "You mustn't worry, Miss Winthrop. I know what I'm doing. Everything will be fine."

She wanted to protest, to tell him everything would most decidedly *not* be fine, especially when Lady Granville returned to London. What she would not tell him was that she feared she could not continue this agonizing charade much longer. How could she keep acting the respectable governess when heated desire smoldered underneath her staid, starched exterior? When she constantly ached for his kiss, for the glorious feeling of his arms around her once more, for another chance to press against his hard, taut body as she had done that unforgettable night?

She could not go on this way. Could he? She didn't know. He'd done a masterful job of concealing his true feelings. It didn't matter. She was no good for him and she could not go on indefinitely torturing herself.

That night, Florinda cornered her brother in the drawing room. "Surely you know people are talking. *Tiens*. What on earth are you doing, letting yourself be seen all over town with your governess? It is most unseemly."

Suppressing a sigh, Granville heartily wished his shallow sister had remained at Penfield Manor with their mother and Regina. He might have guessed she soon would return to London, and she had, in less than a week, declaring herself "bored silly" and "buried in the countryside where nothing ever happened."

"I haven't a care what's unseemly," he told Florinda. "Miss Winthrop is the children's governess. When I take my children to see the sights of London, it's only proper she come along."

"Ha! You're not fooling me," Florinda skeptically replied. "She has wormed her way into your affections, hasn't she? Well, I'm not blaming you, John, men can be such fools. But *mon deux*, so *mal à propos*. I'm only thinking of you, and how your career will be ruined if you don't stop these . . . these *trysts* with a servant."

"Whatever are you talking about?" Granville inquired, his ire on the rise despite himself. "I have never had a *tryst*, as you put it, with Miss Winthrop. The children are always with us.

We are never alone." Here he was, forced to defend himself, a fact that raised his ire even higher.

"All the same, people are talking," Florinda smugly replied. "What of your reputation? How can you expect to win the next election? What if Lady Camilla finds out? Mark my words, you need more than three naive young children as chaperones."

"Then why don't you accompany us?" he asked, fighting the impulse to answer through gritted teeth. "You would be most welcome. In fact, absorbing a little culture might do you some good."

"You think I want to wear myself out tramping through that drafty British Museum? Or visiting those dull, boring Elgin Marbles? Really! And besides, the Season is coming. I shall be much too busy with fittings for my new gowns."

"Of course." Granville shut his eyes a moment and calmed himself down. "Do what you please, Florinda, but kindly don't tell me how to conduct my life."

"I won't have to," Florinda snapped. "Regina is better. She and Mama will be home soon. Do you think for one minute Mama will tolerate your nonsense with the governess?"

"She'll have to."

"Oh, no she won't. You think Mama has no power over you, but she does. You think she won't get her way, but she will. Mark my words, John, she'll do anything to get rid of that governess."

On Lucy's first free day, she hastened to Augusta's. Now, comfortably ensconced in her sister's cozy kitchen, she had just finished telling Augusta how thrilled the children were to be in London and how much she, herself, was enjoying the sights. "Tomorrow we're going to Mrs. Salmon's Waxworks."

Augusta issued a thoughtful "Hmm" and set her teacup down. "When you say 'we' you mean you, the children, and Lord Granville?"

"Well, yes, of course."

"How cozy." Augusta lifted her eyebrows in that knowing way she had.

Lucy gathered her defenses. "There's absolutely nothing between us, I can assure you."

"Do you wish there was?"

"I . . ." Lucy felt a hot blush creep over her cheeks.

"Hmm, so that's the way it is," mused Augusta. Briskly she added, "You're treading a dangerous path, my dear."

Lucy thought to argue, but on second thought, what could she say? She was saved from further comment when Montague arrived. His eyes lit when he saw Lucy. "Welcome home, little Lu." She rose to greet him and he gave her a big hug. "It's good to have you back."

"You're looking uncommonly handsome," she replied. Shrewdly she surveyed his meticulously tailored frock coat, polished beaver top hat, kid gloves, and fancy walking stick. "My, my, all this on a banker's salary?"

Montague's blue eyes lit with amusement. "I see Augusta's been blabbing again. Well, she's wrong. I am not an embezzler, nor have I committed any fraud. They like me at Edgemont-Percival. I receive bonuses all the time."

"Humph," Augusta remarked. "Then can we expect you'll soon pay back the money you took from us?"

"I will, when I get ahead of my expenses."

Lucy took her brother's face in her hands. "Tell me the truth, Montague. I worry so about you. If you are stealing at the bank, you know sooner or later you'll be caught and you *know* the consequences."

Montague clasped her hands in his and looked deep into her eyes. "I give you my sacred word, Lucy, I have not committed any crime."

Lucy searched Montague's handsome face for deceit. She could find none, but then, Montague had lied to her before, many times, and always so convincingly she was always fooled.

True to Florinda's prediction, Granville's mother and older sister returned to London the next day.

"Her ladyship and Lady Regina have arrived," announced Montclaire, a footman who acted in the butler's absence.

Damme. Granville had been comfortably seated in his

study, perusing the morning newspaper, when brought the news.

Montclaire added, "Her ladyship wishes to see you in the drawing room."

"Inform her I'll be there directly."

"Yes, your lordship," Montclaire said with a nod, his several chins jiggling.

Watching the extremely corpulent footman make his retreat with a rolling, laborious gait, Granville felt a pang of sympathy. Montclaire had been employed as a footman at Cheltham House for many years. He hadn't always been this fat, but a voracious appetite for food and, Granville suspected, drink had taken its toll. His mother wanted to get rid of him. "He's an embarrassment," she claimed, "even fatter than Prinny, if that's possible." But Granville had an aversion to dismissing his servants, even when they deserved it. In his opinion, Montclaire did not deserve dismissal, even though he could be surly at times and was not, all things considered, very likable. As it was, the poor fellow would never advance. His massive bulk was against him, and he lacked the skill, charm, and finesse required for the exalted position of butler. If he wished, though, he could stay on as a footman as long as he liked.

"I am surprised," Granville told his mother when he entered the drawing room. "Last I saw you, you were settled in the countryside, declaring you planned to remain indefinitely." He settled on a settee, expecting at any moment she would begin a long harangue concerning his excursions with the governess, which surely her scandalmongering friends would have informed her of by now.

Lady Granville hardly looked up from her embroidery. "I would have left Regina behind, but she's a mite better and did not object to our return. Actually"—she set her embroidery on her lap—"you'll be out campaigning soon. You'll need my help."

Well, he could not deny that. He would not have been elected in the first place had it not been for his father's influence, connections, and money. Now that his father was gone, he did not lack for money but still counted on his mother and her powerful friends.

"Tell me," she went on, "have you started to plan your campaign yet?"

"Er . . . no." The truth was best, he supposed. "Actually I've been spending time with the children. They're delighted with London. We've gone on quite a few outings."

"How nice."

To Granville's puzzlement, the usual biting sarcasm was missing from his mother's voice. There was even a slight smile on her face. Doubtless it would fade when she heard what he had to say next. "We were lucky to have Miss Winthrop along. She adds a lot to the occasion, what with her charm and wit. And of course she's marvelous with the children."

"How very, very nice."

He couldn't believe his ears, yet Mama seemed sincere and was still smiling. They chatted for a while, mostly discussing his campaign for reelection.

"I'll see you at dinner tonight." He rose to leave. "The children will be dining with us, as well as Miss Winthrop."

"How delightful."

Once outside the drawing room, Granville shook his head in puzzlement. Why was she being so pleasant? Why had she not complained about her health? Why had she not mentioned Lady Camilla one single time? Perhaps the countryside had mellowed her and from now on she'd have a different outlook on life. He would surely like to think so.

Lady Granville's smile vanished the moment her son left the room. She was proud of herself. With the utmost difficulty she had squelched her fury and remained pleasant, even after John's infatuation with the governess became obvious. She had rushed back to London for one reason only—to determine whether or not the horrid rumors she'd heard were true. Now that she knew they were, she would take whatever steps were necessary to get rid of Miss Winthrop. She must exercise the utmost caution, though, and continue her pretense of liking the governess.

Florinda joined her, eagerly asking, "You talked to John? Now do you see what I mean?"

"He's besotted with her," Lady Granville grimly answered.

"What shall we do, Mama? Lady Camilla won't wait much longer. And why should she? The new Season starts soon. There'll be plenty of young bucks clamoring for her hand."

"John *will* marry Lady Camilla." Lady Granville clamped her jaw with determination. "Miss Winthrop may be smart, but she's also vulnerable, and assuredly no match for you and me. All we need do is put our heads together and come up with a plan."

Florinda giggled. "She's only a servant, after all. It shouldn't take much to get rid of her."

Chapter Fourteen

*M*ontague Winthrop's considerable pride was wounded when he accepted the position as clerk with Edgemont-Percival & Company, the prestigious bank established in Berners Street in 1782. He felt the position was beneath him, it mattering not one wit that Edgemont-Percival possessed a solid and respected reputation, among its clients some of the wealthiest families in all England. He was compelled to accept, though. His gambling debts were increasing. Because of certain dire threats, they must be paid, and soon. Paying back his sisters would have to wait.

Despite his perceived humiliation at having to work at so low a position, Montague soon became the golden hope of Edgemont-Percival. He possessed a natural aptitude for figures and could carry a good deal of statistical information in his head, including the exact position of the accounts of all the bank's main investors. He formed the habit of arriving at work before the other clerks in the morning and staying on until after they left. His golden good looks, wit, and pleasant disposition were immensely pleasing to the bank's customers. In fact, it wasn't long before certain valued female customers lined up at Winthrop's window, eschewing other windows with shorter lines.

And he was absolutely trustworthy. Who would doubt that gleam of honesty in his candid blue eyes?

Messrs. Edgemont and Percival, the two elderly partners who should have retired years before, found young Winthrop to be a godsend. Neither partner had sons of his own. For years, they had worried and fretted over who would head the bank when they were gone. Now they had Montague.

As time went on, Montague assumed more and more responsibilities and soon was entrusted to the granting of loans. At first, he was scrupulously honest. Then one day he recklessly granted a loan of considerable size to a friend who was a speculative builder. The friend proceeded to fail, leaving Montague faced with either admitting his mistake or covering it up. He chose the latter course. After all, why disturb the partners over a matter that was really quite trivial, especially when he could replace the lost funds in no time? He had noticed early on that stockholders were not automatically informed when all or part of their holdings were transferred. Thus, all he had to do was forge a few documents authorizing transference of certain sums from a few customers' accounts into a "special" account of his own. It was all so safe and simple, especially since he saw to it that the accounts continued to pay dividends on the sums the customers believed they still owned, the correct figures in every instance entered in their passbooks.

Actually he wasn't stealing, simply borrowing.

At the beginning, he planned to pay the money back immediately. No one would be the wiser and he'd never "borrow" again. But the problem was, he started using part of the money to satisfy his gambling debts and, worse, to continue gambling. Had he chosen to terminate his ruinous habit, his debts would have been paid off completely by now, but whenever he decided to quit, he invariably allowed himself "just one more try." Alas, his luck was abysmal. Instead of diminishing, his debts increased.

Now, as he strolled to work along Berners Street on a fine, crisp London morning, Montague reflected that despite his best intentions, somehow the number of accounts he was plundering—er, borrowing from—had increased. Not that any of this was really his fault. Edgemont and Percival kept appointing him executor of newly deceased, wealthy men's estates, so the ultimate blame lay with the partners for placing irresistible temptation in his path. How easy, how safe it was to embezzle huge sums. He could not resist, and why should he? Of course, he would stop soon. Any day now, and no one would be the wiser.

Montague chuckled to himself. Let Lucy and Augusta worry all they wished, he was absolutely confident no one would ever discover his little scheme. They were all so incredibly naive at the bank it was pitiful. That included the two old men, his fellow bank executives, and all those pathetically unenlightened clerks.

So a pox on his sisters and their silly warnings that the penalty for fraud was death. Ludicrous. Only the careless got caught. Most certainly not Montague Winthrop.

In the weeks that followed her ladyship's return to London, Lucy saw much less of Lord Granville. Inevitable, of course. He was a busy man, what with the opening of Parliament and his coming reelection.

Gone were the delightful afternoon outings with Granville and the children. Some days she never saw him at all. Others, she would catch a quick glimpse of him as he, impeccably dressed, ventured forth to Westminster Palace, or some meeting or social event. At those moments her heart would flip-flop and she knew nothing had changed, she loved him as much as ever, if not more.

Lucy and the children were no longer welcome at dinner. For good reason, as far as her ladyship was concerned. Important guests were present in the dining room nearly every night. As Lucy overheard Lady Granville pointing out, "These guests are essential to your career, John. Allowing your children at the table would be a huge *faux pas*. It simply isn't done."

Lucy heard Granville reluctantly agree. Such moments were painful, and becoming more frequent as, slowly but surely, Lady Granville inserted herself into her son's life once again. One disturbing fact Lucy had found: Lady Granville had two faces. One she reserved for the times she addressed Lucy when her son was around. On those occasions she would smile pleasantly and act quite congenial. When Granville was absent, Lady Granville's attitude instantly changed. She glared at Lucy with flat, passionless eyes; her voice became hard and cutting. Although she never spoke a derogatory word, no doubt fearing the consequences should Lucy tattle to her son, it was crystal clear she truly detested Lucy and wanted her gone.

Lucy had no intention of leaving. The children needed her, especially William. In both deportment and scholarly achievements, he had dramatically improved since she first arrived. In another year he would be sent away to school. Meantime, she cringed at the thought that if she left, William might fall into the hands of an indifferent governess or tutor and slip back into his old behavior. She also needed to stay because of her stipend, from which she continued to send a generous amount to Augusta. Were Lucy the type to brood and be resentful, she would have railed at the way Montague allowed his newfound money to slip through his fingers. At first, he had been generous. Lately, though, he wasn't offering so much as a farthing toward Augusta and her children's support. He was gone every night. Lucy suspected what money he had was lost on the gambling tables. She graciously accepted her responsibility, though. Never once did she raise the issue of Montague's selfishness.

There was another reason she was determined to stay, a reason she was not proud of. *John.* She couldn't bear the thought of being away from the man she loved with all her heart.

The new Season began. On the night of the very first ball, Mary and Winifred prevailed upon Lucy to let them stay up late so they might catch a peek at the splendor of their aunt's and grandmother's new ball gowns. The family was gathered in the entry hall, about to leave, when Lucy, holding each little girl by the hand, descended the staircase. "Good evening, your lordship," she began, dipping a proper curtsy. "Excuse me, your ladyship and Lady Florinda, but before you leave, the girls wanted to see you in your ball gowns."

A fleeting frown crossed her ladyship's face. She quickly recovered and remarked, "All right, but be quick. We're late."

Florinda giggled. Clutching an ivory fan in one white-gloved hand, she held up her arms and twirled around. "What do you think, my darlings?" Her evening dress of rose-pink satin billowed about her in graceful folds.

"You look beautiful, Aunt Florinda," Winifred cried.

"You truly do, ma'am," Lucy agreed. "And you, your lady-ship, and . . . you, sir."

He'd been standing by the door, quietly waiting. She had caught her breath at the sight of him. Never had he looked more splendid, standing patiently by the door dressed in full evening wear.

Granville failed to acknowledge her compliment. Instead, he gave her a long, intense gaze. She wondered why he bothered. Compared to the ladies in their gorgeous ball gowns, she felt like a dull, drab little mole. His gaze swept over her, revealing an unmistakable hunger and longing in his eyes. He hadn't looked at her like that since the night in the nursery.

Finally he smiled. It was a wry smile, conveying admiration, keen awareness, and something so deeply indefinable she caught her breath. He bowed. "You, yourself, would look lovely in a ball gown."

Winifred clapped her hands. "Then why can't you take Miss Winthrop to the ball?"

His gaze still locked on Lucy, he solemnly replied, "Perhaps someday I shall, Winifred. Would you like that, Miss Winthrop?"

Before Lucy could even begin to form an answer to his astounding question, Lady Granville, all briskness now, spoke up. "We're late. Good night, Mary and Winifred. See they go straight to bed, Miss Winthrop. Come, John. Come, Florinda." In a twinkling they were gone.

"That settles it," Lady Granville hissed behind her fan. She was addressing Florinda during their first private moment at the ball. Over the strains of a lively waltz she asked, "Did you see how John looked at her? You don't suppose—?"

"That he's already bedded her?" With a brisk snap, Florinda opened her fan. From behind it she whispered, "I would not put anything past that mealy-mouthed little governess."

"She'll ruin everything." Just then, Lady Granville caught sight of Lady Camilla waltzing by, serene and smiling, floating in the arms of one of her many suitors. "Just look. Lady Camilla won't wait much longer, even if John *is* the catch of the Season."

"Something must be done," Florinda whispered back, "but what can you do? You know how protective of her John is. If you dare harm one hair of her head . . . mercy, it's too dreadful to contemplate."

"I don't care about that," Lady Granville snapped.

"You mean—?"

"I mean, Miss Winthrop must go."

"But you cannot dismiss her, John wouldn't hear of it."

"You and I shall find a way," Lady Granville replied with supreme confidence.

"But how—?"

"We watch, we wait, we seize whatever opportunity comes along."

"But what? I cannot imagine . . ."

"Don't worry, Florinda, I predict that in the end our high-and-mighty Miss Winthrop will cause her own downfall."

Later that night, Lucy tapped on Lady Regina's door. Lately she had formed the habit of stopping by. She enjoyed her conversations with Regina, especially now that she was still improving every day. It wouldn't be long before she, too, would be going to the balls.

"So did you see the new ball gowns?" Regina asked.

"Simply gorgeous."

"And his lordship?"

"Dressed to the nines."

"My brother is a handsome devil, don't you agree?"

"Very."

Something in the way Lucy said "very" caused Regina to raise her eyebrows. "You're in love with him, aren't you?"

Lucy was taken aback. In all the times they'd talked, she had scrupulously avoided any mention of her feelings toward Lord Granville. Now, startled by Regina's blunt question, she could find no quick answer and could only stammer, "I . . . I . . ."

Regina pounced on Lucy's hesitant answer like a dog on a bone. "Aha! I thought so. Of course you love him. Tell the truth, now. You adore my dear, esteemed brother and he loves you. Confess!"

Why not be honest? Lucy wondered. Regina was trustworthy and would never tell. "I love him very much."

"And he loves you."

"I cannot speak to that."

"You don't see him proposing to Lady Camilla, do you?"

"Well, no, but I supposed—"

"But it's so obvious. Until dear Mama returned, he spent every minute he could with you."

"But it was the children—"

"Don't be naive, he adores you. I can see it in his eyes."

"Whether he does or not, the situation is hopeless."

Regina thrust out her chin. "It most certainly is not. You're the daughter of a baron are you not? That stands for something. But the important thing is, you two are mad for each other. I wish John could just forget all that garbage about titles, and status, and all that folderol, and marry you."

"Then he'd lose the next election, let alone ruin his entire career. I shall not be responsible for that."

Regina's brow furrowed thoughtfully. "I am not sure he would really care if he lost his seat in Parliament. John possesses a great love of the land. The happiest I've ever seen him is when he's home at Penfield Manor, managing his estate. Left to his own devices, I wonder if he would ever have chosen a life in politics. He didn't have much of a choice, though. First our father pressured him to run for office, now Mama." Regina scowled. "Why can't she let him go? She's worse than ever and the irony is, John is still under her influence. The sad part is, he's under the illusion he's his own man, but he's not."

"Which is why our love is hopeless," Lucy replied. "I cannot imagine his defying your mother's wishes."

Unexpectedly Regina gave a delighted chuckle. "I would love to see him do it, though."

Without thinking, Lucy blurted, "While we're on the subject of frustrated love, I would like to see *you* defy your mother's wishes and run off with Lord Kellems." The moment the words left her mouth, she knew she should have kept silent. "Forgive me. It's none of my business. I should not have spoken."

Regina did not appear in the least offended. Instead, she

broke into a delighted smile. "It's time I told you. Mama doesn't know yet, but I have consented to marry Lord Kellems."

"But that's wonderful."

"We shall probably elope. Mama won't know until after the ceremony."

"That's for the best." *There's an understatement,* thought Lucy. She could only imagine the turmoil that would result if Lady Granville discovered Regina's wedding plans ahead of time.

Regina continued. "Now there's *his* parents to deal with, but it's going to be all right."

"Do they know?"

"Lord Kellems told his mother and father yesterday. I was quite worried, his being the oldest son and all, but from what he says, they plan to welcome me with open arms. As a matter of fact, they have invited us to call tomorrow afternoon."

"Well, I'm thrilled," Lucy replied with utmost sincerity. Never had she seen Regina so happy. "Will you go to Gretna Greene?"

"I think so, although I'm not quite sure . . ."

The two continued chatting, both of them pleased and excited about Regina's upcoming wedding. When Lucy finally got up to leave, Regina turned serious. "Since we're speaking so frankly, can I give you a word of advice?"

"And what is that?"

"Be careful. For years Mama has dreamed that someday my brother will become prime minister. Now you're threatening that dream. Much as I love Mama, I suspect that short of murder, she'd do anything to get rid of you." Regina sniffed with contempt. "And I'm not even sure she'd stop at that."

Lucy replied, "I watch my behavior every moment. With one notable exception, it's been so circumspect Lady Granville could not possibly complain about my conduct, let alone demand I be dismissed."

"I shan't ask you what the notable exception was," Regina said with a faint smile, "but be careful." Deep concern was evident in her eyes.

*   *   *

All the next day, Lucy's spirits were high as she thought of Lady Regina. How wonderful that such a truly deserving woman was at last going to live her own life. That night, as usual, Lucy knocked on Regina's door, eagerly anticipating a merry recounting of the visit to Lord Kellems's parents.

Matilda opened the door. Her countenance appeared more dour than ever, if that was possible. "Come in, Miss Winthrop. She's here, but she's not well."

Lucy knew immediately something was wrong and felt a stab of trepidation as she stepped inside the dimly lit bed-chamber. Regina was lying on her bed, a damp cloth on her forehead, staring at the ceiling. "Ah, Miss Winthrop," she said, "come in, but if you're expecting to hear what a wonderful time I had at Lord and Lady Marsh's home, you are doomed to disappointment."

Lucy swiftly seated herself beside the bed. "You mean—?"

"It was ghastly."

"But I thought you said—"

"That Lord Kellems's parents would welcome me with open arms? What wishful thinking. At the beginning, they were all forced smiles and politeness, but soon I discovered their fury."

"But perhaps you were being overly sensitive?"

Regina replied with a derisive snort. "After tea, they asked Lord Kellems to leave the drawing room so that they could have a 'little chat' with me alone. The minute he left the room, their eyes turned cold." Regina shuddered and rubbed her arms. "I could almost feel the chill. First they asked me if I was aware Lord Kellems was their son and heir. I told them of course I was aware. Then they asked me how many children I thought I could bear."

"Such rudeness."

"That's not all. They pointed out that at my 'advanced age' and considering my health, I might not be able to have any children."

"But didn't Lord Kellems tell you it didn't matter?"

"Of course he did, but his parents pointed out that it didn't matter now, but in the future, after the first glow of love was long gone, their precious son would live to deeply regret he married an older, sickly woman who could give him no heirs."

"But you're *not* old and you're *not* sickly."

"My head hurts." Regina groaned and pressed the cloth to her forehead. "They're right. I was out of my mind to think I could actually lead a normal life and find happiness with a younger man." Bitterly she added, "I was willing to flout my mother's wishes, but his parents, too? It's too much."

"But you love each other."

"He loves me now, but a few years from now? His parents are right. Doubtless he'll bitterly regret marrying an older, barren woman."

"But that's not true." Lucy felt like shaking her. "I'm no expert on love, but if ever I saw a man in love with a woman, it's Lord Kellems with you."

Regina folded her arms with resolve. "It's over. I shall never see Lord Kellems again."

Heartsick, Lucy tried to argue but soon gave up. Stubborn Regina had made up her mind.

After an evening session of Parliament, Granville arrived home and was surprised to find his mother waiting up for him.

"What's the occasion?" he asked, noting the sheen of excitement on her face.

"Wait 'til you hear." She was more animated than Granville had seen her in ages.

"What is it, Mama?"

"It's such a coup."

"For God's sake, out with it."

"The Prince Regent is coming for dinner."

"Here?"

"Of course here. What did you think?"

"That is indeed quite the coup. I'm delighted. However did you manage?"

"Oh, I have my ways," Lady Granville coyly replied. "But don't think for a moment I invited him for my own sake. I did it for you, John. We *must* court his favor. If Prinny's behind you in the next election, how can you lose?"

"Let me count the ways," Granville cautiously replied. "As

you well know, Prinny tends to shilly-shally between the Whigs and Tories, whatever suits his purpose at the time. Need I remind you it wasn't too long ago he formed an all-Tory cabinet?"

"That was then, this is now." Lady Granville wasn't the least deterred. "And even if the Whigs are the opposition right now, he could still support you personally."

Granville placed his hands on his mother's shoulders and gazed with gratitude into her eyes. "No matter what happens, I am most grateful. When is he coming?"

"Next Tuesday evening. That gives me a week." Lady Granville's eyes suddenly went wide with realization. "A week! I must talk to Cook immediately about the menu. And whom shall we invite? The Percys, of course, and the Cavendishes. The Russells do you think? Of course, Lord Shelborne. Oh, dear God, so much to do."

"Calm yourself. Everything will fall into place. It always does."

"The entertainment. My mind has gone blank. What does Prinny *do* after dinner?"

"Well, he likes cards."

"Too dull. We shall need more than cards. Hmm, let's see . . . ah, yes, Florinda can play the piano, which she does at least passably well. No singing, though. Even I must admit she hasn't much of a voice. Ah, I have it. We shall invite Lady Camilla who, as you well know, sings like an bird. And we might even . . . ah, yes, we shall have some tableaux."

"That's fine." Granville was pleased. Despite his popularity with his constituency, he was going to be opposed by the well-liked Lord Ramsey who, Granville didn't fool himself, might very well win. How clever Mama was. She had her faults, but when it came to politics, her perspicacity was uncanny. Providing Prinny an outstandingly delightful evening might well reap huge political rewards.

Or just the opposite, came a fleeting, dark thought, *if anything goes wrong.*

Lucy was in the middle of a history lesson when Becky burst into the classroom. "The Prince Regent's coming to dinner, Miss Winthrop. 'Ere, to this very 'ouse. And her ladyship wants you and the children in the drawing room right this minute."

As the children squealed with excitement, Lucy responded, "That's exciting news." She was curious to know why the children's presence had been requested in the drawing room, especially since Lady Granville took such pains to ignore her grandchildren most of the time. "Do you know why—?"

"The children are to be part of the entertainment. That's all I know."

Lucy, too, was excited. What a marvelous chance for the children to see royalty in the flesh.

In the drawing room, Lucy, trailed by three newly scrubbed and combed children, found not only Lady Granville but Ladies Florinda and Camilla, the two of them huddled together giggling, making plans.

Her ladyship began, "As I am sure you have heard, Miss Winthrop, we are to be honored with the presence of the Prince Regent for dinner Tuesday night. Naturally we shall plan the best of entertainment, including a few carefully planned tableaux."

Winifred clapped her hands and asked excitedly, "Are we to be in a tableau, Grandmama?"

"You most certainly are, my dear." Her ladyship addressed Lucy. "I want you to plan a tableau that will include the children. It must be tastefully done, of course. An historical event, perhaps? I want something that will reflect one of England's many triumphs, which in turn will reflect our infinite esteem for His Royal Highness's remarkable achievements. My seamstress will provide whatever you need in the way of costumes. Bosworth and the footmen will help with whatever you need by way of scenery." Lady Granville leveled a challenging gaze. "Well, Miss Winthrop, are you up to the task?"

Lucy welcomed the challenge. It would be such an exciting night for the children, and educational, too. "We could do a tableau celebrating the victories of 1814."

William piped up, "Better yet, Napoleon's defeat and banishment to St. Helena."

"Splendid, William." Lady Granville beamed. "Just as long

as we pay tribute to His Royal Highness for his courage in res-
cuing us from Napoleon."

Courage indeed, Lucy reflected. Prinny had been much too
occupied with his own selfish pursuits to have had anything to
do with saving England. Such sentiments, however, could
never be voiced, at least not around here. "We shall need a
Napoleon."

"I'll do it," William exclaimed. "I want to be Napoleon and
wear his fancy uniform."

"And what shall we be?" asked Mary.

"Hmm . . ." Lucy thought fast. "You and Winifred shall be
goddesses. I see the two of you diaphanously draped in white
gauze with satin sashes across your chests and letters in gold
reading, 'Goddess of Victory' for you, Mary, and 'Goddess of
Peace' for Winifred."

Both girls clapped their hands in delight.

"We must have a Duke of Wellington," William declared.

"Aren't you the clever one," said Florinda. She and Lady
Camilla had been listening, greatly amused. "I think Bosworth
should be the Duke of Wellington."

Lady Granville nodded her approval. "Good choice,
Florinda. Bosworth has the stature as well as the dignity."

William asked, "And who shall be the Prince Regent?"

Lucy said, "It must be someone very tall and very regal. I
picture him somehow elevated, looking down beneficently
upon the rest." She frowned. "But offhand, I can't think . . .
except perhaps his lordship?"

"He'll be much too busy as host," Lady Granville cut in
sharply. She addressed her daughter and Lady Camilla. "Do
you have any ideas?"

The two young ladies exchanged glances. Camilla asked,
"Why not one of the footmen?"

"I suppose," Lady Granville replied, "as long as it isn't
Montclaire."

Her response brought peals of laughter from the two young
ladies. "Can you imagine the insult?" Florinda cried. "Prinny
would be livid. Montclaire is even more obese than he is."

"Prinny fancies himself quite the handsome dandy," said

Camilla. "I doubt he's ever looked in the mirror and contemplated his own girth."

Her ladyship had not joined in the laughter. "I see nothing to joke about. What do you think, Miss Winthrop? After all, you are the one in charge."

Lucy, too, had skipped the laughter. She could see nothing funny in the ridicule of someone's physical shortcomings. "One of the other footmen? Benson perhaps?"

"He's handsome, but he's too skinny." Florinda's comment brought on more peals of laughter.

"We could plump him out with a pillow," Camilla suggested between giggles.

Lucy waited until the humor had subsided. "Benson it is then." She allowed a wry smile. "Without the pillow."

Florinda smiled, suddenly friendly. "You can count on us, Miss Winthrop. We want to help in any way we can."

Despite her lack of high regard for the Prince Regent, Lucy threw herself into the planning of the tableau. Her ladyship's seamstress was compelled to bring in extra help. For the two little girls they created two long, white angellike gowns; for William, a miniature Napoleon uniform complete with fringed epaulettes; for Bosworth's portrayal of the Duke of Wellington, a red-jacketed naval uniform with brass buttons, white breeches, and a swashbuckling sword borrowed from his lordship.

As for Prinny, Florinda had been true to her word and most helpful. "You know how Prinny dresses," she told Lucy. "I shall ask his lordship if he'd kindly loan us the most magnificent clothing in his wardrobe."

Several times during the week, Lucy remarked to herself that Florinda was being surprisingly friendly. Lucy wasn't sure why. She only felt relief that Florinda was no longer being rude.

The entire household was in a high state of readiness when the big evening finally arrived. Chaos had reigned throughout the day, but by evening the carpets had been beat and relaid, furniture dusted and rubbed, flowers piled in vases. The hall was scoured, and the steps and banisters of the staircase were polished to the brightness of glass. In the dining room, the table was set with the finest of silver and china and the sideboard flashed resplendent with gold and silver plate.

Lucy and the children were standing on the landing when His Royal Highness arrived. When she saw him, she was shocked. She had seen the Prince Regent only once before, several years ago. Back then, he was a handsome man, tall, with a powerful, well-muscled body. Now he was grossly fat. He had chosen to wear the uniform of a field marshal, complete with a sash across his chest covered with medals, including the Order of the Thistle, and the star and bright ribbon of the Order of the Garter. Nothing could disguise, however, his huge girth or several chins.

"Look, Miss Winthrop," Winifred cried, "the Prince is fa—"

"Hush," Lucy cried, placing a quick hand over her small charge's mouth. "It is rude to comment on the physical attributes of others," she whispered, giving thanks His Highness hadn't heard. After all the distinguished guests had arrived, she and the children returned to the nursery where they had their dinner, and the children donned their costumes. Finally they were summoned to the ballroom where a temporary stage had been constructed at one end of the hall, where ordinarily the orchestra played. The small door at the back that the musicians normally used gave handy access. A temporary curtain was stretched across the makeshift stage.

The guests had already gathered in chairs forming semicircle rows around the stage. From the doorway where Lucy and the children stood waiting, Lucy saw the Prince Regent was seated in the middle of the front row, Lord Granville on one side, her ladyship on the other. His Royal Highness looked quite content and seemed to be enjoying Lady Camilla's rather shrill rendition of "Hark the Bird's Melodious Strain." When she finished, Lady Granville stood and announced, "It's time for the tableaux."

Aided by some of her suitors, Florinda presented the first tableau, a splendid depiction of "The Year of the Sovereigns," which commemorated the year 1814 when the Prince Regent was host to several heads of the European countries that had defeated Napoleon. They included Tsar Alexander and his ally, the King of Prussia, Prince Metternich of Austria, and the conquering Field Marshal von Blücher.

Lady Camilla and friends presented the second tableau, "An Ode to His Royal Highness's Favorite Poets, Writers, and Painters." The applause was deafening as the curtain dropped, displaying Lord Byron, Sir Walter Scott, Thomas Lawrence, and Jane Austen. Lucy saw His Royal Highness smiling, applauding hardest of all.

Lucy's tableau was last. After the stage was curtained again, she slipped through the back door and with Florinda's help directed the two footmen who had been assigned the task of placing the scenery quickly on stage.

Lucy beckoned the children. "Come, get into your places," she whispered. Bosworth appeared. "You're to stand right there, Bosworth." When they were all in their places, she peered around. They were missing the Prince Regent. "Where is Benson?"

Florinda peeked out the door. "Don't worry, here he comes. Is everything in place, Miss Winthrop? I must get back to the piano. Signal when you're ready."

As Florinda slipped through the door, Lucy took one last, anxious look around. All seemed in readiness, and if she did say so herself, the scene looked lovely. Banks of flowers framed the stage; in the middle, William in his Napoleon uniform, in a running pose, appeared to be fleeing toward a palm tree where a sign announced, "Island of St. Helena." Chasing him, sword poised for the kill, came Bosworth in full naval regalia, a discreet sign around his neck announcing, "The Duke of Wellington." In pretty poses on either side were Mary and Winifred, in their long, white gowns and gold lettered sashes. But where was Benson? Representing the Prince Regent, he was supposed to be standing behind, elevated on an unseen stool banked with flowers, gazing down benignly on all the rest.

Just then, Benson appeared and started to climb upon the hidden stool. "You had best get off the stage," Bosworth whispered to Lucy. She started to leave, then stopped abruptly. *Something wrong.* She looked at Benson again.

Oh, no, oh, no.

Just then, Lady Granville's voice came through the curtain. "And now I am pleased to present 'His Royal Highness Wins the Day,' a tribute to our honored guest, and presented to you, among others, by my very own dear grandchildren."

"Get off the stage, Miss Winthrop," Bosworth hissed, alarmed.

Numb with horror, Lucy obeyed, quickly slipping through the door. *This isn't happening.* Turning back, she saw the curtain drop away, revealing "His Royal Highness Wins the Day," to the waiting audience.

An ominous moment of silence was followed by a collective gasp, clearly heard over the strains of "God Save the King" Florinda had struck up on the piano. From the hallway, Lucy didn't need to see the stage to be able to picture the disaster.

Somehow, some way, Benson had turned fat. Not just fat but grossly fat. With increased horror, Lucy realized the problem. Benson's breeches were stuffed with pillows. Not a little bit stuffed, but immensely, grossly stuffed, giving him a girth that surpassed that of the Prince's. Those breeches could not be his own. Borrowed from Montclaire perhaps? No matter. What mattered was, the joke had become real. Her beautiful tableau, so carefully planned and executed, had become an ugly, sickening parody of the Prince Regent.

Lucy stood in the hallway, hand pressed to her face in horror. The piano played on for what seemed to her like an eternity, although in reality it no doubt played for only the prescribed minute that the actors in the tableau must hold their poses. Finally the music stopped, followed by a mere smattering of applause, then another ominous silence.

Bosworth burst through the doorway, his face blanched with consternation. "The Prince has been gravely insulted," he announced in a shaking voice. "Who is responsible for this?"

Benson appeared. "Responsible for what, sir?" He looked the soul of innocence.

Bosworth poked at Benson's padded girth. "Who told you to do this?"

Benson hung his head. "'Twasn't my doing, sir. I only do as I am told."

"Then who *told* you to pad yourself to kingdom come?"

Benson flashed a furtive glance at Lucy. "Why, Miss Winthrop, of course. She was the one in charge. Who else could it be? Isn't that right, Miss Winthrop?"

Lucy stared at him, utterly astonished and speechless. When she found her voice, she asked, "Why are you doing this, Benson?"

"It's the truth," Benson retorted. He was about to continue on when a maid came rushing through the door.

"Come quick, Bosworth! The Prince is leaving and her ladyship has just collapsed."

"Good grief, what a disaster," cried the dignified butler before he headed back to the ballroom.

Looking bewildered, the children had gathered around Lucy. "What happened, Miss Winthrop?" William asked.

"Did we do something wrong?" Winifred's eyes were wide as saucers.

Lucy wanted to stay, question Benson further, but her first duty was to the children. She took Winifred's hand. "No, you did nothing wrong, Winifred, in fact, all of you did beautifully. Come, children, it's past your bedtime. I shall talk to you later, Benson."

Lucy led the bewildered children back upstairs. With Becky's help she put them to bed. On the outside, she remained calm, but inside, an icy knot had formed in her stomach. She felt sick just thinking about the repercussions that were sure to follow. Questions spun through her brain. What was his lordship thinking? Was his political career now ruined? Could he honestly believe she would do such a terrible thing? How was her ladyship? Was this just another of her feigned attacks, or was it real this time?

And why was Benson lying? Whom was he protecting, and why? She had her suspicions. *I was led into a trap*, she thought with dismay. Obviously someone had ordered Benson to stuff himself with those pillows. Lady Granville seemed the most likely suspect. She had made her antagonism toward Lucy very clear. Yet, would she have ruined her own exquisitely planned dinner party? Would she have deliberately offended the Prince, thus quite possibly ruining her sons's career? Not likely. No, it could not have been her ladyship. She would never have cut off her nose to spite her face.

That left Lady Florinda. Of course. It all became crystal clear. All along, Lucy had sensed Florinda's deep resentment, no doubt fueled by his lordship's continued refusal to propose to her dearest friend, Lady Camilla. Whether true or not, naturally Florinda thought Lucy was to blame. Lucy, herself, had no idea how much of Florinda's presumption was true; yet she believed the flighty girl was quite capable of doing such a thing. Silly, shallow creature that she was, she had not thought her plan through to the grim consequences. All she'd cared about was making Lucy look bad in front of the Prince Regent. She hadn't thought ahead to how the Prince could doubtless ruin her brother's future in Parliament.

Back in her bedchamber, Lucy threw herself on her bed and buried her face in the pillow. What could she do? she wondered. *Not a thing*, she thought with mute wretchedness. There was nothing she could say or do to prove her innocence.

To stay here now would be impossible.

She would give her notice first thing in the morning.

Chapter Fifteen

*D*ownstairs, the disastrous evening ended early. Bosworth gave a discreet sigh of relief as the last guest filed out the door. His cool dignity swiftly vanished as he immediately cornered Benson in the pantry, and in an action entirely out of character, grabbed him by his neck cloth. "Tell me what happened, you little weasel, and don't lie."

Benson started shaking. "'Twas Miss Florinda. She ordered me to do it, sir—even brought me that pair of Montclaire's breeches so I could stuff 'em with pillows. Said she and Lady Camilla was playin' a little prank. An' she said if I told, I 'ud be out on the street without a character. Then she says I should say Miss Winthrop made me do it."

Bosworth, an upright, moral man who read his Bible every night, knew right from wrong. Most certainly this was wrong. How dare that airheaded Miss Florinda put the blame on a fine, upstanding woman like Miss Winthrop? But much as Bosworth admired and respected the governess, he was well aware she was not the source of the wherewithal that provided him and his family's quite comfortable existence. The sad truth was, Benson wasn't the only one who had no desire to be thrown out on the street without a character.

With a contemptuous little shove, Bosworth loosed his hold on the cowering footman's cravat. "You're a fool, Benson. From now on, keep your mouth shut, and the next time Miss Florinda asks you to do something idiotic, come to me first."

Quaking, Benson backed away. "You won't tell?"

"Get out of my sight," Bosworth bellowed. He felt the utmost sympathy for Miss Winthrop, but when it came down to whose skin to save, he'd save his own.

Lord Granville sat by his mother's bedside. He wasn't sure if her collapse shortly after the early departure of the Prince was real or feigned. Either way, he was concerned. She had worked so hard to create a perfect evening. Now all was ruined. Her eyelids fluttered open. As if from a great distance, she whispered, "Is that you, John?"

"It's me, Mama," he answered gently. "How are you feeling?"

She groaned. "My life is over. I shall never be able to hold my head up in public again."

"I daresay you'll survive." He took her hand.

"But your career."

"If I've lost Prinny's support, I doubt it will be a major blow. My constituents won't change their vote because we showed that pompous ass for what he really is, however inadvertently." The corners of his mouth twitched a smile. "There were some in the audience who found it quite amusing. We should count our blessings no one laughed aloud."

"You cannot say that." She gripped his hand with desperation. "Perhaps we can set matters straight. If we explained to His Highness that it wasn't our fault—that our vindictive governess plotted the whole vile scheme, then—"

"We don't know Miss Winthrop was responsible," Granville cut in.

"You defend her?" A gleam of combat flashed in her eyes. "I want her dismissed immediately. Surely you cannot countenance such low behavior."

"Never in a million years would I believe Miss Winthrop is the one who got old Benson to stuff his breeches."

"It's not funny," she railed. "Who else would do such a thing?"

Granville arose. "Go to sleep, Mama. Rest assured, I shall do what needs to be done."

She leveled a suspicious gaze. "And just what does that mean?"

"Wait and see."

When Granville left, he immediately headed upstairs to the servants' floor. "Granville, you're a fool," he muttered to himself on the way up. "Fool," he called aloud, not caring if the servants heard, accompanying his outburst with a fist thrust against the staircase wall that set the portrait of the first Earl of Granville in a decided tilt.

It occurred to him that in his farcical, ill-thought-out zeal to do the proper thing, he had never visited Lucy in her room. He knew which room it was, though. In fact, he had been acutely aware of it since the day she arrived.

In a state of complete dismay and humiliation, Lucy lay facedown on the bed, her pillow damp with tears. She heard a firm knock on her door. Becky, no doubt, but she was in no mood to talk and called out, "Becky, will you please come back another time?" The door opened. "Becky, I said—"

"It's not Becky."

The sound of Granville's voice made her heart leap, caused ripples of awareness to course through her veins. She flipped over. There he stood in his evening clothes, his presence overpowering in her small, shabby room. Watching as he shut the door, she pushed herself up to a sitting position against her pillow, shoved back her hair, which she knew had to be in disarray, and made a futile gesture to wipe away her tears with the palm of her hand.

"You," she said.

"I." He reached for a fine linen handkerchief and proffered it. "Here, dry your eyes. I've never seen you cry before."

She accepted the handkerchief and dabbed at her eyes and cheeks. "That's because I rarely cry. But after what happened tonight . . ." She could not go on. Her shudder was visible. "I am mortified."

Granville could have chosen the room's one chair to sit upon. Instead, without so much as a by-your-leave, he sat upon the side of Lucy's bed, so close his thigh touched the side of her leg, though neither made an attempt to move. "It was not your fault," he said, the tone of his voice infinitely compassionate.

"Of course not. I would never do such a thing." She threw

down the handkerchief. "But what's the use? They're blaming me, aren't they?"

He took her hand. There was a lethal calmness in his eyes. "I intend to find out who is responsible. I have my suspicions. I doubt I'll have to look too far."

"Florinda?"

"Yes, aided and abetted by Lady Camilla. The two have played similar pranks before."

"I would hardly call it a prank."

"Neither would my mother."

"Oh, I'm sure she's horrified. She blames me, doesn't she?"

He hesitated. "Sometimes we see only what we want to see."

"Your mother hasn't wanted me here from the very first day. I tried not to care, but after this, much as I love William, and Mary, and . . . and"—her throat was constricting—"little Winifred, I cannot stay."

"You can stay and you will stay." He gripped her shoulders. "My mother didn't hire you, I did. And besides—" He paused and closed his eyes a moment, as if his next words were to be wrenched from deep within.

"Besides what?" she prompted.

"That night in the nursery . . ."

"I thought we had closed the door on that night."

He smiled at her, gripping her shoulders tighter, drawing her closer. There was an intensity about him she'd never seen before. "You know damn well I have not forgotten. I wanted you so badly that night I have wondered a thousand times since how I had the willpower to resist. I've tried to convince myself I did the right thing, but—"

"You did."

"No I did not. Ah, Lucy—"

Before she knew what was happening, his lips came down fiercely on hers and his arms went tight around her and the memory of all those warm, passion-filled moments in the nursery came flooding back. How grand to be in his embrace again. Had she not dreamed every night of this moment? And yet . . .

She had vowed not to let her heart rule her head again. She

belonged in Bedlam if she allowed herself to go through the same torture as before.

Suddenly he was lying beside her on the bed, nearly on top of her. It was difficult to move, but she managed to pull her lips away. "Stop," she demanded, "nothing has changed." Her outcry had unleashed a different emotion within her. She realized it was anger. She had been coping quite nicely. How dare he stir the flames of her passion once again. "We mustn't do this."

"It's all right," he replied, "I haven't told you everything."

"You haven't?" Her reply was close to caustic. "What have I missed?"

With an ardent tremor in his voice, he said, "That I love you. That I've always loved you from that day I first saw you in the street outside of Parliament. That since that night in the nursery I've tried to forget you, but I cannot."

He loved her. Her mind went reeling from his words. Still, her anger had not instantly turned to joy. It wouldn't, either. There were just too many barriers between them. "Why are you telling me this now?"

Without hesitating, he replied, "It happened tonight. I've been aware for some time how my mother and sister have been treating you. To my shame, I ignored the situation, telling myself it didn't matter, that you were well able to cope."

"I was, until tonight."

"My eyes were opened tonight. Not only did I perceive the nasty way my family was treating you was intolerable, I saw myself for the first time. What I saw makes me ashamed. For years I've told myself I was free of my mother's influence. Since that night in the nursery, I tried to keep away from you— tried convincing myself that Mama had nothing to do with it, and it was my own supposedly wise decision that I mustn't fall in love with my governess."

"You shouldn't. Your career—"

"Damn my career. From this moment forward, I vow my mother will have no part in running my life. Ah, Lucy . . ."

He crushed his lips on hers again. She lay beneath him, fully aware of his hot, hard body, helpless to stop her eager response to the touch of his lips. *Just like last time,* she thought, *when my mind was strong but my flesh was weak.*

But it would be sheer folly to get involved with this man again. Her choice was clear. Either she surrendered to her passion, thus making a fool of herself and quite easily ruining her life, or she could keep her dignity by showing the courage to reject this vibrant, dashing man whom she loved to distraction. Much as it pained her, there was only one intelligent choice she could make.

Once more she broke away, hitched herself back, and firmly announced, "Sir, I do not intend to melt in trembling surrender this time."

To his credit, he instantly drew away. His eyebrows lifted in amusement. "There's something I haven't told you."

"And what is that?"

"I want to marry you."

It took a moment for the shock of his words to hit full force. When they did, a soft gasp escaped her. "You . . . want to marry me?"

"That's what I said."

"But I'm a governess."

"You're the daughter of a baron, are you not?"

"An impoverished, church mouse poor baron."

"So? Is there really such a chasm between us? You think I haven't thought this through? There's no reason why we cannot make it work. Forget society and its silly artifices. We are, after all, only two people on this vast earth of ours, equal in the eyes of God."

She smiled. "There are some who would say otherwise."

"Do we care what they say? I only know I love you, Lucy, and I don't want to live without you another day."

As they talked, cold, cruel reason took command of Lucy's mind. There was no way around it. There was just no way. "We cannot, John. Not now, not ever."

"But we can. If you're concerned over my career—"

"That's only part of it. Yes, of course, I would worry about your career. Surely you'd never be prime minister if you were married to a governess." He started to answer, but she touched her fingers to his lips. "Hush, let me finish. That's not all. Your reputation, social standing—all would be ruined."

"I haven't a care."

"I care, and the answer is no." This was killing her, but she knew she must stick to the rightful course she had set, no matter how it pained her.

His chin jutted to a stubborn angle. "What if I don't take no for an answer?"

In the back of her mind, an old memory stirred. "You must."

"And why must I?"

"Do you recall the three wishes you granted me?"

"Of course I remember. Your first wish led me to the nursery where I enjoyed one of the happiest evenings of my life."

"Well, my second wish won't be as pleasant."

"You mean—?"

She braced herself. Her next words would be the hardest she'd ever had to say. "I am leaving your employ. My second wish is that you leave me alone. Don't come after me. If by happenstance we should meet, I trust you will treat me as your former governess and nothing more. I want you never, ever to propose marriage again."

Granville's countenance went from self-assured to surprise to downright shock. "You cannot mean it."

"Lest you don't understand, I do love you, John, enough to know I would ruin your life if I accepted your proposal."

"But you would not. I have tried to explain—"

"No." She raised a palm in protest. "My mind is made up. Nothing you can say or do will change it. You must respect my wish. You gave your word."

"I see." Looking as if he'd just been struck, Granville arose from the bed, smoothed his clothing. She could see he was struggling to conceal his shock. "Do you realize what you're giving up?" he asked.

"I've a fair idea."

"Do you? Have you any idea how many women would sell their souls to become Lady Granville?"

"Millions, I'm sure."

"Not to mention the wealth, the privileges."

"Spare me." She crossed her arms over her chest. "Your mother and your sister hate me. That's not going to change, no matter what you say, and quite frankly, I don't care to put up with their enmity for the rest of my life. Then there's your reputation, which you don't seem to care about, but I do. I don't look forward to your receiving the cut direct which you *would* receive if you were to marry me, as would I. We would have no social life. You think it wouldn't matter but it would."

He took his time answering, regarding her with clear, contemplative eyes. "What a conundrum. There are many reasons why I love you, prominent among which are your courage, your high moral character, your refusal to compromise."

"And why is that a conundrum?"

His lips twisted into an ironic smile. "Because it's those very virtues I admire that prevent me from having you."

"I wish it could be otherwise." She was proud of herself. She had said that last with such finality he was sure to know she would not back down.

"In that case, a gentleman always knows when he has lost and accepts his defeat with grace and dignity. And I am nothing if not a gentleman." He moved toward the door and gave a slight, mocking bow. "Wish number two, granted."

"I'm sorry, I know I've hurt you." She gave him a rueful smile. "I doubt you've never been rejected before."

"A first, I must admit, but never fear, you'll not be hearing from me again."

"Thank you," she whispered, grateful that a breaking heart did not show.

"I'll give you an excellent character, of course."

"That would be most kind of you."

"And should you need my help in finding another position—"

"I shall ask for your help."

"So it's good-bye then."

She clenched her jaw to kill the sob in her throat. "Good-bye, your lordship."

The moment he closed the door, the sob she'd held in so long broke through. She made no attempt to hold it back.

*   *   *

Later that night, Lucy knocked on Regina's door and was invited in. As she settled by Regina's bedside, her heart ached at how Regina had changed since her decision to give up Lord Kellems. She was pale and listless, had lost her spark, and was well on her way to becoming a recluse again.

"I have just given notice, Lady Regina. I shall leave first thing in the morning, so I've come to say good-bye."

Regina's first reaction was a mighty, "You cannot leave." Distressed, she pushed herself up and leaned back weakly against the headboard. "You're not leaving over that horrible prank Florinda played, are you? My brother will not rest until he gets her to admit it and gives you an apology."

"That's part of it, but not all."

Regina thought a moment. "It's John, isn't it?"

Over a tightness in her throat, Lucy answered, "Yes."

"He loves you."

"He proposed tonight."

"Really? But that's wonderful." Regina's face lit with pleasure. "Doesn't that solve everything?"

"Your brother would be making the worst mistake of his life if he married me."

"But I know you love him."

How much more could she stand? Lucy felt she must change the subject or disgrace herself by starting to cry. "My mind is made up. Please . . . let's not discuss it anymore. That's not why I came."

"Then why did you come?"

"I came to discuss the love of your life, not mine. I shall speak honestly." Lucy smiled at the irony. "Now I can, you know. Since I've already turned in my notice, I have nothing to lose."

"I am all ears," answered Regina.

"Well, then." Lucy took a deep breath, feeling as if she were atop a cliff overlooking the ocean, ready to dive in. "Regina Weston, you are a fool."

The young woman's eyes widened. "I am? And in what way?"

"Because Lord Kellems loves you with all his heart. And you love him. The two of you belong together, yet you're letting his narrow-minded parents get in the way. Your mother, too."

"But I cannot give him children."

"So what? Did he not make it clear he doesn't care about that? You two could be perfectly happy, yet for some ridiculous reason you've decided to do nothing but lie here in this gloomy room wasting your life away."

As if to protect herself, Regina drew her cover closer about her. "But I am ill. Surely you know—"

"You are *not* ill. Remember when we were at Penfield Manor only months ago? You were taking the stairs, riding horses, getting stronger every day."

"But Mama—"

"No doubt your mother loves you, but can't you see she's smothering you? Oh, I know you're frail. And you'll never be in robust health, but my gracious, that doesn't mean you should spend the rest of your life having doctors probe and prod you, drinking those horrible elixirs and disgusting remedies that don't do you one bit of good."

Regina was listening with great interest. Calmly she asked, "So if you were me, what would you do?"

Lucy was so intent on her message, she could no longer sit still and had to leap to her feet. "I would send a note to Lord Kellems immediately. I would tell him, yes I love you, and I want to marry you, and please come and get me so we can make a dash to Gretna Greene."

"You make it sound so simple."

"It is. Then the two of you could sail to Italy, just as you told me you'd like to go one time. Find a sunny Italian town, Montecatini perhaps, or Venice if you prefer a city. Either way, you two could live in perfect bliss, taking in the paintings, the sculptures, drinking fine Italian wine."

Regina started to laugh. "I am amazed at you, Miss Winthrop. This isn't like you."

Lucy tossed her head. "Oh, it's me, all right. For once I'm speaking out without the fear of losing my position, since"— she smiled ruefully—"it's already lost." She gestured around the room. "Or would you rather spend the rest of your life in this dungeon? The choice is yours." She took another deep breath and sank back down. "There. I've said all I have to say. I do hope I haven't offended you. It's just that I like and admire you very much, Lady Regina. You have compassion, wit, intelligence. I hate to see someone like you continue to live this miserable existence when you could be living life to the fullest with the man you love."

Throughout Lucy's discourse, Regina had listened with intense interest. Now, in a subdued voice not at all like her, she said, "No one's ever talked that way to me before."

"It's time someone did."

"You're very brave. I appreciate your frankness."

"It's because I care."

"Perhaps you're right. I . . . shall think upon what you said."

"Please do."

A few minutes later when Lucy said her final good-bye and left, she felt sick with disappointment. True, Regina had listened, yet she'd shown no indication she'd been the least swayed by Lucy's passionate words.

The next day, in the small kitchen of her home, Augusta gazed at her newly arrived sister in amazement. "You mean, Lord Granville actually asked you to marry him?" Lucy nodded. "And you refused?"

"Don't tell me you're disappointed," Lucy replied. "As I recall, you once referred to him as 'your perfect example of upper-class decadence and sloth.'"

"He is, of course, but"—Augusta's eyes grew warm with sympathy—"I know you love him. It must have been extremely difficult to say no."

How difficult? You will never, ever know. Although Lucy's heart was devastated and she felt numb inside, she made an effort to sound bright and chirpy. "We would never have been happy. For one thing, his mother would always hate me. For another, I doubt his peers would ever forgive him for marrying beneath himself."

Augusta sniffed. "He'd be marrying up, not down."

"So *you* say, dear Augusta," Lucy replied, grateful for her sister's loyalty. "However, I should imagine he'd be snubbed by all society for the rest of his life should he marry a mere governess. He'd come to resent me, I know he would, and I couldn't let that happen." She breathed a pensive sigh. "So here I am, jobless and penniless again."

"And that girls' school you'd planned on?"

"Far down the road I fear, considering Montague hasn't even begun to pay me back." Lucy squared her shoulders. "But no matter. Tomorrow I shall start looking for another position."

"You'll find something quickly, just as good if not better," Augusta predicted.

Her prediction proved wrong. Early afternoon of the next day, just as Lucy was about to set forth to search for a position, Mr. Arthur Baker, a bald, timid little man who worked as a clerk at Edgemont-Percival, arrived at the modest cottage on Harford Lane with terrible news.

Hat in hand, he nervously announced, "Ladies, I hate to be the bearer of bad tidings, but your brother has been taken to Newgate Prison."

"Oh, no," cried Lucy and Augusta simultaneously.

Baker nodded grimly. "The police arrested him this morning at the bank. In front of everyone. Dear me, it was all quite dreadful. Before they took him away, he asked that I come here and inform you of his . . . er, incarceration."

"What do they accuse him of?" asked Lucy, both stunned and sickened.

"Apparently Winthrop has been looting customers' accounts on a grand scale. Some of the clerks were suspicious, you see, and after giving a thorough check to some of his accounts . . . well, the result is, the police were called."

"How much did he steal?"

"When I left, the partners were making a frenzied search of Winthrop's office and security boxes. They are quite shaken. It appears he may have embezzled over a hundred seventy thousand pounds."

Both Lucy and Augusta gasped with horror.

"It's enough to cause the bank to close," Baker went on. "I dread tomorrow after the news leaks out. It appears some customers have lost their life savings."

After the bank clerk departed, Lucy and Augusta hugged in

a tearful embrace. "Is it as bad as I suspect it is?" Lucy asked, fearing the answer.

"They'll hang him," came Augusta's cryptic reply.

A cold knot formed in Lucy's stomach. "We must do something. We cannot let him die."

"I shall fight for his life with every breath that's in me," Augusta declared in her usual stalwart fashion. "He deserves prison, perhaps, but my little brother shall *not* go to the gallows." She donned her cloak and bonnet. Shoulders back, fire in her eyes, she announced, "I'm off to Newgate. No, I don't want you along, Lucy, you'll just be in the way. I do have certain influential friends, you know. Surely he can be released to my custody. With a little luck, we shall have Montague back by sunset."

Chapter Sixteen

*I*n a state of sick anxiety, Lucy spent nearly the entire afternoon waiting by the parlor window, hoping that at any moment she would see the old carriage coming along Harford Lane, Augusta driving, Montague by her side.

It was nearly dark when Augusta returned alone.

"They won't let me see him." Augusta removed her cloak and bonnet and cast them dejectedly aside.

Lucy's heart sank. "Did you learn anything?"

"Only that Montague was taken from the bank and brought before the magistrate at Marlborough Street. When the magistrate heard the facts, he determined there was sufficient evidence to commit Montague to the custody of the warden of Newgate. He's to be held over for trial at the next session at Old Bailey." Biting her lip, Augusta sank wearily into a chair. "They took him to Newgate in a common wagon. He must have been mortified. You know how proud he is."

"What happened next?" Lucy braced herself.

"He was taken to the keeper's office where he had to pay an admittance fee. That's the last I know of him directly, but from my experience with Newgate, I can easily surmise what happened next. He would have been ironed at ankle and groin in the fetter's room. After he was shackled, he would have had to shuffle behind the turnkey down those dark, cold flagstone passageways until he reached the felons' quarters. It's all quite horrible. When the turnkey opens that heavy iron door, the most dreadful, nauseating stench sweeps out. Inside, there's only a flickering light from a few candles. All you can see is a straw-strewn cell filled to capacity with desperate-looking men."

"And now our Montague's among them?" Lucy asked in horror. "I cannot believe it. What can we do?"

Augusta drew herself up with resolve. "I shall go to Edgemont-Percival first thing tomorrow. They liked Montague. Surely Mr. Baker was wrong about the hundred seventy thousand pounds. That seems a ridiculous figure. Surely it's a lesser amount, in which case, if I throw myself on the partners' mercy, they might consider dropping the charges."

"It's worth a try." Lucy was aware they were grasping at straws.

The next day their hopes were dashed when they found nearly the entire front page of the *Morning Chronicle* devoted to the embezzlement. Nothing was left in doubt. The amount stolen indeed exceeded a hundred seventy thousand pounds. Prominent, respected banker, Montague Winthrop, was shortly to be placed on trial for the monstrous crime.

On a separate page, a notice had been placed by the partners:

"The very unexpected situation in which we suddenly find our House placed by the extraordinary conduct of our employee, Mr. Montague Winthrop, has determined us, for the present, to suspend our payments."

"Dear God, they've closed the bank," Lucy told Augusta. "You had better not go anywhere near Berners Street or they'll tear you apart."

She was right. The bank numbered among its clients many tradesmen and small investors who rapidly realized their life savings had been wiped out. By that afternoon, an angry mob had formed outside the bank. Stones were thrown. Police were summoned. Messrs. Edgemont and Percival barely escaped with their lives as they were escorted through the rioting crowd.

"What can we do?" asked Lucy that night. She had never felt so helpless.

Augusta's countenance was bleak. "I shall do everything I can, but I fear there's no way Montague can escape going to trial."

*   *   *

"Crier, make the proclamation."

"Oyez! Oyez! Oyez! If any can inform my lord, the King's justices, the King's sergeant, the King's attorney, on this inquest to be taken, of any crimes or misdemeanors committed by the defendant at the bar, let them come forth and they shall be heard. God save the King!"

Montague's trial had begun. *What am I doing here? Nothing seems real,* Lucy thought as she sat next to Augusta in the Old Bailey Sessions Hall. The aroma of herbs strewn on the courtroom floor and the nosegay of fragrant flowers sitting atop the judge's bench filled her nostrils. Augusta had told her the reason why the herbs and flowers were there: to disguise the stench of Newgate Prison next door.

How could flowers be in bloom at a time like this? came her anguished thought. She craned her neck to catch a glimpse of her brother, brought to the courtroom in chains. She could see only the top of his golden head as he sat, head bowed, before the judge and jury. She felt desperately tired and no wonder. In the scant three weeks since Montague's arrest, she and Augusta had exhausted every possible means of setting him free. Their efforts had been in vain. Even Augusta's many connections with prison officials and those prominent in the advocation of prison reform proved fruitless. Not a soul sympathized. The general populace considered Montague's crime so heinous that no one would consider helping him escape the gallows.

The evidence was devastating. Through investigations of the *Morning Chronicle*, it was already known that Montague had "kept up several establishments" and spent large sums on his mistresses. The attorney general who was prosecuting the case began by making mention of that fact. Next, a parade of clerks from Berners Street were summoned to testify that Montague had knowingly and on many occasions forged their signatures on documents that were produced in court. Further damning testimony was provided by Messrs. Edgemont and Percival themselves, now both bankrupt and ruined. They supplied detailed and irrefutable evidence of Montague's guilt.

The trial was not lengthy, with good reason. There was no provision in English law permitting an accused person to testify on his own behalf, nor could the prisoner cross-examine witnesses.

After the court reporter summarized all the evidence, the jury, having been instructed by the judge, withdrew to deliberate. They were out less than an hour. When they returned, their verdict was not unexpected.

"We find the defendant guilty as charged."

Until that moment, Lucy had held out hope. In her heart she could not believe the dear little boy she remembered so well could be found guilty of anything. True, he had shown some signs of his weaknesses, yet he had been so sweet when he was growing up, an angel with his blue eyes and blond curls. He never got into fights and would play quietly by himself for hours. Generous and loving, he had often brought her and Augusta flowers plucked from the garden, clutched tightly in his chubby, dimpled little hands. Rarely did he have to be punished, and then never a whipping. Just sending him to his room would suffice.

Lucy faced the ghastly reality when the judge donned the "black cap," a square of black silk about nine inches across, and in somber tones proceeded to announce Montague's fate.

"Montague Thomas Winthrop, you are sentenced to be taken hence to the prison in which you were last confined and from there to a place of execution where you will be hanged by the neck until dead and thereafter your body buried within the precincts of the prison and may the Lord have mercy upon your soul."

Montague's execution was set to take place in just five days.

In the condemned cell at Newgate, Lucy and Augusta were at last permitted to see their brother and say their final farewells.

"I am so sorry," Montague fervently cried as they hugged.

He looks so terrible, thought Lucy, noting how thin and haggard he'd become.

As they seated themselves at an ancient wooden table in the middle of the cell, Montague declared, "I deeply regret what

I've put you through. What a fool I was." He dropped his head to his hands and started to sob.

Augusta reached to comfort him. "It doesn't matter now."

"But it does." Montague raised his head. His red-rimmed eyes held a haunted look. "I *did* steal that money, against all your advice. I deserve to die."

Augusta's chin jutted out. "You do not deserve to die, Montague. There's the outrage in this justice system of ours. You did indeed break the law. You should be punished. But death? Outrageous. You did not kill anyone. Such a sentence is an atrocity."

Montague wiped his eyes and made a valiant effort to pull himself together. "Is there any hope at all?"

Lucy clasped his arm. "There are still appeals to be made. You can rest assured we are doing everything we can."

Montague gave a despondent laugh. "You have all of three days."

Augusta raised a clenched fist. "I vow we shall keep on fighting."

"To the bitter end," Montague replied with a wry smile. "And speaking of the bitter end, will you be there with me?"

Lucy asked, "You mean . . . ?"

"At my hanging." Montague seemed to have gathered his strength and said lightly, "They'll be hanging twelve of us, you know. No murderers. Thieves, the lot of us. It won't be a pretty sight, but if you could manage to be there, somewhere in the crowd, it would give me the strength . . ." He choked and could go no further.

To die, came Lucy's anguished thought.

"You can count on our being there," said Augusta. "But you mustn't give up hope."

"No, dear sisters, I must not give up hope." Resignation lay heavy in his voice. "Thank you so much for your help. Know that I love the two of you, more than words can say. And know that I'm terribly, terribly sorry and would give the world if I could take back what I did."

"Oh, Montague," Lucy cried in an anguished voice, "we would do anything—"

"All I ask is that you be there. Your presence will give me

great comfort. Even if I don't see you, I shall know that you are somewhere in the crowd."

Later, as Lucy and Augusta returned to the little house on Harford Lane, they were close to despair. "He's showing courage I never knew he had," Lucy said. "It breaks my heart."

"Tomorrow I shall make another attempt to see Lord Sidmouth," Augusta declared. "As you know, so far he has refused to see me. As for Lord Darwood, it appears he's out of the country."

"My prayers will go with you tomorrow."

"It's our last hope."

Not entirely, Lucy thought, and not without bitterness. Loath though she was to ask, she knew of one more person who might help. The very thought of going to him, imploring his assistance, filled her with trepidation. Still, if Augusta did not succeed tomorrow, and all other possibilities were exhausted, Lucy knew what she must do.

The day after his devastating, and quite humiliating, rejection at the hands of Miss Lucy Winthrop, Granville had received a tempting invitation. On the spur of the moment, Lord Darwood had decided to embark upon a holiday in France and asked his friend, Granville, if he would care to come along.

"We shall wallow in those Paris fleshpots, old boy."

Ordinarily Granville would have refused. In the past, he'd had no interest in participating in the excesses of the decadent French. Now his heart was hurting, he wasn't sleeping well, and the idea of escaping from his current deep malaise was so appealing that before he knew it, he was strolling with his friend along the Champs Élysées.

He had known better than to expect that the naughty delights of Paris could ease his pain; still, he hoped they would at least provide a distraction. But despite the endless wine, women, and song that Darwood found so entertaining, Granville soon found himself restless and bored. It was obvious his wounded heart was not going to mend, at least not this way. *Lucy.* He thought of her constantly, yearned for her without end. Soon he realized his mistake in trying to run from memories that refused to be left behind.

He said his good-byes to Darwood and France, and left for home.

Now, having just returned to Cheltham House late the night before, Granville made himself comfortable in his study where a stack of old newspapers awaited his perusal. As he dug to the bottom for the oldest-dated *Morning Chronicle*, he idly wondered if anything of interest had occurred in London during the three weeks he'd been gone.

He had hardly begun to read when Bosworth knocked and stepped in. "Sir, Miss Winthrop is here and wishes to see you."

"No."

Noting the butler's startled expression, Granville immediately regretted his involuntary, explosive reply. But Good Lord! If a horse had kicked him in the stomach, he could not have received a more sickening jolt. What could the woman possibly want? Was it not enough she had rejected him, broken his heart? The least she could do was leave him in peace. "Inform Miss Winthrop I cannot see her. Er . . . I have pressing matters to attend to."

"Very good, sir." Bosworth left but shortly returned. "She won't go away, m'lord. She said if you still refuse to see her, I'm to tell you she is here to collect her third wish."

Curse the woman. And curse those three wishes he had so foolishly granted. Come to think of it, curse Darwood, too, for talking him into such idiocy in the first place. Still, since he had given his word, he was obliged to see her. "Send her in, Bosworth," he remarked through lips pressed thin.

When she appeared, he stood, braced himself. "Good morning, Miss Winthrop. To what do I owe . . . the honor?" *Good God, what has happened?* he asked himself, inwardly horrified. The last time he'd seen her, but a scant month ago, she had looked the picture of health and vivacity with bright eyes and rosy cheeks. Now, not only had she lost considerable weight, she was pale and drawn; her cheeks were gaunt; there were dark circles under her eyes. The plain black bonnet and gown she was wearing did not help. Had someone died?

Somber-faced, she greeted him, then asked, "May I sit down, m'lord?"

Making sure he was the very soul of courtesy—distant, remote courtesy—he indicated the chair on the other side of the desk. He sat and waited for her to speak again.

She bowed her head a moment, as if gathering her strength. "Of course, you've heard about my brother, Montague."

"I have been abroad and just returned last night." He nodded toward the stack of unread newspapers. "Haven't the faintest notion what's been going on in London."

"So you don't know," she said, her voice heavy with despair. "Then I beg you hear me out." With pained reluctance, she proceeded to inform him of the dreadful facts surrounding Montague's arrest, ending with his trial and sentencing. "He's to be hanged in two days." Her voice broke. She bit her lip. "We've tried everything to obtain a reprieve, but to no avail."

Granville's first impulse was to rush around the desk, wrap his arms around her, and offer whatever solace he could. He would have done so, too, except just in time he recalled that second, crushing wish wherein she made it clear that if by happenstance they should meet, he was to treat her like his former governess and nothing more.

He remained behind his desk.

"I am terribly sorry, Miss Winthrop. I've heard you speak highly of your brother several times and recall how happy you were when he took the position in the bank. Now this. I am shocked and saddened. But surely he has friends who are working for his reprieve?"

Lucy shook her head. "No one wants to help. When you read those newspapers, you will see how the populace is incensed and out for blood. I cannot say I blame them. People lost their life savings because of Montague. He should be punished, but—"

"Not with death?"

"Exactly. So you see why I am here. I never thought I would use that third wish, but here I am, come begging."

"But what would you have me do?"

"Only His Royal Highness can help us now. Only he can grant Montague a reprieve. The trouble is, both Augusta and I have tried everything we could think of to arrange an audience with Prinny, but so far we've gotten nowhere."

"So you are asking . . . ?" The incredible truth had dawned, but he wanted to hear it from her own lips.

"I am asking that you speak to the Prince Regent for us. Oh, m'lord, it's our last chance." She clenched her fists, visibly trembling in her intensity. "Augusta and I love Montague dearly, despite his faults. We cannot bear to think of our dear brother dying such a horrible death."

He let a long, silent moment go by, then softly asked, "Do you realize the enormity of what you're asking?"

"He's my brother. I cannot—"

"You cannot let him die," he finished for her. "Miss Winthrop, I can only imagine how distraught I, myself, would be if a loved one of mine were facing the gallows. Horrible. I do understand. But you must realize, you're asking the impossible."

"In what way?"

"If you will recall, the last time Prinny was in this house, he was subjected to vile insult. Both my mother and I wrote long letters of apology, *abject* apology I should add. However, neither of us has been given the courtesy of a reply. What that tells me, Miss Winthrop, is that should I be foolhardy enough to appear as a supplicant before our Prince Regent, I would doubtless get tossed out on my ear."

Her whole body sagged. She looked stricken. "Then you won't—?"

"It's not a matter of won't. It would be useless to try, that's what I'm trying to convey to you."

Bravely lifting her chin, she declared, "It's my third wish."

He braced himself. This was appalling, seeing her grief and suffering. "If memory serves, we had agreed your three wishes must be within reason."

"And my third wish is not?"

He knew his next words would be devastating, but he had no choice. "No, it is not. You are asking the impossible."

"I see." Pale and shaken, she rose unsteadily to her feet. She swayed for a moment as if she were going to collapse, then took a deep breath and drew herself tall. Leaning her head back, she gazed directly into his eyes. "Then I shall trouble you no further, sir."

He wanted to reach out to her, to say, *Lucy, come back, I'll try, I'll do what I can.* Such a course of action would be foolish, though, and entirely futile.

She left without another word, leaving Granville in a torment of regrets. But despite his profound concern, he knew he had made the only sensible decision an intelligent, prudent man could possibly make.

Chapter Seventeen

*O*n the day of Montague's execution, Lucy awoke before dawn, her first thought, *How can I possibly get through this day?* Augusta had already arisen. Hardly a word was exchanged as the two moved like silent ghosts around the small cottage, dressing in black, readying themselves for what without question was to be the most terrible day of their lives.

Grief-stricken Nell had risen early, too. "Now don't worry about the children. You must eat some breakfast before you leave."

"I couldn't down a bite," Lucy said.

"Let's just go." Lucy had never heard such despondence in Augusta's voice.

In darkness they hitched the horse to the ancient carriage. As they went along Bridge Street toward Newgate, Lucy finally broke the bleak silence. "Do you remember his first little dress coat? How adorable he looked?"

Augusta nodded. "Do you remember the day he got lost in Green Park?"

"You were frantic. Remember how overjoyed we were when we found him?"

They fell into silence again, the bittersweet memories too much to bear. Eventually Lucy remarked, "I have never been to a hanging."

"And I have been to far too many," Augusta replied.

"Tell me what happens."

"You don't want to hear."

"Yes I do. I need to be prepared for what's going to happen to Montague."

"The crowd will gather early. In fact, no doubt thousands are already there. I warn you, there will be a holiday atmosphere, everyone jovial and laughing. A hanging is quite the gala event, you see. The gallows is on wheels. It would have been hauled out by a team of horses last night and placed in front of the Debtor's Door. Around seven-thirty this morning the prisoners will be led from their cells into the Press Yard where the sheriff and prison chaplain will meet them. The hangman's assistant will bind their wrists in front of them and place white nightcaps on their heads."

"Why nightcaps?"

Augusta shrugged. "They're used as hoods. It's simply the custom. Next, the prisoners' leg irons will be removed by the prison blacksmith. They'll be taken out through the Debtor's Door. I warn you, there will be a huge roar from the crowd when it spies them. Cheers, applause, gibes, and insults. Next, the prisoners will climb the steps up to the gallows and—"

"Stop. I can bear no more."

"You'll soon see for yourself," Augusta answered grimly.

In minutes they had arrived at Newgate Prison, found a place for the horse and carriage, and worked their way through the huge assemblage until they could go no farther in the loud, milling crowd. "So that's the gallows," Lucy said softly as she gazed upon a long, elevated boxlike structure, over which extended two long, parallel beams from which nooses were hanging.

"That's right, miss," said a small, unkempt man with rheumy eyes who stood next to her. "They can hang 'em twelve at a time. A'course 'taint nothing like the old days at Tyburn. Now, there was the place to be if you wanted ta see a good hanging." He boastfully stuck out his chest. "I once saw twenty-four souls, all a'dangling at the same time." He cocked his head. "This your first hanging?"

"Yes." She could hardly get the word out.

"Well, you see what they do, miss, is the prisoners mount the stage. That's when they get the hood put over their head, then the noose around their neck. All along the top is a trapdoor, an' when the hangman gives the signal, it's released from below. Then down they plunge. If these poor souls are lucky, they won't be gettin' short ropes today."

"What do you mean, short ropes?"

"Some executioners, them with a mean streak, prefer the short rope. That means the convicts have but a few inches to drop, so they don't die right away, but kick and squirm for a while." Gleefully the man added, "They writhe in agony, you might say. Quite the spectacle. Better sport than boxing or the races, if you ask me."

Lucy felt herself start to go light-headed. She clutched Augusta. "Quick, let's move away."

They managed to move closer in, just as the Debtor's Door opened. A mighty roar went up from the crowd as, one by one, the prisoners were led to the gallows and forced to climb.

Over the tops of a thousand heads, Lucy saw that Montague was third in line.

"Oh, he'll never see us," she cried in desperation.

"Wait," Augusta answered. "He'll be on top soon. Then we'll wave."

Twelve nooses awaited as the prisoners lined up along the platform. Montague, his hands bound in front of him, looked as if he were moving in a dream as he halted before the third noose from the end. Until then, he'd had his eyes cast down. At last he looked up and his gaze swept the crowd.

"He's looking for us," Lucy cried. "Oh, he must find us!" She raised her hands, high as they would go, as did Augusta. Montague looked in their direction. Suddenly an expression of recognition lit his face. He smiled, a poignant, grateful smile that tore at her heart. "You found us. God be with you, dear brother," she cried. She knew there was no way in the world he could hear her, but if he could just read her lips, he would know. And even if he couldn't, at least he knew she and Augusta were there. *Such small consolation at a time like this.*

"At least he sees us." Tears streamed down Augusta's face. It was the first time Lucy had ever seen her cry. Lucy looked at the other prisoners. Some were praying; some, like Montague, stood stoically awaiting the end, ignoring the taunts and gibes of the unruly crowd. Among the condemned was a trembling young woman. One of the hangman's assistants tied a

rope around her lower skirt for modesty's sake. A young boy—
he could not have been over fourteen or so—sobbed hysteri-
cally, fighting his execution every step of the way.

Montague's attention was soon distracted as the hangman
pulled the white nightcap over his face, then dropped the noose
over his head.

The end was near. Lucy and Augusta clutched each other. "I
cannot bear this," Lucy cried.

"Neither can I, but we must," Augusta answered.

"Pray he doesn't suffer." She gazed for what would be the
last time at her dear brother as he stood, hands tied, hood over
his head, the noose in place, waiting to die.

She waited, her heart pounding in her chest. If she lived to
be a hundred, she would never, ever know a moment as ghastly
as this one. Any second now, Montague and the others would
plunge through the trapdoor . . .

"Halt the execution!"

A uniformed member of the King's armed guard strode up
to the gallows. Clutching a roll of parchment in his hand, he
called imperiously, "By order of the Prince Regent, I hold here
a reprieve."

"Who's to escape the noose?" asked the hangman. Surprisingly he looked pleased.

The guardsman unrolled the parchment. "One Montague
Winthrop has been reprieved."

A roar went up from the crowd, a mix of hoots and jeers,
yet cheering, too. Lucy hardly heard. She stood frozen, not at
first comprehending the enormous significance of the announcement. Then jubilation set in. A cry of relief broke from
her lips. "He's saved, he's saved!" She and Augusta hugged
each other, doing a little dance of joy.

Augusta grabbed Lucy's hand. "Come, we must get to
him." She had to shout to be heard over the still-deafening roar
of the crowd.

They fought their way forward. By the time they reached
the gallows, only eleven prisoners remained. Montague was
nowhere to be seen.

"Where is Montague Winthrop?" Augusta inquired of the
hangman.

"He's been taken back to the prison, madam."

"But hasn't he been set free?"

The guardsman frowned and looked discomfited. "Not exactly." He pointed. "You had best speak with his lordship. He's the one responsible for Montague Winthrop's reprieve."

Lucy looked where the hangman indicated.

There stood Lord Granville.

"You?" she gasped.

Granville bowed slightly.

"But where is Montague?" asked Augusta.

Granville shook his head with regret. "You must understand, I did the best I could. At least your brother's life has been spared, but I was unable to secure his freedom."

"What will happen to him?" asked Lucy.

"He will be transported to New South Wales for life."

"But that's on the other side of the world."

"Sorry, Miss Winthrop, it was the best I could do."

Augusta spoke up. "But at least Montague is alive and hopefully will remain so for quite some time. And where are your manners, Lucy? We owe Lord Granville a debt of gratitude. It's obvious he went to great lengths to obtain Montague's reprieve."

Lucy saw immediately that Augusta was right. "Lord Granville, I do want to thank you. He's not going to hang and I am astonished—grateful—giddy with joy." She clapped her hands with delight and could hardly stand still. "Oh, my mind is all a jumble right now, I'm so happy over Montague."

"It was nothing," Granville said.

"Nothing? I cannot believe that. How did you ever gain an audience with the Prince Regent, especially when you said—?"

"It was much easier than I supposed," Granville interrupted with a careless shrug. "In fact, His Royal Highness was quite amenable to my cause, no trouble at all."

"But how can I repay you?"

"No need. Really, Miss Winthrop, what I did was nothing, requiring little effort on my part. It's payment enough to see that your brother has escaped the gallows."

"But—" she began, but Granville backed a step away, obviously anxious to end the conversation.

"Good day, ladies. I have a pressing engagement. I wish you good fortune, Miss Winthrop, in whatever endeavor you may choose."

Without another word, he disappeared into the crowd.

How curious, Lucy thought, that despite her extreme happiness over Montague's reprieve—surely the most joyful moment of her life—she felt as if cold water had just been dashed in her face. Judging from his cool demeanor, it was obvious Granville didn't care to talk to her. In fact, he could hardly wait to remove himself from her presence. He surely must have had an easy time obtaining Montague's reprieve; else, it was obvious he would never have lifted a finger to help.

Two days later Lucy and Augusta were still recovering from their agonizing experience at Newgate. They would be forever grateful that Montague had been reprieved; yet now they faced the grievous knowledge that they would never see their brother again.

Augusta discovered that Montague had been taken to the hulks, those obsolete Royal Navy ships that lay downriver on the Thames at Woolwich. Damp, rotting, and pestilence-ridden, the hulks housed, among others, prisoners who were waiting transport to New South Wales. Sometimes they had to wait for months, living belowdecks in stench and squalor with the most depraved kinds of criminals. They could receive no visitors.

"At least he's alive," the sisters consoled each other. But what would be Montague's fate in a convict colony halfway around the world?

Lucy knew she must get back to her normal life. It wasn't easy. Not only did Montague's fate haunt her every waking moment, she had been hurt deeply by Granville's unfriendly aloofness that day at Newgate. True, he had saved Montague, but obviously at no cost to himself. He had made that fact abundantly clear.

In the late afternoon Lucy was making plans to resume her search for a position, starting the next day, when she heard a knock. Since Nell was busy in the kitchen, Lucy went to open it. She gasped when she saw who it was.

"Lady Regina."

Not only was Lucy shocked to find Granville's sister at Augusta's humble front door, she was amazed to see the young woman standing without support, alone. She was thin and frail as ever, without an extra ounce of flesh on her bones; yet she seemed encompassed by a healthy glow that hadn't been there before. She wore a smart traveling dress of green satin pelisse and a matching bonnet from which poked her saucy red curls. Beyond, Lucy saw the neighbors were out again, gawking at a luxurious coach and four. Not Granville's coach this time, but one just as fancy. The heraldic arms on the side seemed to feature an "M."

Lucy wondered if the "M" stood for the Earl of Marsh, Lord Kellems's father.

"Well, aren't you going to ask me in?" Regina asked in her inimitable presumptuous manner.

Lucy gathered her wits about her. "But of course come in. I am delighted to see you."

Soon the two were settled in the parlor, Regina expressing her delight that Montague had escaped the noose. In return, Lucy complimented her guest on her glowing appearance. "Might I ask what has put that sparkle in your eyes?"

Regina clasped her hands together in delight. "I took your advice. Lord Kellems and I are eloping."

"Right now?" Lucy asked, astounded.

"This very minute." Regina burst into triumphant laughter. "Oh, I am so happy. Did you see Lord Kellems's coach out front? He's waiting for me. He wanted to come in, but I had some things I wished to say to you in private."

"To me? I cannot imagine what."

"Just listen, my dear Miss Winthrop. Do you remember the last time we talked?"

"Of course. The night I left Lord Granville's employ. I fear I was rather too frank with you."

"You were frank all right, but I'm so glad you were. You opened my eyes that night. For the first time I truly realized I was letting others run my life."

"Your mother."

"His parents, too."

"But that was weeks ago."

"It took a while. You see, I knew I should leave, but I was still a coward, in need of something or someone to push me over the edge."

"And you found what you were looking for?"

"Two days ago I found the strength I needed to break away. It was my very own brother who gave it to me."

"But how?" Lucy asked.

"Are you aware of his sacrifice?"

"What sacrifice?"

"I mean, what he had to do in order to obtain Montague's reprieve."

"He claimed what he did was nothing, that he'd had no trouble at all."

"He lied."

"What do you mean?" Lucy felt utterly bewildered.

Regina explained. "That day you came asking for help in reprieving Montague, and John turned you down, he came to my room after you'd left. He was devastated. Common sense told him he had no choice but to refuse you. Yet, he had seen your desperation and couldn't bear the thought he hadn't offered his help."

"But I understood. I could not expect him to sacrifice his entire career for a criminal who was obviously guilty, as well as someone he didn't even know."

"But sacrifice he did. He'll never be prime minister now."

Lucy took a quick breath of utter astonishment. "But why?"

"He could not ignore his conscience and the feelings he has for you. That being so, he vowed he would do his utmost to help in any way he could. Then Mama found out." Regina rolled her eyes skyward. "You should have heard the row. The servants were ducking for cover. Mama informed him if he dared to defend a criminal who had committed such a heinous crime, he would lose all his support in Parliament. John said he didn't care. Then Mama told him Prinny was in Brighton and that the only way John could possibly persuade His Royal Highness to offer a reprieve would be if he crawled clear to the Royal Pavilion on his hands and knees. John said he didn't care about that, either, and he'd gladly do it."

"You mean . . . he went to Brighton?"

"Yes. Talk about a mad dash. Brighton and back in a day. I asked John how on earth he managed to persuade the Prince Regent to issue the reprieve. He wouldn't say, other than to intimate that Prinny had been quite dreadful to him, and John had almost literally to crawl and beg. I suspect, too, a certain amount of money and a few parcels of choice land changed hands."

Lucy shut her eyes, momentarily lost in her burgeoning awareness of the cost of Granville's generosity. Opening them, she asked, "Is his career truly ruined?"

"Unquestionably." Regina leaned to give Lucy a comforting pat on her hand. "Don't feel bad. Much good has come from his sacrifice. Your brother's life is saved, is it not? Not only that, when I saw John stand up against Mama—unequivocally this time—I knew it was time to make my own stand. I sent a note to Lord Kellems. He was ecstatic." Regina flopped out her palms. "So here I am, on my way to Italy where we shall marry and live happily ever after."

"Not Gretna Greene?"

Regina grinned. "It's really not much of an elopement. John not only knows, I have his blessing. As for Mama, she can come visit us in Italy if she wants." She grew serious. "The last time we talked, you were brutally honest. Now I shall be brutally honest with you."

"Go ahead." Lucy's thoughts were spinning. She was ready for anything.

"For heaven's sake, stop fretting about dire consequences that aren't going to happen and marry my brother. You won't ruin his career, it's already ruined. As for Mama, this last time around he most definitely put her in her place. Now she's meek as a mouse and doesn't dare criticize. He's even removing her from Cheltham House. He owns a lovely townhouse in Brighton where he's sending her to stay, permanently. I daresay Mama will survive. Knowing her, she'll soon be the leader of Brighton society."

"So his mother is gone."

"And Florinda soon will be. She's gotten herself betrothed."

"That's a blessing, I suppose, but that still doesn't change the fact I'm only a governess."

"Who cares? You are an exceptional woman, Miss Winthrop. Daughter of a baron—witty, charming, brilliant, and with such *savoir faire*. Mark my words, you'll make such a perfect Lady Granville, people will swiftly forget your former station."

"I . . . I shall think about it."

"Please do."

They chatted a short while, until Regina stood and announced, "Well, my dear Miss Winthrop, I am off to Italy."

The ecstatic lilt in her voice was catching. For the first time since Montague's narrow escape from the gallows, Lucy laughed aloud. "I'm so happy for you. May you and Lord Kellems have a most wonderful marriage."

Lady Regina took both Lucy's hands and looked deep into her eyes. "Don't forget what I said."

How could she forget? Lucy asked herself after Regina had gone.

"How could I have been so dense?" she later asked Augusta.

"We should have known," Augusta replied. "Reprieves don't just drop off the trees. God knows what groveling Granville had to do in order to get Prinny to approve."

"And yet he did."

"Lord Granville must love you very much."

Lucy didn't answer. In deep thought, she was making plans.

The news of Granville's role in Montague Winthrop's last-minute, miraculous reprieve had spread swiftly. As Granville expected, his party's retribution for "coddling a dangerous criminal" was not long in coming. Contrary to what he had expected, there was no cut direct. His friends remained his friends; yet those in power made sure he understood that the office of home secretary was no longer his, and most certainly not any possibility of his ever becoming prime minister.

Oddly enough, instead of mourning the loss of what could have been an illustrious career, Granville felt as if a heavy burden had been lifted from his shoulders.

Now, as his coach pulled up to the entrance of the Palace of Westminister, he felt jubilant. Today was the last session of Parliament. Soon he would be free to return to Penfield Manor where he would manage his estates to his heart's content, in peace, with his children . . . without Lucy.

A familiar heaviness descended upon him. He might tell himself he'd be happy, and he would, to a certain extent. Yet since Lucy Winthrop left, an irredeemable sadness dwelled inside him. He would have to live with it. It would never go away.

Granville descended from his coach. Approaching the gates of the palace, he caught sight of the small, trim figure of a woman standing by the front gates. She wore a brown redingote with matching bonnet. Her hands were buried in a large fur muff that she held primly in front of her.

His pulse did a wild leap when he saw who it was.

Lucy.

He drew closer. When she saw him she smiled, and said as he approached, "Good afternoon, m'lord."

"If it isn't Miss Winthrop," he replied, striving to conceal his shock at seeing her again. He searched for something innocuous to say. "You appear to be standing at the exact spot where you stood when we first met."

"I am aware of that." She glanced down at the cobblestones. "It was exactly here. I planned it this way."

"To what purpose, might I ask?"

Her lips twisted into a winsome smile. "Call it a sentimental gesture, in fond memory of the day we met."

"Why would you care?" He was deeply puzzled, and more than a trifle annoyed. Was she toying with him? Was it not enough she'd broken his heart?

She answered, "I care a great deal."

"I find that hard to believe."

"Will you listen?" Exasperated, she dropped her arms to her sides, one hand clutching the muff. "I have a question to ask."

"Ask away." To save face, he added, "But be quick. The debates start soon."

"It concerns my second wish."

"What?" He was so startled he could not think.

"My second wish," she repeated, "where I made it clear that if by happenstance we should meet, you were to treat me—"

"Like my former governess and nothing more," Granville testily interrupted. "Yes, yes, I remember. So?"

She drew in a deep breath, as if she was about to say something of great import. "I'm not sure of the rules, but I'm wondering if it's possible to rescind a wish."

"The second wish?"

"Yes, I've changed my mind."

He could only stare at her wordlessly before he finally asked, "What does the genie say?"

"The genie says it's quite all right."

"Well, then, I suppose it is."

"Not only that," she went on, "the genie says if I rescind a wish, the rule is I may replace it with another."

"Do tell." How could he sound so calm when inside wave after wave of shock was slapping at him?

"My replacement wish is this." As if gathering her resolve, she looked skyward, down at the cobblestones again, then square in his eyes. "Will you marry me, Lord Granville?"

For a moment he could only stare at her in astonishment. Then reason took hold and he asked in a near monotone, "May I ask why the change of heart?"

"I spoke to your sister. You lied to me. She told me what you did for Montague."

"So you're grateful? Is that it?"

"Gratefulness has nothing to do with it." Eagerly she plunged ahead. "You see, I had thought that a marriage between you and me was utterly impossible."

"And now?"

"Lady Regina says I needn't worry about your career any longer."

"Ah, yes, my great career." He glanced skyward. "May it rest in peace."

"And your mother . . . oh, dear." In dismay she clapped her hand over her mouth. "I didn't mean—"

"That dear Mama should also rest in peace?"

"I'm making a mess of this, aren't I?" She bit her lip. He could see her confidence had slipped away. "Forgive me. I should not have come here. You are probably betrothed to Lady Camilla by now. Good-bye, m'lord."

She started to move away, but he angrily clasped her arms. "Am I so shallow I could offer you my love, my heart, then turn right around and marry someone else? What do you take me for?"

"I didn't mean—"

"Marry Lady Camilla? Are you insane?" He wanted to shake her. Instead he gripped her tighter. "I adore you, Lucy Winthrop. You're the only woman I shall ever love. When I asked you to marry me, it was because I wanted to spend the rest of my life with you. I wanted to love you—take care of you—have children with you."

Locked in his viselike grip, she suddenly smiled. "But that's just the way I feel about you." She gazed up at him, her expression lit with love. "You and I are going to have a wonderful life."

Unmindful that he was standing in front of the Palace of Westminster and some of his most stuffy, censorious colleagues were passing by, Granville issued a whoop of joy, lifted Lucy Winthrop off her feet, and swung her around.

Her fur muff went flying just as Lord Darwood arrived. With a slight smirk, he retrieved the muff and politely returned it as the near-oblivious couple stood, arms around each other, gazing into each other's eyes with newfound joy and wonder.

Darwood continued on, shaking his head. He ought to be laughing at his lovesick friend, yet was suddenly struck by a deep pang of envy. The man appeared to be truly in love, a most desirable but nearly unobtainable condition.

Lucky devil, that Granville.

Epilog

New South Wales
October 5, 1821

My Dearest Sisters,

Five years have passed, and it is with great joy that I
am at long last able to write you. I could not write
before now. Because of the despicable crime I
committed and the horrendous events that followed, I
felt I was of little worth and thus it would be best all
around if I simply disappeared from your lives forever.

Before I tell you why I am writing now, I must relate
my remarkable adventure since that day I nearly
hanged and was miraculously reprieved. As you surely
know, I was taken to the hulks where I spent several
months in conditions too dreadful to describe. Finally I,
along with two hundred desperate souls, was put
aboard the ship The Lord Melville. On September 15,
1816, we set sail for New South Wales via the Cape of
Good Hope.

Conditions aboard the ship were little better than the
hulks—actually worse, if you consider the constant
seasickness we suffered. We were kept belowdecks in
fetid quarters, bound in chains. Only for a brief period
once a day were we allowed on deck for a bit of fresh
air and exercise. A pall hung over us knowing we had
no future other than to be thrown into another
abominable prison when we arrived.

After five months at sea we landed in New South

Wales in February of 1817. Imagine my joy when I discovered that because of an acute shortage of labor, instead of being sent to prison, I was assigned to work as a plowman for Mr. John Burton, a farmer, in Ross. Now, dear sisters, I know you will find this hard to believe, but for the next three years I worked long, hard hours, diligently and without complaint. I knew if I misbehaved, I would be sent to the notorious road gangs or the dreaded penal station at Port Arthur. But my reasons for remaining a model prisoner were not entirely to save my own skin. Since that ghastly day at Newgate when I was nearly hanged, I greeted each precious day grateful to God that I was still alive. Each day I vowed I would regain my faith in myself, lead a good life, and never hurt anyone again.

God was good to me. After three years with Mr. Burton, and a perfect record, I received my Certificate of Freedom. At the same time, I married a lovely girl named Margaret Fenton. She was also a convict, only sixteen when she was sentenced to death for the theft of five yards of printed calico. Later her sentence was commuted and she was transported on The Lord Melville, *as was I. We were granted forty acres of fertile land. I built a small house, and have farmed for the past two years with some success, mainly growing flax. Soon, I plan to purchase a dairy property, and more acreage.*

Thomas, our first child, was born a week ago. Up 'til then I had been too ashamed to write to you, but when I took my son in my arms for the very first time, I felt such a swell of pride, such hope for the future, that I knew it was time to let you know that your brother is no longer a wastrel but a citizen of solid standing in the community, honest and forthright. He will remain so the rest of his life.

Please know that leaving England nearly broke my heart, yet I can honestly tell you that my precious family and I are alive, well, and happy in this new land.

One of my fellow convicts wrote this poem on our

long, hard journey aboard The Lord Melville. *He's not
Keats, by any means, but the sentiment expressed shows
exactly what was in my heart both then and now.*

> *Far away—oh, far away—*
> *We seek a world o'er the ocean spray!*
> *We see a land across the sea,*
> *Where bread is plenty and men are free,*
> *The sails are set, the breezes swell—*
> *England, our country, farewell, farewell!*

*Are you well, dear sisters? I think of you every day.
Augusta, are you still the champion of good causes?
Lucy, are you a governess still? I do hope this letter
finds you happy in whatever endeavors you have
pursued. Forgive me for letting five years slip by
without a word. Needless to say, I shall be most humbly
grateful if you could find it in your hearts to answer my
letter.*

> *Your loving brother,*
> *Montague*

"Lucy, why are you crying?" Granville felt a sense of alarm
as he gazed at his wife, sitting in the drawing room clutching
a letter, tears spilling from her eyes.

She smiled and held the letter out. "Augusta just brought
this. Montague at last. Oh, John, these are tears of happiness."

When Granville finished the letter, he sat by his wife and
took her hand. "Five years . . . so much has happened."

She nodded brightly. "He doesn't know I'm Lady Granville
now."

"Or the mother of five children. My three—"

"And our two sons," she finished, glowing with pride. "All
of them healthy and happy."

Granville went on, "He doesn't know about the girls'
school you started and what a success it has become. Although
how you've managed, and still become a leader of society, I
shall never know."

"I have another wish." A faraway expression gleamed in Lucy's eyes. "Someday I would like to sail to Italy."

"Ah, yes, where we would visit Regina and Lord Kellems and find out if they are as radiantly happy as her letters indicate. Of course they must be with a daughter and a son."

"I shall be overjoyed to see for myself," Lucy replied. "And then . . . oh, I know wishes don't all come true, but then someday I would like to sail around the Cape of Good Hope and on to New South Wales where we could visit with Montague and see his farm, and Margaret, and his children—he's sure to have more by the time we arrive." She laughed and shrugged. "Oh, I know it's an impossible wish."

"Not at all," Granville briskly replied. He put his arms around his beloved wife. "We'll see what the genie has to say."

Allison Lane

THE NOTORIOUS WIDOW
0-451-20166-3
When a scoundrel tries to tarnish a young widow's reputation, a valiant Earl tries to repair the damage—and mend her broken heart as well...

BIRDS OF A FEATHER
0-451-19825-5
When a plain, bespectacled young woman keeps meeting the handsome Lord Wylie, she feels she is not up to his caliber. A great arbiter of fashion for London society, Lord Wylie was reputed to be more interseted in the cut of his clothes than the feelings of others, as the young woman bore witness to. Degraded by him in public, she could nevertheless forget his dashing demeanor. It will take a public scandal, and a private passion, to bring them together...

To order call: 1-800-788-6262